For Phil and Brendan Godfrey

PART ONE

*H*ERA

Chapter One

I have a story for you. It's a simple story, old as the gods yet as young as each new generation which tells and retells it. It is a tale of immortals, acted by mortals, and told by a borderline character plying between their two worlds. That's me. The messenger of the gods. My name is Hermes.

It is the day after the fire which gutted Camden library. A monsoon-like cloud has recently opened above London and plunged the city into an abrupt gloom. The gutters are running like mountain streams, and the rain is falling faster than the street drains can carry it away. Passing cars and buses throw great arcs of water at each other, and at Jessie Parker, who is walking along the street towards her house. When she left home a few hours earlier, she decided not to bring the car. Now she is laden down with heavy bags, and rain is running down her face into her eyes, and down her arms into the shopping bags. Her long, red plait is drenched and hangs down her back like a heavy rope. Jessie has got it wrong again.

As she opens it, Jessie's front door jams on a large brown envelope, two inches thick, which is lying inside on the mat. It is something which happens regularly, but the driving rain makes it particularly irritating today. Jessie reaches a wet hand round the door and tugs at the package. The paper tears as she wrenches it free and tosses it further into the hall, but it doesn't bother her. She knows what's in it and has no respect for it. As she slams the door behind her, one of two umbrellas which are leaning in the corner falls across the mat. Jessie stares at it as she puts down the shopping and takes off her sodden jacket. She often stares like that at the two umbrellas when she comes in out of the rain, but somehow she never sees them when she's on her way out. The jacket drips on to the hall carpet. On the doormat, the rest of the mail is beginning to soak up the run-off from the plastic carrier bags. Jessie props up the umbrella beside the letter-cage which is also leaning in the corner. It has been there for two years, waiting to be screwed on to the door.

Jessie rescues the mail, brings it into the sitting-room and drops it on the table beside the shopping list that she forgot to take with her when she went out. She screws it up and throws it into the bin before she can be tempted to read it and find out how many things she has forgotten.

About half a mile away, Patrick Robinson is anticipating problems. He has allowed indecision to hinder him an instant too long on the road opposite the burnt-out library, and one of the two policemen standing at the door has noticed him. The camera beneath his overcoat gives him, he knows, an odd sort of pregnant bulge, and the old black hat that he always wears does not suggest respectability. The water that drips from its drooping brim is, he notices, a little muddy. As he

DOWN AMONG THE GODS

Kate Thompson

A *Virago* Book

First published by Virago Press 1997
Published by Virago Press 1998
Reprinted 1999

A CIP catalogue record for this book is available from the British Library

ISBN 1 86049 495 1

Typeset in Perpetua by M Rules
Printed and bound in Great Britain by
Clays Ltd, St Ives plc

Virago
A Division of
Little, Brown and Company (UK)
Brettenham House
Lancaster Place
London WC2E 7EN

crosses over the road, he pushes the hat back from his face, and casually undoes the buttons of his coat. He has already taken photographs of the building from the back, where the damage is most evident, and now he needs to get inside. But he doesn't like the look of the policemen. His press card won't stand up to close scrutiny.

Patrick scissors over the police barriers and all their warnings of danger. The two officers in their yellow mackintoshes stand still and watch him. The sight of the camera has done little to gain their respect. They have not failed to notice the hat.

'Press,' says Patrick to the nearest of them.

'You're a bit late, aren't you?'

'I work for the weeklies.'

The constable stares hard. Patrick flashes him a brilliant smile which masks a bitter contempt for all figures of authority.

'Do they suspect arson?'

The officer shrugs. It is a mistake. Dislodged raindrops run down inside his collar and trickle coldly down his back. He sighs, deeply. 'Go on,' he says, 'but don't touch anything.'

Some other sort of distance away, high up on Mount Olympus, perhaps, or deep within the human psyche, the gods look on. We are all but forgotten now, reduced to quaint images on flaking frescoes, unlikely characters in story books for the very young, historical oddities in classic texts.

Not that we mind. It is just such ignorance which renders entire populations helpless. Worship is one thing but power is another. Unrecognised and unopposed, the gods are free to wreak havoc throughout the mortal world. We are alive and well, believe me, and we are having a ball.

The only opposition we have to worry about comes from each other.

Jessie drips across the living room and lights the gas fire. She cannot remember the last time she was so wet. Everything is wet, including the evening paper which she lays in front of the fire to dry out. It's the early evening edition, but the *Mail* photographers have been quick about their business and the front page carries a photograph of the gutted library. Jessie has already heard that news. She has heard it from every shop-keeper and passing acquaintance in the High Street, and she prefers not to think about it. The library has always been a source of comfort to her, and these days she seems to need comfort more than ever before.

During the last three months, two things have happened to change her life for ever, both of them drastic and irreversible. First she turned forty. Then, just three weeks later and quite unexpectedly, her mother died of a heart attack. Jessie has been left with an overwhelming sense of having been cheated, abruptly orphaned and thrown into a premature middle age. And now that the library has gone, she can't even consult the psychology shelves about what is happening to her.

She stands for a moment, staring at the photograph, then goes back out to the hall. Despite her absent-mindedness, Jessie is not untidy. She collects things; the house is cluttered with little milestones from her life, but it is always clean and, in its own way, orderly. She goes through now into the kitchen and unpacks the shopping. Throwing away the list hasn't helped. As the carrier bags empty she becomes aware, one by one, of the things that she has forgotten.

The wind changes direction and hurls a battery of heavy raindrops against the kitchen window. It reminds Jessie that she is wet through and needs to change. She shakes the water from the plastic carriers and opens the bottom drawer beneath the draining board. It is already full of carrier bags, overstuffed and stiff. Jessie keeps them because she wants to be environment friendly and re-use them, but she never remembers to take them with her when she goes out. For a moment she stands and looks at the multi-coloured mess still expanding gently into the unaccustomed space, wondering if her forgetfulness is a sign of mental decay. There is always something else on her mind, and it worries her, because she feels that, at the age of forty, she ought to have given it up. It is something that she has never told anyone and never will. Whenever she is alone and not working or reading a book, Jessie's mind runs for her a constant picture show. She is a fantasist. The scenarios change, and the characters and the details, but the central theme is always the same. Jessie creates, repeats, and recreates for herself, the perfect romance.

Patrick wanders through the remains of the library building, among sodden cinders and buckled shelving. It is not the magnitude of the damage which fascinates him, but the small details, the books that have somehow remained intact, the little patches of untouched paintwork, a beam which hangs above his head and ought to fall but doesn't.

After some time of being lost in wonder, Patrick realises that he is being watched. Over in one corner, a group of forensic experts are huddled together beneath a pair of umbrellas in some kind of debate. Standing guard beside them is another mackintoshed policeman, and he is following Patrick's every movement with his eyes. Patrick smiles and raises his camera in explanation. The officer's hostile gaze doesn't alter. Gritting his teeth against a rising anger, Patrick turns away and examines his camera. It is the single most valuable thing that he owns, and his only source of livelihood. Despite his care, a few drops of rain have made their way on to the front of the lens. He reaches into an inside pocket and takes out a soft cloth wrapped in a plastic bag. The policeman watches. There is something about Patrick that he doesn't like, and Patrick is fully aware of the fact. He cleans the lens carefully and puts the cloth away. Then he begins to take photographs.

Jessie sits beside the gas fire with her feet up. A pot of tea stands on the table at her right hand. Rain still batters against the windows, but Jessie has changed out of her wet clothes now. She is warm and dry and satisfied. Life is not without its pleasures.

She leans back and sips her tea for a few minutes, relaxing into her most recent romantic fantasy. It is set in North Wales, where she has gone to get away from the pressures of the city and write, at last, that earth-shattering novel. This time round, he is a destitute musician, damaged by life, his tent blown down in the gale which skirls around her cottage. She is warm and cosy beside the fire when the knock comes at the door. He is not too tall, not too dark, not too handsome, and very, very wet.

Jessie didn't always have the same type of fantasies. In her tomboy phase she was a heroic, warrior-woman type, striding into battle alongside the men and emerging triumphant. This was when, unknown to herself, she worshipped Artemis, the great huntress of Olympus, chaste and proud. Women in her favour are generally strong and competent, unabashed by the male disapproval they often encounter. Later, as Jessie moved into maturity, she became, in her fantasies, phenomenally beautiful, quite irresistible to men, and quite often willing to be rescued by them. This was during the rule of Aphrodite, the goddess of desire. More recently, however, were Jessie to know enough to take notice, she would see that her fantasies are driven by Hera, queen of Olympus, mother or step-mother to most of the gods. The men Jessie dreams of now are without exception needy and ill-used by the world. She restores them to their wholeness by endless kindness and patience, and by unconditional love.

It was this aspect of Hera that Zeus exploited when he failed to win her in marriage by any other means. He turned himself into a bedraggled cuckoo, which she took into her protection. She is mother, after all, and nurturer, ever willing to take the fallen and luckless to her breast.

Jessie finishes her tea, and turns to the letters which are lying beside the teapot on the table. The first one is a tax renewal form for her car. The second is a subscription reminder. The third is a letter from her sister in Uruguay. It is brief and businesslike, relating to their mother's will and the sale of the family house. Jessie puts it down. When her father died, it was her mother who took care of all the technical details. Now it is Jessie's turn to deal with them, and she finds them difficult to manage. In retreat, she glances down at the latest edition of *Time Out* which protrudes from beneath the evening paper, drying nicely now. At her ease, after dinner perhaps, she will turn to the Lonely Hearts column and read through it slowly and carefully. She will read it a little guiltily and furtively, as though she just happened upon it by chance. She has never answered an ad and she never will. It would be beneath her dignity. But she reads them all the same, and gets fuel for her fantasies, and is comforted by the knowledge that she is not the only one who is alone.

The heavy brown envelope is still waiting to be opened. It is about as attractive to Jessie as a lump of cold dough. She doesn't need to open it to know what is in it, but it will have to be faced some time.

The covering letter reads:

Dear Jessie,

Here it is. If anything it's marginally worse than the last, but I have every confidence in your manipulative abilities. Let me know what's required as soon as you've read it. Good luck,

Lydia

She puts aside the letter and turns to the first page of the manuscript. 'Life Drawing' by Frances Bailey. Jessie drops it back on to the table and it makes a sound like a hefty slap. She struggles with familiar frustration for a while, then absorbs the slap and pours herself another cup of tea. The work is bread and butter and it is necessary. But if she had time and space, she would show them all how to write. About this she has no doubt.

In the library, the hostile policeman has turned his attention towards the forensic team, who have made some new discovery and are doing something with tweezers and plastic bags. Patrick has taken all the photographs his editor will use, but he isn't finished yet. He wants a few for his own collection.

He takes one or two surreptitious shots of the forensic

team at work, then begins kicking carefully through the cinders, amusing himself. He photographs plastic chairs in the children's section, shrivelled into grotesque formations. He photographs a set of shelves, still standing, with an entire row of book spines, all perfectly preserved, all pitch black. He prods with his toe at a half-burnt coffee-table book on the floor and persuades the sodden and wrinkled pages to turn. *The Living Model: How to bring paper to life and life to paper.*

The effects of the fire upon the book are fascinating. The nude figures, randomly mutilated, remind him of the damaged remains of Roman statues. He squats on his heels and examines the book more carefully. The closer he looks at the drawings, the more fascinated he becomes. He is remembering a time, long ago, when he was good at this.

Patrick has always been convinced that he could have been an artist. Throughout his life, whenever he has thought about it, he has been determined to return to drawing, and to painting, and to doing something with his growing file of unusual negatives. During rare moments of reflection, Patrick knows that the life he is leading is a deepening rut. What he needs is some kind of a boost, a kick-start to get him going and give him a new direction. He contemplates taking the book away with him, to give him inspiration, but when he looks up, he finds that the policeman is watching him again. He shrugs, a little more tetchily than he intends, and focuses the camera on the book.

Jessie picks up the paper and opens it at random. The Inner City Polytechnic is advertising evening classes for adults. It could be just what she needs to freshen her up, get her out into the world and meeting some new people. The first of the classes to meet her eye is Life Drawing.

Patrick uses up half a roll of film on the book, then stands up and begins to wander back towards the entrance to the library. Not far from the doors, beside the blistered desk, is a large pin-board covered, half covered now, with green baize. A diagonal line crosses the board. In the lower right-hand triangle there are charred papers and blackened pins. The higher left-hand triangle, however, is intact. The fire had reached exactly so far and no further. The pin-board is a standing testimony to the arrival of the fire brigade.

Patrick finds the right distance and photographs the board. Then he moves in, to get a close-up of a partially burned paper. As the focus clears, he finds that he is looking at the words 'Life Drawing'. He lowers the camera and reads the heading. 'Inner City Polytechnic. Evening classes for adults'. He takes out his notebook and pencil.

Jessie tears out the ad and pins it beside the phone.

That's my bit done for the moment. It was easy enough. Coincidence, hunches, synchronicity, those things are all my department. Some people have called me a trickster because of this aptitude I have, but no one has to listen to me if they don't want to. For those who desire it, however, I can produce the most extravagant series of coincidences which will keep them happy and mesmerised for as long as they like. So, if you're bored with life and have a suspicion that you might, underneath it all, be the new Messiah, just whistle me up. I'll produce all the evidence you need to convince you that it's true.

And if, after all that, you are still having difficulty identifying me and my area of influence in human life, you might know me by my absence better than by my presence. Those are the times when the magic is missing from life, you're down on your luck, without inspiration. Everyone has those days, weeks, years even, when nothing is worth looking at or thinking about. The world seems grey and meaningless. If you recognise what it is that's missing at such times, then you might be close to knowing me.

Chapter Two

Zeus, having charmed Hera with the old cuckoo trick, resumed his own shape and raped her. She was shamed into marrying him, and from their union Ares, Hephaestus and Hebe were born. Zeus, however, was not content with wedlock. As a result of his philanderings with various nymphs, Apollo, Artemis and Athene were born. And that wasn't all. He fathered, they say, the Fates, the Seasons and the Muses. There's a rumour that he fathered Persephone as well, who went on to marry his brother, Hades. And then there was me, of course. Hermes.

Hera was in a state of perpetual jealousy. She found ways of getting her own back, though, and despite their constant bickering, she and Zeus maintained some kind of balance up there on Olympus. But when Zeus extended his amorous attentions to a mere mortal, it was more than Hera could stand.

The unfortunate woman's name was Semele, daughter of King Cadmus of Thebes. By the time Hera found out about the affair, Semele was already six months into her pregnancy by Zeus. Hera determined that her offspring would never see the light of day. Disguising herself as an elderly neighbour, Hera convinced Semele that she must discover the true nature of her mysterious lover. This she did, but what mortal can look upon the face of a god and survive? Confronted by thunder and lightning, the poor woman burst into flames and although I arrived on the scene almost immediately, there was nothing I could do for her. In sudden inspiration, however, I whipped the foetus from her womb and stitched it into Zeus' thigh.

It was a gamble, but it paid off. The foetus reached full term and emerged, horned, crowned with serpents, the newborn god of wine. His name was Dionysus.

All the old stories. They never really happened of course. They're just myths, that's all.

∽

Patrick stops in for a pint on his way to the class. It is early in the evening, and the pub in the alley beside Griffon Square is almost empty. At one end of the long, dark bar, the landlord is making distant responses to the chatter of a middle-aged woman who is slumped against the counter. He takes Patrick's order and pulls him a pint, still muttering in a solicitous way in response to the woman's complaints. It seems to Patrick that she is looking for an opportunity to weep, and he takes his glass over to a seat beside the window, carefully avoiding her sideways glances. It is his belief that women, all women, exist in one of two steady states: on or off, infatuation or recrimination. He will deal quite happily with the first, but has spent a large part of his existence finding ways of avoiding the second. It's not that he doesn't like women. He does. There is little that he enjoys more than spending an evening with a woman who loves to flirt as much as he does. But since his experience of relationships has been that the one state is invariably followed by the other, he never allows such an association to go any further. His past relationships seem to him like quagmires that he has successfully dragged himself out of. And if his life is a little marshy right now, it is at least his own. He doesn't have anyone else's problems and resentments to worry about. Patrick has promised himself, or someone that he assumes to be himself, that he will never again enter into an emotional involvement.

He finishes his pint and looks out of the window at the alley, wishing that he had chosen another pub. The woman's presence fills him with unease and his need for a second pint is almost cancelled out by his reluctance to approach the bar again. He is not at all sure what he is doing there in the first place, and begins to fear that he may have taken leave of his senses. The money that he paid out at enrolment left him uncomfortably short for most of the week, and he wonders if it's too late to change his mind and ask for a refund. He has a deep mistrust of coincidence and can't understand how it is that it has succeeded in luring him there. For a few minutes he struggles with a suspicion that borders on paranoia. Then the drink begins to take effect. He returns for the second pint, keeping his back to the woman, who is continuing to build on her stockpile of anguish. Half-way down the glass, he lets out a massive sigh as the tension within him melts away. Now, for an hour or two, he will be ready for anything.

The room where the class is held is large and airy. Six fluorescent tubes obliterate the soft daylight which lies against the windows. Patrick screws up his eyes against the glare for a minute or two and decides to keep his hat on.

As he looks around, he realises that the other students are not the young enthusiasts he had imagined. On the whole, they are as clumsy and uncertain as he is and mostly of around the same age or older. He follows the stragglers as they pick up their drawing-boards and collect sheets from the thick slab of butcher paper that the college has provided. As he sets up his board, an elderly man with a worried expression takes the place beside him.

'I thought it was going to be apples and bananas,' he says, 'or flowers, that sort of thing. Someone told me she's the model.' He tilts his head in a rather obvious way towards a girl who is chatting with the teacher. 'She's not going to take her clothes off, is she?'

For reply, Patrick winks. But when the model does come to stand before them, he finds that he, too, is slightly embarrassed. On the opposite side of the room, so is Jessie, and so is every one of the other students. The model, on the other hand, is not in the least ashamed. She is ashamed about a lot of things, but her body isn't one of them.

Patrick glances at her a few times, then picks up his pencil and looks more closely. She is standing now in the centre of the group, her arms folded, her eyes averted. He runs his eyes over her body and makes gestures over the page with his pencil, but he is not yet ready to draw. He is playing with his feelings for a moment, trying to provoke some sense of desire. It occurs to him that he has noticed desire lately only by its absence, and he wonders if he ought to worry about it. At the age of forty-two he should be still going strong. A small anxiety stirs at the back of his mind, an association between alcohol and loss of sexual drive, but before it can become clear, something begins to happen. Patrick's pencil meets the page and he is drawing. To his surprise, he moves almost immediately into a smooth synchronism of hand and eye that he recognises from years gone by. Accurately, but with a minimum of care, he sweeps the pencil across the page and the figure begins to emerge, almost as though it had always been there and awaiting liberation. He is away.

Across the room, Jessie has noticed the man in the black hat and registers with interest the hungry look on his face as he studies the model. She watches him now for a little longer as his expression changes and registers the intensity of his concentration. She begins to sketch pale lines on the forbidding whiteness of the paper in front of her and realises as she does so that she hasn't the slightest idea what she's doing.

Everyone is drawing now except for the elderly man, who seems to be having some sort of a problem with a pencil-sharpener. When the teacher, on her first round of the class, steps quietly up behind him, he jumps and holds up the offending object in a profession of innocence. It is full of broken lead.

Jessie's attention alternates between her page, the model and Patrick. She likes the hat. It is somehow suggestive of loyalty and comfort. When he steps back to get a perspective on his work, he pushes it back from his forehead and clears his face of its shade. She has a feeling that she knows him from somewhere, and she searches his face until he becomes aware of her eyes upon him and glances up. Jessie smiles. Patrick wonders where he has seen her before and how it is that he hadn't noticed that she was in the group before now. He raises his eyebrows to her and smiles back. Jessie looks down and continues with her drawing, just as the teacher reaches her elbow. It seems that as far as her drawing is concerned, there is nothing to smile about. The teacher sighs a little wearily and, on her own sheet of paper, shows Jessie some of the basics. Jessie listens attentively and nods, and returns to work with a little more enthusiasm. But occasionally her eyes slide from the model towards Patrick and she is pleased to notice that his attention is also divided. She draws his hat on the head of the figure taking shape on her page. It is considerably more recognisable than the model. When the class takes a short break, she holds it up for Patrick to see. He laughs, pulls the hat down over his brow and peers out at her from underneath it.

The elderly man is packing away his pencils as the model takes up another pose, on her knees this time, and facing Jessie. It would be difficult now for her to avoid looking at Patrick even if she wanted to. She works with half her attention and is surprised to find that after a while her drawing is beginning to look something like a human being. The teacher, however, is not of the same mind. Jessie screws up her face in exaggerated anguish and looks over to share it with Patrick. He is already watching. Their eyes meet.

Beware of love at first sight. It is far from being simple. The advantage of being the gods' messenger is that I have, as it were, a foot in both camps. I can see what's going on from all angles, which no one else can, not quite.

There's a lot going on here. There are, in fact, four different encounters involved. For a start we have two mortals, each in their own way lonely and needy. Given a chance they might come to like each other quite a lot. But that in itself wouldn't be causing the extraordinary jolt which they are both experiencing. The strange sense of recognition that they share is very common among those who are attracted to each other, and sometimes it's so strong that people get the sensation they have known each other for ever. It's in fashion these days to attribute this to meetings in past lives, a hypothesis for which I am always willing to provide evidence for those who seek it. What I'm seeing right now, though, is a meeting, a fairly strong clash in fact, between two of the immortals. Jessie and Patrick have never met. It is impossible that they should recognise each other. But Hera and Dionysus have known each other for ever. Dionysus is giving Patrick strong messages to back off, and Jessie feels a similar desire to disengage and retreat. But there are still two more pairs of co-ordinates here. Jessie, like many over-regulated people, has long had a fondness for Dionysus, and tends to be attracted to him again and again. And Patrick, despite his resolutions, has not succeeded in breaking free of the childish longing to hand over responsibility for himself to someone who is willing to take it. Which is why, in the past, he has attracted Hera to himself, again and again and again.

Jessie looks away, hoping that she doesn't appear as flustered as she feels. Patrick covers a momentary confusion by going over some lines with his pencil but it's a while before he is able to concentrate again on his drawing. They have both been abruptly besieged by an inner conflict which neither of them is able to understand. For the rest of the class they are acutely aware of each other but each carefully avoids meeting the other's eyes. When the model finally relaxes and gets dressed, Patrick's attention is taken by the teacher who is full of enthusiasm and encouragement. Patrick is flattered. He is beginning to believe that his creative faculty might be intact.

Why shouldn't it be? Every human being is potentially a genius. But anyone with creative aspirations needs to be aware that Dionysus is a brilliant mimic, and one of the best impressions he does is that of the muse. He will serve the imaginative individual up to a point, but the gods are not handmaidens to humanity. The time inevitably comes when they cease to serve and demand to be served instead.

The drawings on Patrick's board are good, without doubt. But the creative impulses, the ideas and enthusiasms which are at present passing through his mind are mirages. They, like so many before them, will vanish before he can reach them.

The teacher issues a general invitation to the class to meet in the Red Lion for a drink. Patrick agrees readily and, without thinking, looks around to see if Jessie is coming. But she has already gone. The drawing that she did of the model wearing his hat is just visible among the crumpled papers she has thrown into the bin. The sight of it gives him a slight jolt and he turns back to the bustle of the class, packing away. Carefully, he rolls up his own drawings and tucks them under his arm.

As he walks down to the pub, the sky is as dark as a city sky can be, and a light fog blurs the edges of the buildings. The trees in Griffon Square are beginning to drop soft scatterings of autumn leaves on to the pavement. It is the kind of evening that Patrick loves, mysterious and calm, as though awaiting the arrival of drama. He remembers Jessie's face clearly and that strange, ambivalent meeting of their eyes. It remains with him along with the general excitement of renewed possibilities as he scuffs through the fresh leaves.

But by the bottom of the first pint he has forgotten her.

It is late when he gets home from the Red Lion. He has no car and no money for a taxi so he has to walk. For a while he had a bicycle and he remembers that time as being pretty much perfect. But the bicycle was, inevitably, stolen and he hasn't been able to get the money together for another one. He will, sooner or later. Just as he will, sooner or later, find the impetus to break free from King's Cross.

The house where Patrick lives is on a main thoroughfare where three lanes of one-way traffic pass almost continuously.

There are stairs down to his basement flat and something rustles among the rubbish bags that he keeps forgetting to bring up to the street for the dustmen. He pauses on the steps. Two heavy lorries rumble past, and in the relative silence that follows Patrick is aware of a sense of anxiety as he goes on down and fits the key into the door. For some reason that he cannot understand, the flat has begun to feel menacing to him in recent months. He doesn't believe in ghosts or evil spirits but it seems to him that the flat is inhabited by some sort of malign presence which constantly threatens his peace of mind. Reason, Patrick's defence against anything unknown, is becoming increasingly powerless to protect him.

He passes quickly through the hall and into the larger of his two rooms, which is where he sleeps and occasionally cooks. The darkness is solid after the street lights, but not as empty as it ought to be. Patrick strikes a match. It flares and leaves a blind white spot in his vision, then gutters and creates dark shapes which sway and lean towards him as he crosses the room. The hairs on his back stiffen and tingle as the match burns out, and he quickly lights a second one and touches it to the two candles on the mantelpiece. As they kindle and the light expands, the room takes on a less forbidding quality. When he first moved here, in exodus from his last relationship, he bought a bolt of cheap grey fabric and hung it around the walls using a borrowed staple gun. It was a way to cover the crumbling plaster, and he had not thought of it as being any sort of a decorative achievement. It did, though, have some unusual and pleasing consequences. The cloth hangs over the recesses on either side of the fireplace, leaving perfect alcoves where the clutter of his life can lie concealed. And instead of bringing these curtain pieces right into the corners, he rounded them where they are attached to the ceiling, so that the room appears to be oval in shape. All the sharp edges are hidden.

Patrick puts a match to the gas fire and as it heats up its red light begins to overpower the candles. He sits down for a moment or two to calm himself before starting into the night's work which lies before him. For the first time in all the years he has lived here, it occurs to him that the round, warm space he has created is a womb. But it is a womb which has outlived its purpose. Now it is trying to expel him.

Chapter Three

The hatred between Hera and Dionysus is long-standing and bitter. For when Hera's first attempt to get rid of Dionysus failed, she did not give up. As soon as he emerged from Zeus' thigh, she ordered the Titans to destroy him. They did their solid and pragmatic best. They tore Dionysus to pieces and boiled him in a cauldron, but his grandmother Rhea rescued him and delivered him back to Zeus, who entrusted him to Persephone, the queen of the underworld. She in turn brought him to King Athamas and his wife, Ino, who reared him in the women's quarters, disguised as a girl. But Hera was not to be deceived. When she discovered what they had done, she rewarded Athamas and Ino with madness.

∞

Jessie would have liked to linger on after the class to see whether there was anything happening but instead she drives across town, in the opposite direction from her home. She has agreed to meet Lydia to discuss Frances Bailey's novel with her, and little short of accident will stop her from keeping her promise. Jessie has, she believes, got her priorities in order.

She knows London well. There isn't much traffic around, but by habit she zips the little car through side streets and alleys, taking the shortest route. The drawing has done her good, stimulated an unused part of her brain and woken her up.

Something else has woken her up, too. She frowns to herself in the car, remembering the man in the hat. Her visual memory isn't good and she can't recall his face, but it will be a long time before she forgets the feelings that his hungry gaze produced.

But along with those feelings, and the reciprocal hunger, comes the all too familiar emergence of guilt. Jessie's father was a Methodist minister, and her mother was his even more Methodist wife. They believed in the one, true god, and did their best to defy all the others that they dimly sensed lurking in the shadows. They did this in themselves by instilling rigid and indissoluble discipline. To rid their children of the symptoms of original sin, they used shame.

Towards the end of his life, Jessie's father began to get an inkling that he had somehow been conned. The one god idea is intriguing, but has consistently failed to get past humanity's tendency to worship something outside itself, and to be consequently overtaken by that which it worships. The Church, despite the remarkable insight of its originators, soon became just another of the deities in the pantheon, and although she occupied a seat on Olympus for quite some time, she has clearly not succeeded in her bid to overcome the rest of us.

But her father's reversal came too late for Jessie to be affected by it. She accepted and obeyed her Methodist teachings, even when they ran against the passions that were steadily gaining strength within her nature. Her rebellion began relatively late in life, when she left home to go to university.

Did she change, then? Hardly.

Human beings do not change, though they do, from time to time, change their allegiance. This can happen at any time during their lives, but there are certain critical points when everyone is, in terms of the gods, up for grabs. The most important of these is adolescence.

With rare exceptions, children accept with little question the gods that are favoured by their parents. It is not until the teenage years that there is a monstrous reshuffle, which is agonising for them and those around them. Because now the gods close in and vie for power. The individual in the midst of it is prone to all kinds of unpredictable passions, enjoying inflations of character as one or another of the deities takes possession, then suffering desperate depressions as they are dropped again. The adolescent swings between the safe, parental gods and the inducements which the new ones are offering, while their parents find themselves lying awake at night wondering how it is that their placid and reliable child has been transformed overnight into a demon. In rare cases, this uncertainty remains with an individual, who spends his or her life in a state of unpredictability, pursuing now this interest, now that, forever on the point of finding their heart's true path, forever failing to do so. Most people, however, come through the phase of adolescence and settle. They come to some sort of decision about their life.

At least, that's how it appears from their standpoint.

Jessie's decision to study literature was an acceptable one to her parents. What she did during her years of college would not have been, had they known about it. For as soon as she was free of their restrictive influence she entered her postponed adolescence and moved straight into the inner-city whirlwind of the seventies. Jessie was ready to join the party. Her red hair and unpretentious air of innocence ensured that she was never short of suitors. She fell in love easily, and out again, amazed by her own sense of abandonment, her readiness for anything. Those were heady times. She never knew where she was going to wake up, or with whom, or with what kind of hangover.

The gods were having a ball. Dionysus was there, his latest campaign just beginning to pick up strength, and Apollo, the god of music, during his rock and roll phase. And wherever you find those two together, there also you will inevitably find Aphrodite, goddess of desire, and her unruly son, Eros.

He's popular on earth, Eros, particularly with the manufacturers of greetings cards. The Romans called him Cupid, and maybe that's the name by which he's better known. A cutesy little cherub with dimply buttocks and a dainty bow and arrow. Where would the world be without him?

But what people don't remember is that he has another side to his nature. He never got a seat up here on Mount Olympus; too irresponsible, it was decided. So he stays down below, getting into all kinds of mischief in darkened rooms across the world. It's not Aphrodite who is responsible for rape, child abuse, prostitutes and rent boys. She had little, if any, part to play in the sudden and terrifying emergence of AIDS.

Jessie pulled up short and returned, slightly shamefaced, to the fold. The Methodist title was rejected for ever, but the Methodist ethic remained.

'You know what bothers me?' she says to Lydia, as they settle before the fire in the untidy clutter of her flat.

'No. What bothers you?'

'What bothers me is that I get no acknowledgement for what I do for Frances.'

'You get paid.'

'I know I do. That's not the point. Frances would be nowhere without me, and that's a fact. She can't write good English to save her life. I mean, there I am, basically ghost-writing her stuff and she's never even thanked me, let alone given me any public recognition.'

Lydia moves her chair away from the fire at the same moment that Jessie draws hers closer. Lydia is one of those people who never seems to be cold. Jessie is somehow never quite warm.

'Would you want it?' says Lydia. 'Really?'

'Oh, I don't know. It's the principle of the thing, I suppose.'

Lydia pours vodka from a new bottle into two glasses. 'Frances probably has to ignore you, Jessie, for the sake of her dignity. If she admits to what you do then she also admits that she doesn't do a great job herself. I have a suspicion that she believes all writers work like that. They just deliver the baby and give it to someone else to clean up. Quite a lot of them do, these days, you know?'

'Well, it bothers me,' says Jessie.

'It didn't used to. You used to love it.'

'I suppose that's true.'

In the silence that follows, Jessie is surprised to discover just how much it does bother her. Her literary faculties are jammed full, bunged up with things that she wouldn't even read, given the choice. The work had seemed to be a perfect way of earning money while she waited for her own inspiration, but it hasn't turned out that way. No inspiration has come to her since the year she was on her own between Alec and John.

Alec was Jessie's first long-term partner, when the frenetic relationship with Aphrodite and Eros came to an end. He lasted four years. After him, there was John, who lasted a year and a half. Since him, there has been no one. No one serious, anyway.

The two men were about as different from each other as it is possible to be. Alec was grave and studious and self-absorbed while John was light-hearted and irresponsible. But they had two things in common. They were both heavily dependent upon alcohol, and they both left her.

Jessie knows why. She was too eager and too possessive. With both men she made the fatal mistake of putting aside all other interests and investing herself totally in the relationships, so that they meant too much to her both before and after they broke up. She was bitterly hurt on both occasions, and resolved never to make the same mistakes again. She isn't even entirely sure, despite her idealistic and romantic dreams, that she wants the opportunity to prove it. There are aspects in each of the relationships that she misses and remembers with nostalgia, but the highest point of her life during those years was the time after Alec had gone and before John arrived, when she was writing. Nothing that went before and nothing that came after can compare with the vitality of those eighteen months. Her life was illuminated by a creative spirit that seemed to guide every waking hour and every step she took. Her mind was as sharp as a razor, constantly active, and she woke early to write before work, and stayed up late into the nights in feverish production. The fact that nothing came of it, that her novel was never finished and her poems still lie unread in the drawer of her desk didn't matter at the time, and still doesn't matter to her now. It was the process itself that gave meaning to her life, and it is that which she still awaits, with fading hope. Now that she thinks about it, she has no reason to believe that it will ever return. It is three years since John left and the inspiration that tried to emerge at the time lost out against the necessity to get paid work to cover the debts he left her.

Jessie studies Lydia in the gentle light thrown out by the fire and the reading lamp which sits on the mantelpiece, its face turned to the wall. Lydia is always so certain about life and what she wants from it. She doesn't seem to be subject to doubts and depressions the way Jessie is, and because she doesn't fall prey to inertia she doesn't need anything or anyone to free her from it.

Jessie straightens up and sighs, wrenching herself out of the tightening grip of self-recrimination. 'Funny coincidence,' she says. 'Life drawing.'

'What?'

'Life drawing. I've just been to a life drawing class.'

'Oh?'

'I saw it advertised in the paper about a minute after I opened the manuscript. So I thought, why not?'

'Indeed,' says Lydia. 'Why not?'

'It was good, actually.'

'I'm sure it was.' But life drawing is one of the many things which tend to raise Lydia's feminist hackles. 'I bet you there were no male models, though.'

'Not officially,' says Jessie, and grins to herself in a way that is offensively familiar to Lydia.

'Oh, no,' she says, 'not again.'

Lydia considers herself to have broken free of the shackles of male/female relationships. She's not gay, as a number of threatened men have suggested; she has no sexual relationships of any sort. This she considers to be the height of individual attainment, complete freedom. But she is, in fact, every bit as shackled as Jessie is. Her mistress is Artemis, the chaste huntress, goddess of the Amazons. This accounts, though neither of them knows it, for the slight ambivalence that has always existed between herself and Jessie. Lydia likes Jessie, and would count her among a small handful of her best friends. But there is also something about Jessie which makes her uneasy, and particularly when she's involved in a relationship with a man. Were she to be totally honest with herself, she would admit that her jokes about Jessie's propensity to fall head-over-heels in love are based upon a deep disquiet. There is a good reason for this. Artemis has no great liking for Hera, but she can take her or leave her. When it comes to Aphrodite, however, there is no love lost, none at all.

It goes back a long way. It goes back for ever, in fact, but probably the story of Hippolytus and Phaedra would be the best place to look, to know what is happening here. They won't, though, either of them. They might have read Euripides and they might not. If they have, neither of them remembers.

Lydia has never tackled Jessie face to face about her romantic associations. Their conversation comes to a temporary halt, however, and for a while they both gaze into the fire, uncomfortably aware of something which lies, or hovers, in the air between them.

Patrick has, as he often does, left everything until the last minute, and he works through the night to get his photographs ready for the next morning.

There is no electricity in the basement. The meter and most of the wiring had been ripped out before he moved in. His darkroom, originally the flat's kitchen, is powered by a wire run down from the flat above, which is occupied by a varying number of rowdy but well-disposed rent boys. Patrick suspects that they may be paying for his gas as well, because he has never had a bill, so he helps them out with the occasional fiver when times are lean.

As he mixes chemicals, Patrick remembers the woman with the red hair. He isn't quite sure whether the look she gave him was a come-on or a get-off. He plugs in the kettle for coffee to drink while he works. Whatever she meant, it makes no difference. There's no way he's going to get involved again.

The night draws on. As the prints come out of the wash, Patrick spreads them to dry in the soft, grey room next door. They cover more and more of the floor space as the hours go by. Apart from the ones of the library, almost every photograph has Irish associations. There are pictures of weddings, football matches, and touring musicians. The negatives of the life drawing book and the plastic chair gargoyles remain unprinted, and join a collection in a personal file which is growing to unmanageable proportions.

All the photographs he needs are eventually spread out. The week's wages, for his milk and coffee and Weetabix, his bags of chips and his beer and naggins of whisky. There will be enough to replace the photographic paper, visit the launderette and pay bus fares. No sleep, though, and no dreams. By the time morning comes, Patrick is liverish and dazed by exhaustion. He is not prone to hallucinations, but it's as good a time as any to give him a reminder of a dream he had long, long ago and which woke him, sweating, in the early hours of the morning.

He was still young, still strong enough to resist the rapidly increasing influence of Dionysus upon his life. I offered him, in his dream, a glimpse of what was happening to him, a true picture of the god that was slowly but surely enslaving him. He opened his eyes and sat up in bed, but failed to rid himself of the monstrous image which gripped him with terror for several days. Had he looked more closely at the dream he might have picked up the signs of who he was dealing with. The demon was draped with vines, after all, and carried a great staff topped with a pine cone. Dionysus goes nowhere without his thyrsus, every Greek knew that. But every Irishman doesn't, and Patrick chose not to enquire. Instead he took to his heels. And ran, of course, in the wrong direction.

Patrick wonders briefly why it is that the image from that dream should have started recurring lately. It has some sort of uncomfortable connection with the anxiety he feels about the flat these days, and his fear of the darkness. The dream troubled him a lot when he first had it, but he had presumed that it was forgotten. It was, after all, only a dream.

Only a dream. A message for you, for you alone, privately in the night. A message from Hermes, messenger of the gods, guide of souls, bringer of dreams. When the postman arrives with a letter for you, do you shake your head and close the door in his face? 'Only the postman, dear.'

It reminds Patrick, none the less, of the time when the Muses still lived on the hill, or on the horizon, or just over it. And it seems to him that they could be there again if he only knew how to start looking. If he had a bit more money, he could print those special negatives and put together an interesting exhibition. But his deal with the *London Irish Weekly* is pretty regular. He works on commission, and occasionally gets orders for extra copies from readers, but on the whole there is little room for expansion. And if he can't increase his income, then he has to look at his expenditure to see if he can lower it. But that, like his press card, will not stand up to close scrutiny.

He begins to gather the dry prints. Hope is a scarce commodity these days. It is crazy to waste it. In rare, quiet moments like this one, eight hours since the last pint and several hours before the next, Patrick knows that he is in an awful mess.

Chapter Four

When Queen Ino's attempts to hide Dionysus failed, Zeus asked me for assistance. I turned Dionysus into a young goat and gave him into the care of the nymphs who live on Mount Nysa. They were delighted with him; fed him on honey and took care of his every need. It was here that he invented wine.

As Jessie is leaving the house on her way to the second of the art classes, she remembers, for once, to bring an umbrella. The memory triggers a chain reaction, and she has gone back to the kitchen and released the plastic bags from their restriction before she realises that she's not going shopping and has no use for one. Back in the hall, she remembers that she is driving, and therefore has no use for the umbrella, either. But as she parks the car in Griffon Square, she finds that she has forgotten to bring her pencils.

On the other side of the square, beneath the autumn trees, Patrick is standing in an agony of indecision. His left hand is in his trouser pocket, rubbing a small collection of coins against each other. He knows exactly how much is there. Two pints. Two pints to last him through the evening, through the night and up until the delivery of his photographs tomorrow. If he drinks them now, he will miss them after the class and the night will be that much longer. But if he doesn't drink them now, he won't have the courage to attend the class at all. There is, as always, a reason for a mortal's dependence upon the gods. Patrick, without the help of Bacchus, is a social cripple.

'You coming?'

Patrick jumps, yanked out of his inertia. Jessie has recognised him by his hat. She is breezy, clearly pleased to see him. It helps.

They fall into step along the side of the square and across the road towards the college.

'I almost missed you in the mist.'

'Missed me in the mist, did you miss?'

Jessie giggles. 'How do you know it's miss, eh?'

'Ah. Am I being presumptuous?'

'Yes. Actually it's Ms.'

'Ah. Ms.'

'Ms.'

'Mzzzzz. Ms what?'

Jessie gives the swing doors a shove. Patrick watches them close. He is in, now. No going back. Jessie has gone on, but he catches her up. It's easier to enter a room full of people if you're with someone else.

'Jessie,' she says, as he draws alongside.

'Ms Jessie?'

'Just Jessie. And you?'

'Patrick.'

She glances at him approvingly. 'I love the hat.'

The hat says something, but not a lot. There is nothing else about him that gives any clues as to what sort of person he is. Patrick is a boozer and he lives a bit rough, but he's not a bum. He shaves and washes every day in the leaking bathroom at the back of the house. He sets aside money for the launderette and even washes his sheets. That much self-respect remains to him.

But not much more. The class is a torment. He cannot recapture his free-flowing hand of the week before, and each line that he draws is tortuous and strained. He is acutely embarrassed by his efforts and is flustered when the teacher arrives at his side.

'Can't seem to get a feel for it this week,' he says.

'Why do you say that?' she says. 'It looks fine to me. What's the problem?'

'Well, it's a bit stiff, isn't it?'

'I don't think so. Not at all. You really have a good eye, you know. You have a great feel for perspective.'

She moves on. Patrick is astonished. The truth, though he still can't see it, is that his drawings this week are every bit as good as they were the last. It is his opinion of himself that is different.

The teacher's praise bucks his spirits. He catches Jessie's eye for the first time that evening and gives her a nod. She returns it, feeling the conflict returning, that strange mixture of attraction and antagonism. It makes her uncomfortable. She has a strong suspicion that he's dangerous.

She's wrong, though. If you were to ask me, I'd say that Patrick's worst fault is his cowardice, his inability to face the things that go wrong in his life and the reasons for them. He isn't dangerous at all.

But Dionysus is.

As the class draws to an end, Patrick draws a quick cartoon on a discarded page. It shows a humanised pint glass, very macho, winking down at a coy, feminine half-pint. He holds it up for Jessie to see, a question in his eyes. It takes her a minute to work it out, but then she gets it and laughs.

Now it is Jessie's turn to feel flattered, and it is this that has impaired her judgement. In normal circumstances, she would have been appalled by the tasteless and stereotypical images in the drawing. As it is, she has a vague sense of unease as she returns the borrowed pencils, but it passes as she strolls through the college with Patrick and out into the misty street. She likes Irish men. Always has.

'You're obviously not new to this game,' she says, as they walk towards the pub.

'What game is that?'

Jessie brushes damp leaves with her feet, suddenly uncertain. She decides not to laugh. 'The drawing,' she says.

'Oh, that.'

'You're very good at it.'

'No, not really.'

'You are.'

Patrick glances at her. He is always hungry for praise, but right now he is hungry, above all else, for a pint.

Jessie reads the look as being slightly contemptuous. She believes herself in general to be a good judge of men, but she is having a great deal of difficulty reading this one, and he fascinates her. 'You've obviously done it before,' she goes on.

Patrick sighs. 'Yes.' They are almost at the pub, and his attention is already inside it. But Jessie is looking over at him, expecting him to say more. Her eyes are bright in the mist-filtered light from the street lamp on the corner. She is inquisitive. For a moment, despite himself, Patrick is drawn in. There is something showing there, in Jessie's eyes, that he recognises. Something that he has lost.

It is the ability to listen to me.

A few of the other students are gathering at the bar but Patrick, with some casual engineering, keeps himself and Jessie a little separate. Again Jessie is flattered, seeing it as a gesture of exclusivity, but in that she is mistaken. Given the choice, Patrick would always make for the crowd. When he steers her away from them it is to ensure that he won't get into the embarrassing predicament of having to buy a round.

'What are you drinking?' he says.

'Oh, I don't know,' says Jessie. 'What are you having?'

Patrick pauses, as though for deliberation. 'Guinness, I suppose.' He is long enough out of Ireland now to find London Guinness palatable.

'Sounds good,' says Jessie. 'Guinness, then.'

As Patrick turns towards the bar, Jessie remembers his cartoon and adds, 'A pint.'

For an instant, Patrick suffers a mental seizure. He isn't at all sure why he chose to team up with Jessie in the first place but he did it on the assumption that the most he would have to sacrifice would be a half-pint. Now, if she doesn't recipro-cate, he's going to go thirsty. He looks at her carefully, trying to sum her up, and is surprised to find that she really is quite good-looking. Certainly not the feminist type, but probably not too traditional, either. The seizure passes and he turns back to the bar.

Jessie, meanwhile, in her increasingly mesmerised state, has taken Patrick's long, searching look to be one of reappraisal and final approval. She knocks back her pint with admirable speed and orders two more. Dionysus, always on the lookout for converts, begins to forget Hera and take a bit more interest. Patrick is getting relaxed. A woman who drinks like that, he thinks, might be worth getting to know.

Patrick's chances with Jessie are good, but Dionysus is on a non-runner. He has wooed her before, quite temptingly at times, but in the long run he can never win. She worked her way through most of the available drugs during her university days, but discovered in the end that she doesn't have the constitution for them. A few jars once or twice a week is about all she can manage. Any more than that and she gets the spins, or throws up, or gets paralysed by migrainous hangovers and swears off the booze. And when she is off it she doesn't miss it at all.

'Do you suppose,' she says, 'that we'll get a chance to draw a male model?'

'A male model?'

'Yes. Or will we have the same one all the way through?'

'It's a good question. I hadn't thought about it really.'

'Nor had I. But I have a friend who thinks about things like that. She thinks it's an issue of some concern.'

Patrick has an image of an Amazonian ball-breaker. He has no time for Artemis at all. 'Does she?' he says.

'Well, it is a bit one-sided when you think about it. I wouldn't mind getting a shot at doing a man.'

Patrick hesitates. He senses that the kind of response his King's Cross drinking companions would expect to a remark like that might not go down too well with Jessie. 'Yes,' he says. 'I suppose it would make a change. Could be a bit awkward, though, couldn't it?'

'Why?'

'Well . . .'

Jessie can barely keep her eyes off Patrick's face. It is causing him acute discomfort, not only because there is something slightly predatory in the way she looks at him, but because he is beginning to suspect that he wouldn't put up too much resistance to being preyed upon. Jessie is nothing like the women that he normally finds himself drinking with.

Most of them are members of the bacchae. They are maenads, as besotted with Dionysus as Patrick is himself. And if they are licentious it is because they take pleasure in being licentious, not because they have any further design. Patrick has rarely felt threatened by them. This woman is different. This woman is coming dangerously close to drawing him in.

'You wouldn't do it, then?' she says.

'What, model?'

'Yes.'

'No way.'

'Why not? There's nothing to it.'

'Not much, there isn't.'

Jessie looks him up and down, approvingly. 'I can't imagine what you'd have to hide.'

'Thanks very much,' he says, but it passes her by.

'I don't understand why men are so shy about their bodies,' she says.

'Would you do it, then?'

'Ah,' says Jessie. 'Touché.'

She gets up to go to the Ladies and Patrick thinks about what she has said. The rent boys would do it, no problem. They'd do almost anything for enough to buy a few snorts. But as he thinks about it, he isn't sure that he would really like to know what evidence of brutality might lie beneath their denim jackets and tight jeans. The bright lights and loud music of their flat is in apparent contradiction to the subdued darkness of his own, but the demonic figure which continues to haunt his rooms is somehow associated with them as well.

And now, he realises with a sinking heart, he will have to go back there. He has work to do in the darkroom before tomorrow, and however much he dreads facing it, he dreads even more the prospect of losing his week's wages. He empties his glass and leans back in his chair. The art teacher nods to him from a table nearby and he returns the greeting. He had forgotten that the others were there. The murmur of voices is comforting and he is strongly tempted to stay, but he has no more money. Jessie has still not come back, and he considers slipping away quietly. She is, without doubt, a danger to him. But before he can make his decision, he spots her making her way back towards their table. She is carrying two more pints.

Chapter Five

When Dionysus reached maturity, Hera found him again, and recognised him despite the effeminate appearance that his upbringing had given him. As she had punished his first foster parents, so she punished him also: by driving him mad. It didn't have the desired effect, though. It merely made Dionysus doubly dangerous and sent him off on a wild and violent rampage across the world.

That was the first of his campaigns.

Knowing nothing of the gods, or the terms on which they operate, Patrick has accepted everything that Dionysus has offered him. In the early days it was escape, ecstasy, euphoria. Later it was exaggerated self-confidence and the courage to break away from the despised establishments of family and education. More recently, Dionysus has offered Patrick little more than protection from the unacceptable reality of where his allegiance has brought him. But at every step, sacrifice has been exacted. First it was the irreconcilable breakdown in his relationship with his parents, followed by a progressive decline in confidence, failure to keep contact with friends, the loss of women that he might have loved, and the child that he has never seen.

Yet Patrick knows nothing of sacrifice. He sees these things as the unavoidable actions of a world that has never understood him, and from which he has come to expect nothing better. He doesn't consider his life to be tragic. In sour moments he blames society, or the institution of the family, or the insufferable nature of women for the state of his existence. But in general he considers himself lucky to have escaped the suffocating mediocrity of middle-class life and the humiliation of being registered as a state statistic. His has been a life spent in hiding, in fear of exposing his underlying vulnerability, his unquestionable guilt, his inadmissible pact with Bacchus. And he has hidden with great success: from the Inland Revenue Department, from jilted lovers, from the mother of his child, and above all from himself. He has always, just, succeeded in keeping one step ahead.

'I shouldn't really drive,' says Jessie as they leave the pub, 'but I'm going to.'

'Three pints,' says Patrick. 'That's not much, is it?'

'It is for me,' says Jessie, 'but to hell with it. Can I take you home?'

Patrick has learnt, over the years, to think quickly. He thinks quickly in order to defend himself because he believes that he is in need of defence.

He almost says, 'No thanks, my car is just around the corner,' but he catches himself in time. Patrick is not entirely honest, but he tells lies only under extreme pressure. What he does say surprises him slightly, because it is against at least one of the wills that is currently operating within him.

'Which way are you going?'

'Camden.'

'I'll come as far as Camden with you, then. I can make my own way from there.'

They will, in fact, have to pass through King's Cross, or close to it, to get to Camden, but Patrick will not ask Jessie to drop him off. There are no respectable residential areas anywhere near it that he can claim. Camden is a gamble. From its nearest point he will have a short walk home. From its furthest, he will end up footsore.

Jessie drives competently, despite the drink. She drives fast, like all Londoners, and accurately.

'So what part of town do you live in?' she says.

Patrick stalls. 'Actually, I'm not too happy where I am at the moment.' He pauses, and before Jessie can ask him why, he says, 'Good God!'

'What?'

'Did you see that? That guy on the motorbike?'

'What about him?'

'Sending up sparks from the foot-rest. Didn't you see?'

'No.'

'Phew. He's had a few I'd say. Either that or there's someone on his tail. Did you ever have a motorbike?'

'No,' says Jessie, 'I never did.'

'Shame. You've missed out.'

When Jessie pulls up in Camden High Street a few minutes later they are still, somehow, talking about motor bikes, despite the fact that Jessie has no interest in them whatsoever. Patrick looks out and up.

'You don't live here, do you?' he says.

'No. I'm going to get a Chinese. Want one?'

Patrick passes Chinese restaurants almost every day in the course of his travel around the city. He passes Indian, Greek and Italian restaurants, all issuing the smells of wholesome meals. Yet he never gives any thought to what he is missing. Those places are beyond the range of his pocket, out of reach, out of mind. But with Jessie's offer, Patrick suddenly wants a Chinese take-away more than anything he could possibly imagine.

Jessie picks up on his hesitation. 'I'm buying,' she says.

'I'll give it to you next week.'

'What do you want?'

He shrugs. 'Anything. What are you having?'

'I'll get a few different things. We can share.'

She slams the car door and disappears behind the half-painted window of the take-away. While they were in the pub the night air cleared, and a few dim stars are now pene-trating the smoggy aura of the city. Further up the street a group of Bengali boys are leaning against a bus shelter and an elderly man, drunk and wavering, is negotiating the pave-ment towards them. As he draws level he stops and says something. Patrick watches. The sound of passing traffic can be heard through the closed windows of the car but the old man's voice cannot. The boys stare frostily at him for a moment or two, then one of them moves forward and drops a glinting coin into his outstretched hand.

The scene fills Patrick with anxiety, but not because of the confined space of the car or the rough appearance of the boys. More dangerous to him by far is the sudden appearance, as if from nowhere, of kindness in the world. His psychic barriers, which have taken him a lifetime to erect, are beginning to crack. If he allows himself to believe that care and intimacy exist then he will have to admit that he wants them, needs them, is barely surviving without them. He will also have to admit that he has had them in the past and lost them. And if that happens he will be at the mercy of regret.

He buttresses the walls before the cracks can grow any wider. When Jessie returns to the car with yet another plastic carrier, she finds Patrick cold and distant and wonders if she has said something to offend him. Jessie searches her mind for a way of breaking into it, but there seems to be no point of contact. There is a dark silence between them as they drive the few blocks to her house.

'This yours?' he says, as he follows her in through the front door.

'Yes.'

'What, all of it?'

Jessie laughs. 'Yes.' She turns on the fire and puts the food in front of it to keep warm, then goes into the kitchen for the bottle of whiskey and two glasses. Patrick winks at her, and takes it upon himself to pour.

'Want to have a poke around?' says Jessie.

'I'd love to, if you don't mind.'

The house is a fairly basic three up and three down, with a small glass extension built on to the back as a conservatory or potting shed. Patrick wanders through the rooms on the ground floor with his glass in his hand. Jessie's tastes show themselves more clearly in her house than they do in her dress or her choice of car. There is nothing of opulence in the surroundings but there is a certain elegance. The rooms are decorated in colours that are soft but rich, and everywhere there is fabric. All the floors have faded but welcoming rugs. Every chair has a cushion. The sofa and the armchairs are draped with Indian bedspreads or old velvet curtains in warm colours. Patrick sighs, envisaging himself stretched out on the floor in front of the fire, reading one of the books which line at least a wall of each room.

He wanders through the living room and on to the front of the house where Jessie has her office. An Indian batik covers most of one wall, and the others are hung with Japanese prints in simple frames. Closed up on the desk, beside a pile of papers, is something that looks to him like a small, portable sewing machine.

Jessie has come quietly in behind him. 'Grub's up,' she says.

'Right,' says Patrick, 'I'm coming.' He points to the thing on the desk. 'Do you make your own clothes, then?'

Jessie looks puzzled for a moment, then bursts out laughing.

'Where have you been living?'

Patrick smiles but as a defence it is incomplete. He has made a blunder and for an instant Jessie catches a glimpse of his underlying vulnerability. It produces an extraordinary effect in her. She has a barely resistible urge to put her arms around him and hold him tight, make it all all right.

Hera has caught a glimpse of the mortal soul that she's trying to prise free.

But Patrick has closed up again and taken cover behind a stern expression of indifference.

'It's a computer,' says Jessie. 'I suppose it does look a bit like a sewing machine.'

'I haven't seen one like that before, that's all.'

Jessie leads the way back to the living room where she has spread out the meal on the floor in front of the fire. They are both a little awkward as they sit down to eat but Jessie is confident that it'll pass. She has had enough to drink, but she tops up Patrick's glass.

The gods repeat their dramas perpetually, not only in the lives of successive generations, but even within single, mortal lives. Some people seem to make the same mistakes over and over and over again.

Jessie is one of them. If Lydia knew what was happening here she would be tearing out her hair in exasperation. Another Alec. Another John.

Patrick eats carefully, warmed by the whiskey, determined to make the most of the unaccustomed luxury. Jessie is pleased to see that his manners are impeccable, even by her standards.

Patrick's father was not a brawny, bog-blown Connemara man, much as he would have liked to be. He was born in England of second-generation Irish parents, and brought up there. Four years studying English in Balliol college had a strange effect. It rubbed the last of the Irish edges off him, but also turned him into an aspiring poet, besotted by the bucolic mysticism of Tagore and Wordsworth. He was lured back to the west of Ireland by a romantic dream of rustic simplicity, and soon fell prey to the undemanding sympathy of tall black pints and golden chasers. He was often absent, if not physically then mentally, and he left the running of the household and most of the farm as well to Patrick's mother. But when he was there he would quote Yeats bombastically from his place at the head of the table while the family, growing in size and unruliness, picked slugs from their cabbage. He had turned his back on English civilisation and despised convention in any shape or form, but even so his conditioning had left certain indelible marks. His fist on the table sent potato skins flying. 'For God's sake, boy! Do you still not know how to hold your bloody knife?'

The memory is far from Patrick's consciousness, along with all other memories of childhood. But he is looking with interest at his fork. He uses a knife to butter bread and a spoon to eat cereals. Fish and chips he eats with his fingers, straight from the bag. He can't remember the last time he had use for a fork. He isn't even sure that he has one.

'I use it for my work,' says Jessie.

'Hmm?'

'The computer. I used to do typesetting for a couple of small publishers, but these days it's mainly editing.'

'Ah. You work at home, then?'

'Yes, mostly. What about you?'

'Oh, I'm all over London, me. I'm a photographer.'

'Funny, that,' says Jessie. 'I had a feeling you were into something in the artistic line.'

'I'd hardly call it artistic,' says Patrick. 'It's pretty boring stuff, really. Just keeping half the London Irish in touch with what the other half are doing. I do a few things for myself as well, though. Get some more creative shots.'

'Can I see them some time?'

'Yes, when I get round to doing a bit of work on them.'

Jessie hesitates for a minute, then plunges in. 'I do a bit of writing. At least, I'm not doing much at the moment, but it's what I want to do.'

Patrick nods, politely.

'I think it's the most important thing in life,' Jessie goes on, 'to have some sort of creative outlet. It doesn't matter what you say or what you paint or photograph, it's what you bring to it yourself. Do you know what I mean?'

Patrick isn't sure that he does, and his mouth is too full to reply, so he nods again, to be on the safe side.

Jessie has stopped eating and is prodding the food on her plate absently. 'I think that writers and artists, the good ones, that is, the original ones, have found what it is we're all looking for.'

Patrick isn't looking for anything as far as he knows, but his mouth is empty now, so he says: 'And what's that?'

'Authenticity. I think that's what happiness is. The discovery of your own authenticity.'

'Nice word,' says Patrick. But happiness for him is this moment, the meal and the warmth of the fire and the pleasure of a woman who is bothering to try and impress him. And it doesn't last. When they finish eating, he becomes restless. Jessie puts on a Tracy Chapman tape and refills his glass, but he turns to the washing up, despite her protests. He is becoming seriously worried about the time, and the walk ahead of him, and the work. Jessie clears the table, humming along with the tape. As she throws empty cartons into the bin beneath the sink, her shoulder brushes against his. Patrick is also seriously worried about that. He is rapidly getting out of his depth in this situation and is anxious to get out of it. He steps aside to give her more room, not too obviously, but obviously enough.

And she notices the threatened look in his eyes as he explains that he has to go, and why. She masks her disappointment carefully as she accompanies him to the door. They stand together, a little awkwardly, on the front step. The night is fresh and inviting.

'Can I drop you home?'

'No. No thanks. I love walking, actually. Especially at night.'

Jessie decides not to push it. Patrick takes a step towards the street. 'Thanks for the meal. I'll pay you back next week.'

'Don't be ridiculous. My pleasure.'

'No. I'll pay you back.' He walks down the steps. 'Goodnight.'

'Goodnight. Call in if you're passing.'

'I will.'

But he takes no note of the number on the door of the house or its position in the street. He doesn't even notice what street he is in, but walks with the aid of a sort of automatic pilot towards the High Street and across the canal.

Within half a mile, the walking has warmed Patrick up, so that the cool night air is soothing rather than threatening. The streets are quiet; a lot quieter than the ones in King's Cross where many of the citizens are just now starting into their working hours. Patrick looks up towards the sky but it is polluted by the light which rises from the city and the smoke from households which defy the smoke-free zones. He is uncomfortably full and not half drunk enough. It is one of the problems he always has with food. Eating soaks up too much drink, and deadens the effect.

'Damn!' he says to the night.

Patrick can't stand to be in debt. He is unconventional but not unprincipled. There is no doubt in his mind that he will have to come up with that fiver. He mulls over the problem most of the way back to King's Cross, calculating and budgeting and fidgeting with coppers like worry beads in his pocket. He cannot understand how it is that wherever he goes he finds himself, sooner or later, in debt, if not financially, then emotionally or morally. It is almost as though he were jinxed.

Ahead of him a group of young men are straggling along

the street, laughing and shouting. He crosses over to the other side, and as he does so he gets his bearings and remembers a short-cut home. He sighs, straightens his back, and strides out more purposefully.

But behind him, Hera is once again slighted. She has been after this one for years in one way or another. Several times she has had him eating out of her hand but in the end he has always given her the slip.

Jessie suffers for it. The fact that Patrick was unwilling to stay cannot, by any reckoning, be considered her fault, but she is being punished just the same.

The gods are not renowned for their compassion.

Jessie lies awake, despite the heavy meal and the drink, and watches the occasional fan of light which crosses her wall as a car passes. She tells herself that she had no intention of sleeping with Patrick, and that things are working out as well as she would want them to. It is true, but not entirely, and it doesn't dispel the pain of disappointment that lingers and keeps her awake. She replays the evening, again and again until it dissolves into a jumble of conflicting images as she sinks towards sleep.

And dreams that the moon, which lies so distant and cold in the sky, is making love to her.

Chapter Six

And what about those who follow me? Does anyone? Who, in their right mind, follows a mere messenger?

A little more, perhaps, than a mere messenger. I have a number of other duties, too, out there in the ill-defined region of borders. People have always had a certain amount of difficulty in giving me a clear identity, and I have gathered quite a collection of titles over the years.

When I was young, very young in fact, I made a little set of reed pipes and played a tune on them for my brother, Apollo. He was delighted, and offered me the golden staff with which he herded his cattle and the patronage that went with it; god of all herdsmen and shepherds. I told him that it wasn't enough, and that I wanted to learn the art of augury from him as well. He said that he couldn't teach me himself, but he told me where to learn. So I gave him the pipes and he gave me his staff, and I set out for Parnassus where the Thriae live. There, as he had promised, I was taught to tell the future by studying the action of pebbles in a basin of water.

As time went by, I expanded on the theme. First there was divination by knuckle bones and later . . . well, one thing follows another . . .

∞

Patrick, so far, has had a bad day. A very bad day. It was three o clock in the morning before he got back from Jessie's place. The flat above was as dark and silent as his own, and he stood for a full five minutes on the basement steps before he could find the courage to go down there. When he did the work went badly, and not only because he was exhausted. Again and again throughout the night he found Jessie's face drifting into his mind, and images of the meal, and the comfort of her house. At times they were so strong that they seemed to distort the projections from the enlarger and some of the prints turned out badly and had to be done again. Worse than that, when he comes to sort though the photographs in the morning, he realises that he has forgotten to develop one of the most important rolls of film. It is still in his coat pocket.

The *London Irish Weekly* is no longer run on the shoe-string budget that it was when it was first starting up and Patrick came to work for it. It has increased its circulation steadily both in London and abroad, and is picking up more advertising every year. But Brendan Haymes, the editor, sees no reason at all to inform Patrick of the fact. This isn't the first time that Patrick has let him down.

He is understandably annoyed. Patrick and Ray, the reporter he usually works with, had two good evenings out of the events that the forgotten film covers. One was the opening of a series of Irish plays in the King's Head and the other was a gathering of the O'Mahoney clan from all over the world to celebrate a wedding between two distant branches of the family. The theatre article can run as it is, but the O'Mahoney gathering was to take up a half-page spread, most of it pictures of the better known members of the family. Brendan is unlikely to get others, especially at such short notice. He refuses to pay Patrick for work that he hasn't delivered.

As Patrick walks back towards King's Cross, it begins to rain. Women out on the streets put up umbrellas, unfold plastic raincoats, pull up pram hoods over their sleeping infants. Patrick falls into a furious rage. The bitch will have to do without her fiver. She can afford it after all, with her car and her fancy house and her bloody computer. He should have known better than to go with her. Amazing that he hadn't more sense, didn't see what was coming. That was a nifty move, stopping off to buy that meal. If it hadn't been for that he'd have been nowhere near her house, nowhere near her and her filthy schemes. It's always the same when men get mixed up with women. Things start to go wrong.

And there's the ghost of Hippolytus, hovering around again.

'Can I really do what I like with it?' says Jessie.

'Go ahead,' says Lydia. '*Carte blanche*.'

'Are you sure? Shouldn't I speak to Frances about it first?'

'No. She won't object.'

'Even when I send her the ashes?'

Lydia laughs. 'She's getting worse, isn't she?'

'Much worse.'

'Just lazy, I expect. Too reliant on you. How are things, anyway?'

'Great. I had Patrick round for dinner last night.'

'Patrick. Wait, don't tell me. He's a Celtic prince from County Fermanagh who followed a ley line right to your door.'

'Wrong. I already told you. I met him at the art class.'

'Did you? Oh, god. What's he like?'

'I don't know, really. Too early to tell.'

'I'll tell you, then. He's a loser. The ones you go for always are. Get rid of him.'

Jessie laughs. 'Shall I tell you about him?'

'No,' says Lydia. 'Not before, not during and not after. I've heard it all before. Never again.'

'I see,' says Jessie. 'Like that, is it? Well, that's one topic of conversation up the spout.'

'Maybe it'll encourage you to keep track of some others, then. This time.'

'Oh, come on, Lydia! I'm not that bad.'

'I hope not,' says Lydia. 'Keep in touch, won't you?'

Jessie sits and looks at the phone for some time after she puts it down. The conversation has irritated her, but what bothers her more is the suspicion that Lydia may be right. Because what is the use in going through it all again? The yearnings, the efforts to make it work, the inevitable disappointment when it doesn't. For a moment she is tired, older than her years, utterly cynical. But there is always hope, there must be. She just needs a bit of help, that's all.

For a few minutes she flips through the thick manuscript, but she is unable to give it her attention. She doodles with the pen on the covering letter, writing her name, writing 'manuscript' and 'buggeritbuggeritbuggerit' in her best handwriting. She could start on a story now, or a poem, something to express her frustration before it turns into despair, but as always, there is a good reason not to. No time, no energy, no point. She puts down the pen and reaches up to the top of the bookshelf where she keeps her pack of Tarot cards wrapped in black silk. She puts them out on to the rug and spends a moment or two lighting candles and incense, before settling down to business.

I am summoned, and I come.

It is a long time since she has consulted the cards. The broad elastic band that encircles them has decayed; it snaps softly as she takes it off. An edge of the silk has been bleached to a blotchy grey by the occasional morning sunbeam which reaches high enough to touch it. She weighs the package in her hand. It is so, so familiar. There was a time, once, when people came to her for readings. At first it was fun, a bit of excitement for herself and her friends, but gradually it began to become more serious. News of her abilities spread, and strangers with unhappy faces started arriving at her door, offering money for readings. Jessie called a halt to it all. She had no desire for that kind of responsibility, and besides, she was never really sure whether she believed in it or not.

She still isn't. None the less, she is filled with a familiar feeling of apprehension as she unwraps the cards. The silk slips through her fingers like an undergarment. Disuse has stuck the cards together, but they free themselves up easily enough as she works them this way and that in her hands. As she shuffles, she takes great care to keep the faces of the cards turned away from her. She has no desire to influence their placement, even unconsciously. To be even more certain, she closes her eyes and, still shuffling, concentrates hard on the issue which is uppermost in her mind.

*

I don't need this solemnity. It bores me, to be honest. I get impatient.

But it makes Jessie feels better about the business. 'Tapping in', she calls it, though into what she has never sought to enquire too closely. Not until the moment feels perfect does she begin to deal the cards; five of them, in a simple cross formation, face up. She puts the rest of the pack aside, drapes the blemished silk across it, and studies her reading.

On the left, the card representing Jessie herself: the Empress. Down the middle are three cards, past, present and future: ten of swords, two of cups and two of swords. On the right, representing Patrick, the Fool. Upside down.

Jessie's heart sinks a little, even before she begins to analyse the cards. She remembers why she gave up reading them for herself. It is easy to be objective about someone else's situation, but not at all easy to be clear-sighted about one's own.

She doesn't like the look of the Fool. She never could make up her mind about reversed cards, whether or not to use the extra, and usually opposite set of meanings that could be assigned to cards that appear upside down in a reading. Sometimes she used them that way and sometimes she didn't. Now, almost without thinking, she reaches out a hand and turns the Fool the right way up. And completely changes his meaning.

I'm gone. Bloody mortals! Why did she ask if she didn't want to know? If she wanted to play it like that, she should have just picked out the ones she wanted.

The candle gutters noisily, as though a door somewhere has opened, or a window. Jessie gets a chilly feeling. She stopped smoking five years ago, but at times like this, she wishes she hadn't. It is a bewildering reading, and not at all what she had been hoping to hear. Her right knee creaks as she gets up off the rug and searches out a book from the higher shelves of the bookcase. *Tarot and the Modern Psyche*. She brings it with her into the kitchen, where she fills the kettle and switches it on. The book is divided into two sections. In the first are the long, Jungian explanations of the archetypal significance of the cards and the different stages of the querent's life journey that each of them represents. In the second, shorter section, are the quick and easy meanings; a sort of shorthand. Jessie justifies her faith in the Tarot, such as it is, on the basis of the first set of interpretations, but when it comes down to analysing a reading, she invariably uses the second.

The Empress: A mature woman, wealthy and fertile. Earth-goddess. Fruitfulness. Satisfaction.

True enough, Jessie supposes. She has everything she needs, and more. The kettle boils. She makes an instant coffee.

The Fool: Freedom from responsibility. One who follows pure intuition. Divine agent. Innocence.

Almost despite herself, Jessie's eye wanders over the next two lines:

Reversed: Irresponsibility. Inebriety. Drunkenness. Delusion. Dementia.

She skips over it, turns to another page. She knows this next one well.

Eight of Swords: A dangerous oppression. Restriction of vital forces by another. A losing battle.

Jessie nods. Of that, at least, there is no question. That was the state of past relationships. She doesn't normally take sugar, but she piles two heaped spoonsfuls into the mug. She needs something comforting.

Two of Cups: A new relationship. Blossoming feelings. A fresh start.

Ten of Swords: Defeat. Humiliation. The end of a long conflict.

Jessie sips the sweet coffee, then turns back the pages and reads it all through again. She would like to pretend that it made no sense. But it does. Both her serious relationships began with blissful harmony and degenerated into irresolvable conflict. In the past she had come to believe that there was no such thing as love, that all sexual relationships were a sort of power struggle which one or other player inevitably lost. But she had forgotten that, and fallen back into the romantic idealism of her younger days. She isn't at all happy at being reminded.

For a while the sweetness of the coffee is comforting, but in the end it becomes too much and Jessie pours it away. She remembers the brief feeling that she had of Patrick being dangerous, and wonders if it is true, if she oughtn't to listen to her instincts and to this reading. The house feels cold, and vague shadows flit about the corners of the rooms. Jessie has a strong desire to leave it.

*

Gregory has a lot in common with Jessie. He is around the same age, craves monogamy, and is still single. He is a tried and trusted friend, but a little more than that. Lydia is a friend, too. Gregory is an ally.

He is alone that evening, and welcomes Jessie with open arms when she arrives on his doorstep. Her heart is already being lifted as she follows him through the hall and up the stairs to his flat.

'Notice anything?' he says, and gestures broadly around the small living room.

Jessie stands at the door and looks around carefully. Gregory goes over to the kitchen area and puts on the kettle. The room is softly lit, softly furnished, living and breathing with dozens of plants. It looks to Jessie exactly as it always has. She racks her brains to spot the difference, but she can't.

'Fraid not,' she says, at last.

'Right,' says Gregory. 'Nothing's changed.'

Jessie laughs, and all her tensions melt away.

'How about you?' Gregory goes on.

'Oh, not much,' says Jessie, but it is with an air of mystery that Gregory knows well.

'Aha,' he says. 'Out with it.'

Jessie smirks and settles herself into a comfortable chair beside the fireplace. 'Well, he's a bit too tall, a bit too dark . . .'

'And absolutely gorgeous,' says Gregory.

'I don't know. That sort of thing is subjective, I suppose.'

'Absolutely gorgeous subjectively, then,' says Gregory. He brings her over a muddy-looking cup of coffee and sits on a bean-bag on the other side of the hearth. 'They always are, the ones you get.'

'I haven't got anything, Gregory. And even if I had, I'm not sure that I'd want it.'

'That sounds serious. Are you sick or something?'

'No. Actually, it's not me so much as the Tarot.'

'What?!' Gregory sprays coffee on to the rug as he bursts out laughing. 'What do you mean, the Tarot? What's the Tarot got to do with anything?'

'Well, it said . . .'

'What?'

'It said that I couldn't win.'

Gregory doubles up with laughter again, and Jessie, suddenly struck by the absurdity of it all, joins him. After a while, Gregory regains temporary control. 'You need a pack of cards to tell you that?' he says. 'Why didn't you come to me?'

They laugh again until they are laughed out, then Gregory says, 'They never last, we both know that. But you can't give up. Never say die. Tell us what happened.'

Jessie sips the coffee. Gregory doesn't buy jars of coffee, he buys drums of it. It is the cheapest on the market and looks and tastes like powdered clay. But it has the effect that Gregory wants. He speeds through his life with a minimum of sleep. He is one of those people who is never bored, always up to something or other. Jessie sometimes wishes she had half his energy.

'We went for a few pints, then picked up a Chinese take-away.'

'Your place or his?'

'Mine.'

'Candles?'

'Come off it, will you? That's a bit too blatant for me.'

'Not for me.'

'I know. That's why you always scare them off.'

'Is it? Why didn't you tell me this before?'

'I did. A hundred times.'

Gregory sighs. 'I suppose you did. Never mind. Go on, anyway.'

'That's all. He's a photographer. We chatted a bit and then he went home.'

Gregory is crestfallen. 'Why?'

'I don't know. He said he had some work to do.'

'Maybe he did.'

'Maybe. I don't know anything about him. He could be spoken for, you know?'

'Maybe he's gay?'

'Don't get your hopes up.'

'Why not? He's no use to you if he is.'

'I suppose not. But I don't think he is. I think he's just cagey.'

Patrick wakes in the early hours of the morning, from a recurring dream in which he is imprisoned in a soundproof bubble, unable to communicate with the outside world and slowly suffocating. Wide-eyed in the pale city darkness he listens to the rustle of rats in the rubbish bags and the distant wail of a siren. He reaches out for the radio beside his bed, but it is already turned on. While he slept, the batteries have gone flat.

The gas fire is on low, and Patrick has a sensation that there is no air in the room. He fumbles around on the floor until he finds matches, then he lights the candle. A lorry passes along the road above, and after it there is the long, low drone of a descending plane.

Patrick pulls on his trousers and brings the candle to the

darkroom, where he plugs in the electric kettle. Then he goes out into the back yard, to breathe the cool air. A single light burns on the top floor of the house, but there is no sound.

A light rain is falling into the yard. Patrick turns sideways onto his back door, to ensure that nothing can come out of the flat and take him from behind. Increasingly, the daily six or seven pints that Patrick can afford are not enough. He has to spread them out, often starting earlier in the day than he would like in order to set himself up for work. He is just getting by.

The few pints he keeps for the evenings are the best. Taken together they relax him, and if the right sort of crowd is in the pub he can even feel quite exuberant. But it doesn't last. On the nights when he can't afford the luxury of a bottle to bring home, he finds himself struggling to keep his back turned against the enemy.

He knows that he will have to get out of this place before it drives him mad. Jessie returns to his mind.

Hera can be devastatingly attractive to men. Who would not love to have their slippers put on, their bath run, their meals brought hot to the table and cleared away afterwards? Who is there who does not, from time to time, long to hand over responsibility for their lives and all their problems to someone who appears to be ready and able to take it all on?

Hera will do all this, and more. She will listen to troubles and give sound advice. She will rub aching muscles, attend at the sickbed, repair damaged pride. And all that she asks, for all that she does, is one small thing in return.

Obedience.

Patrick recoils from Jessie's image. If he does get out it will not be that way. Never again.

Chapter Seven

Dionysus, perhaps because of his half-caste status, has a constant need to prove his divinity and gain recognition both among the other gods and among mortals. The powers that be, whether in the form of the king or the government, seek to repress him and to that end they imprison him. But being sent underground has no effect on Dionysus other than to make him more powerful than ever. He bursts forth, and under his influence his followers turn upon the authority of the state and tear it to shreds. The fact that he has done this successfully in the past makes no difference. He acts, as do all the gods, according to his nature.

As the gods' messenger I have been asked, many times, if there is any way of becoming free of their influence. Given my nature, it isn't easy to offer a straight answer. Various methods have been tried. The Indian yogis, for example, have discovered that if you sit in the same place for long enough and refuse to move, the gods will eventually get bored and go away.

∞

Jessie has tried it, on more than one occasion. She has even done a course in TM, where they charge you £250 for your own personal piece of gibberish which will keep your mind busy while you are refusing to move. Whenever she has done it, Jessie has found meditation beneficial, but in the end she always slides. It takes too much effort, too much willpower and too much time. Besides, she knows of one or two cases of people who have become completely addicted to it.

Patrick, however, is in no danger there. He has never, ever tried meditation. Any form of reflection or contemplation is anathema to him. It is crucial to his survival that he does not stop and think. To this end he keeps himself permanently occupied in one way or another, and when he has nothing else to do and no more money to spend in the pub, he listens to the radio.

The radio is Patrick's companion in life. But this week every few shillings will count, so he forgoes renewing the batteries. It is a tough, tough week. The price of fixer has gone up by half a pint, and the shop he usually deals with has run out of the paper he needs, so he has to get a larger and more expensive size and cut it down. It works out cheaper in the long run, but the long run has never had a place in Patrick's budget.

On Friday evening, he and Ray go to a traditional Irish concert in Clapham. By ten o'clock, Patrick has spent all the money he brought with him and is ready to go home, but Ray has heard about the stray film and insists on lending him twenty quid. By the following morning, what is left of it is jingling in Patrick's pocket, and buys him a couple of pints and a sandwich before the football match he has been sent to cover.

As he is coming home that evening, he runs into Paul, one of the boys who lives above him.

'How's it going, Patrick?'

'Not so bad. And you?'

'Grim. Any chance of a fiver?'

'Sorry. I haven't even got the price of a cup of coffee.'

'Haven't you?' says Paul. 'That's rough. Come up and have one with us, will you?'

Patrick has only once been in their part of the house, and that was when he went in to fix up his electrical connection. At that time Paul wasn't there, nor were any of the boys who now share the house, but its orientation was the same. One by one the lads move on and are replaced by new ones, homeless and stranded in London, glad to meet up with friendly faces and willing, for want of alternative, to join them in their trade.

All the lights in the house are on, even though it isn't yet dark. The stereo is on, too, and in another room, the TV. In front of it a boy that Patrick hasn't met before is sitting cross-legged on the floor wearing nothing except Doc Martens and a pair of underpants. He is carefully decorating his legs with tiger stripes, using a thick, black marker. Behind him one of the grids of the gas fire is leaking, sending up a roaring yellow flame which blackens the wall above it as far as the ceiling.

Paul goes into the kitchen. Patrick stands adrift and looks at the TV, but the noise of the stereo drowns out the words of the actors. The boy turns round, and is a little startled to find that he has company. 'Who are you?' he says.

'Patrick. I live downstairs. And you?'

'Corrie. I like your hat. What you doing here if you live downstairs?'

'Just called in for a cup of coffee. Is that OK?'

'Oh, yeah. I'll put the kettle on.'

He goes to stand up, but Patrick says, 'No, it's all right, Paul's making it.'

'Oh,' says Corrie, 'you with Paul, then?'

'Yes,' says Patrick. 'No. I've just come in for a cup of coffee.'

'So you keep saying,' says Corrie. He holds the marker out to Patrick. 'Will you do my back?'

'We've got no milk,' says Paul, coming in from the kitchen. 'Do you mind Marvel?'

'Bloody Marvel,' says Corrie. 'Rehydrates instantly into eight pints. Special discount packs available for haemophiliacs, guaranteed HIV negative.'

'Shut your face, Corrie,' says Paul. Patrick follows him with some relief as he goes back into the kitchen.

The two pints that Patrick drinks before the life drawing class are his first of the day and his last of the week. It means that he will have to go straight home afterwards, but in many ways that's not a bad thing. He hasn't got the fiver for Jessie, and this will give him a good excuse to avoid her.

But as he comes into the classroom, she spots him and waves. He tries to look away but it's too late, she is already coming across the room towards him. And despite all the resolutions which have accompanied him throughout the week, he is surprised to find that he is delighted to see her.

'How are things?' he says.

'Great. And you?'

Patrick sighs. 'Bound to get better, I suppose.'

'Nothing too bad, I hope,' says Jessie, with a concern that appears genuine to both of them. There is nothing Hera loves better than a man who is all at sea with himself.

'No,' says Patrick. 'Nothing I can't take care of.'

The teacher calls the class to order and the model takes up a pose. Jessie has bought a new charcoal pencil in the hope that it might make her a better artist. For the first few minutes she does a great deal of loose sketching and rubbing, then eventually screws up the paper and starts again. The teacher gives her a dirty look. She, in turn, looks over at Patrick for support but he is, to all intents and purposes, engrossed in his own drawing.

But it's not going well at all. His attention is being pulled again towards Jessie and there is nothing he can do to stop it. He feels like a foolish teenager, aware of Jessie's every movement even when he is looking elsewhere.

And Dionysus is getting angry. He has been, perhaps, a little over-confident about his hold on Patrick, who is clearly wavering. If Hera gets her claws into him, there is a chance, just a chance, that Dionysus will lose him. He shoves Patrick's focus as hard as he can towards the paper in front of him but it isn't working. The drawing makes no sense to him at all. He looks up and meets Jessie's eyes. She behaves in a way that would drive Lydia frantic, and herself, too, if she could gain any degree of objectivity. She doesn't quite flutter her eyelashes but she looks up from beneath them in an engaging manner. Patrick responds with charming smiles and quick, sneaking glances.

The atmosphere between these two is so thick that it is permeating the room. There is no one in the class who is not aware that something very powerful is going on.

At the break, Jessie comes over to look at Patrick's drawings, but he turns them round before she gets there. She tries to turn them back but he resists, stands in her way, and on a sudden impulse, puts his black hat on to her head.

Afterwards he can't imagine why he has done it. Something has gone beyond his control. The model is posing again and he starts to draw, but he is becoming paralysed by conflict.

One of the Zen masters once said, 'When walking, walk. When sitting, sit. Above all, don't wobble.' Patrick is wobbling now, torn between the desire to go along with Jessie in anything and everything she might propose and the opposing desire to flee.

But he draws. And the next time he stands back to look at his work, he turns numb with shock. The body he has drawn is a good representation of the model. But the face belongs to Jessie.

He is suddenly afraid that he is cracking up. As quietly as he can, he rolls up his drawings and slides out of the door without a backward glance.

Women. They ruin everything, and they always have done, right through his life. No matter how hard he tries to steer clear of them, they just can't seem to leave him alone.

As he passes the Red Lion, the door opens and a sweet waft of warm, beer-scented air slips into the street. He almost follows it, is on the point of turning into the doorway and making a fool of himself when he remembers that he's broke. He catches himself in the nick of time.

At the next corner there is a litter bin strapped to a lamp-post. Patrick shoves the roll of drawings into it in rising anger. The twenty-five quid is the worst of it. It has been wasted but it's the last time it'll happen to him. He won't take any more foolish gambles like that. It was just a crazy dream to think that he could ever get going as any kind of an artist. And why the hell should he want to, anyway? He has a perfectly good life, a good job, a comfortable place to live. Above all, he is his own man, a free agent. There is no one to tell him when to come in at night or when to get up in the morning. If he wants to work, he works. If he doesn't, he doesn't. Why sacrifice all that for the sake of some stupid fantasy? London is crawling with mugs who are trying to be artists.

He will never, never again allow himself to be diverted by coincidence. It's dangerous, it leads people into all kinds of illusions and false avenues. He can't understand now how he came to be deluded in that way; so easily, too. He has always believed that a man must remain in command of his own destiny.

Patrick stops abruptly. Normally he keeps his aggressive instincts locked securely away along with the rest of his emotions, but in a sudden rage now he thumps the wall with his fist, bruising the side of his hand quite badly. The bitch, the fucking whore. She has his hat.

He doesn't know how long he has had that hat and he has managed to forget who gave it to him. But it is more a part of his identity than any other thing he owns. He measures out the rest of the street, each step a curse, but there is no way out of this. She will have to keep it. Nothing will induce him to go back.

Jessie has been completely thrown off kilter by Patrick's behaviour. One minute he was flirting like Don Juan and the next he disappeared. She masks her disappointment as well as she can and participates in the rest of the class but she's sure that she looks a fool. She is wearing the guy's hat and he is gone. He didn't even acknowledge her as he left.

She can't take the hat off, either. The floor is dusty, and the chairs are all stacked at the back of the room, too far away to travel unnoticed.

Her drawings, she realises, are atrocious. All she has got out of the classes has been her flirtation with Patrick, and she has already let herself go too far. On the third time of meeting, he has succeeded in knocking her for six, and it's clearly time to get a grip on herself. She brightens and finishes her last drawing with more assertiveness than usual. The teacher notices and nods her approval. When the class is over, Jessie circulates and introduces herself to some of the other members of the group, feeling slightly ashamed that she hasn't done it before now. As she makes her way down to the Red Lion with the others, she stops off to leave her drawings and the hat in the car. It isn't until she is inside the door of the pub that she realises how much she had been hoping that Patrick might have been waiting for her there. But by the time she gets to her second gin and tonic, her spirits are lifting.

Is there any god greater than Dionysus? Imagine a world bereft of his gifts and condemned to eternal sobriety. Who else among the Olympians has the power to soothe all griefs and lift the soul towards joy? To coax tired feet into dance and weary voices into song? To wind down the over-stimulated mind and wind up the listless one?

For an hour and a half, Jessie loses herself in laughter and companionship. When she leaves the pub, she is light-hearted. It is not until she catches sight of the black hat in the passenger seat that she is brought back to Hera's heel with jarring speed.

'Fuck him!' she says. She almost flings the hat out into the street and there are times afterwards when she wishes that she had. But it wouldn't have made any difference. Patrick isn't to blame for what she's going through, even though he might take credit if he knew. The problem that Jessie has is with Hera.

Chapter Eight

Dionysus was, is, will always be on campaign across the world. This time around, he has some new avenues of influence. Vines do not grow in the large modern cities, and nor do mushrooms, but marijuana plants do, and so do small chemical factories and large dealership networks. Dionysus, in all probability, has never been so powerful before. He has taken over the centres of all the major Western cities and, along with his cohorts is marching outwards, through the suburbs and into the rural areas. As well as his old and reliable alcoholic beverages, he is armed with smack, crack, coke, acid and Ecstasy. He looks set to prove once again that he is entitled to his seat among the greatest of the gods. And Hera is furious.

∽

The next day brings a bonus for Patrick. Brendan pays him for this week's work and takes as well the belated theatre and O'Mahoney photos. He also pays for some extra photos he used several months ago that Patrick had forgotten about. It isn't that he has any particular sense of obligation towards Patrick, even though he pays him less than he should. If it was left to him, he'd give Patrick the shove at the first opportunity. But he isn't so keen to lose Ray. And Ray has given him a talking to.

Patrick binges. He calculates the money he needs for the week and brings the rest of it with him to the local. There he spends a rare, uninhibited evening with his squatter neighbours, buying drinks for them and enjoying for a brief interval, the illusion of wealth.

It isn't until the next morning that he remembers the twenty quid he owes Ray. But he has no regrets, not even during the liverish gloom of the following morning. There are easy ways of dealing with liverish gloom. Regret is a different matter.

Jessie, too, gets a surprise this week. The estate agent phones to say that there has been a good offer for her mother's house in Bromley and he advises her to accept. She phones Maxine in Uruguay and they agree to go ahead with the sale.

Jessie has never had much truck with Ploutos, the god of wealth. Her promiscuous days were lived out in squats and cheap rented accommodation in and around the Angel, and most of the people she mixed with had a similar disdain for money. Jessie herself always had a small income from her grant, and later from temping as a typist, but most of her circle of friends were on the dole. It never seemed to matter that there wasn't much money about. If one person didn't have it, another did. There was always just enough.

After she split up with Alec she came into her first inheritance, when her father's widowed and childless sister died. It was enough to put down a deposit on the Camden house and buy a good computer. The work was satisfying and kept her afloat but she never saw it as a means to getting rich. Getting rich is not among her ambitions.

But this news has taken her by surprise. Her share in the price of the house will be enough to make her dream of rural bliss into a reality. At this moment, the thought is a little too terrifying to take on board.

The sale of the house has other consequences as well. The contents have now to be sorted out and disposed of. Maxine is too far away to be of any assistance. Over the phone, she earmarks one or two things that she wants to be kept for her. The rest is up to Jessie.

Before she sets out for the house the following morning, she puts Patrick's hat and her drawing pencils into the car. She has no idea how long it will take her to organise the contents of the house, and she doesn't want to waste time going back to Camden if it gets late. As she drives, she is constantly aware of the presence of the hat on the back seat, and catches herself enjoying, for a moment, a feeling of power, as though possession of the hat in some way gave her possession, or at least part possession, of the man. The feeling excites her, but it also sickens her slightly and gives her a sense of foreboding. She remembers all the swords in the Tarot and wonders if she ought to bow out gracefully before the going gets rough.

By the time she reaches her parents' house she is feeling pessimistic and dispirited. The sight of the padlocked gates and weeds already beginning to push up through the gravel in the driveway do nothing to improve her mood. Jessie has buried her mother and dealt with all the business of closing down her accounts and her life. It was she who cleared out the perishables in the kitchen and had the electricity disconnected but even so, the finality of the closed-up house takes her by surprise. The last of her father's cherished line of spaniels died two years ago but Jessie had somehow never noticed the absence of a dog until now.

She parks the car outside the gates and climbs over the wall, brushing the brown and bedraggled flower heads on the laburnum bush which was the first thing her mother planted when they moved into the house. One of the panes of glass in the back door has a crack that she has never noticed before but there is no evidence that anyone has tried to break in. The door sticks slightly as she pushes it open, already swelling with the cold and damp. The house is not welcoming.

Jessie is surprised at how distressed she becomes as she wanders through the silent rooms. For an hour or two she makes no decisions, just soaks up what remains here of her parents' lives and what remains here of her own. The job before her is not only much bigger and more complex than she had imagined, it is heart-breaking as well. As she sits beside the empty fireplace, wondering where to start, the art class returns to her mind, and Patrick, and his black hat still sitting in her car. For an instant she slides towards the comfort of fantasy, dwelling on the potentials that exist in the situation. Then, abruptly, she collects herself. It has all been an escape; a device to avoid the discomfort of the reality that is here, the finality of death and the necessity of coming to terms with it. She has no artistic ability and no aspirations, either. The only reason she is going to the class tonight is to have the opportunity of meeting Patrick, who is clearly even more neurotic than she is. The cards were right: she has no need for that kind of engagement. If the man wants his hat, he knows where to get it. But it won't be in the life drawing class tonight and nor will she.

Once the decision is made, Jessie feels happier and more

competent than she has in months. She stands up and starts at the beginning, taking all the ornaments down from the mantelpiece. Maxine has asked to keep the pair of globes that stood at each end of it, one of the earth and one of the night sky, so she puts them to one side. There is a little box inlaid with mother-of-pearl that she was always very fond of and she puts that aside, too. The rest – the clock and the Staffordshire figures of shepherds and shepherdesses – can go into the auction. The next time she comes, she will have to bring cardboard boxes.

The work is not painless but most of the decisions are easier than she had expected. She eats the packed lunch she has brought and works through until the light leaves the sky and makes it impossible to do any more.

On her way home, at just about the time that the life drawing class is beginning, Jessie drives past the pub in Islington which Patrick has just entered. By his own standards, he has taken a grip on himself over the past week. For the first time in months he has got ahead with the photographs. There will be nothing for him to do when he gets home except sleep. As he starts into the four pints that he has saved for the evening, he is relaxed, almost happy.

They have forgotten each other. You might think that now our two immortal players might give each other a grudging acknowledgement and call it quits. They have, after all, plenty of other places to express their hostilities. Up and down the country, most countries in fact, they are battling it out in the more usual arenas, the embittered households where fractured families struggle on between bickering recriminations and hefty silences. But no. Hera is not about to let any opportunity pass her by. She has another job for me, and a tough one, this time.

Should I refuse? Tell her to stuff it? Don't be tempted to misunderstand me. I, like the others, act according to my nature. I carry messages. I bring dreams. And I have a few other areas of influence as well. The divine dramas tend, on the whole, to continue along their familiar courses but there is quite often the chance for a nifty gamble. I'm not going to miss out on the chance to make a little ground.

Jessie brings home another take-away, ignoring its uncomfortable connotations, and eats it in the kitchen. The recent distractions have been slowing up her work and, as she clears away the rubbish, she sets herself the target of finishing the three chapters that she still hasn't done in the first half of the Frances Bailey book. It will be a late night but the second part of the book won't need so much revision and she will be able to sleep with an easy mind.

But Jessie is besieged, abruptly and without any warning, by a poem. Not one that she has heard or read but a new one, one of her own which demands to be written.

Although Jessie can find no time for serious writing in her life she does manage the occasional poem. She has a slim, tidy folder in the locked drawer of her desk where her small collection is kept. No one but herself has ever seen it.

It is probably just as well. The poems are not good. The content is genuine enough but Jessie's style is derivative and stale. She does have a voice of her own, fresh and strong, but she hasn't yet found it. She is, however, one of the few people left in the world who still buys books of poetry. What's more, she reads them.

*

Patrick neither buys nor reads poetry. He despises it. He believes that his hatred of poetry stems from his father's didactic force-feeding during his childhood, but that's not the real reason. Patrick hates bad poetry because it is pretentious and boring. He avoids good poetry because it has the power to shatter his defences and blow his garrisoned heart wide open.

The only other thing that can do that to him is music. He avoids that as well, keeping his radio tuned to the talk channels, but there are still times, occasionally, when he is caught off guard. Recently, in the local supermarket, a piece of well-performed Brahms somehow infiltrated the muzak system and crept up on Patrick in the dairy department. He was looking at the price of cheese when a wonderful, melancholy phrase burst in upon him, injected sweet agony into his cerebral fluid and paralysed him with tears. For a few moments he struggled manfully, trying to make sense of the orange block in his hand. Then he put it down, left his basket where it stood on the floor, and beat a hasty retreat to the nearest pub.

I must assume at least part of the blame, or the credit, for Patrick's discomfort. It was I, after all, who invented the first musical instrument. It was a lyre made from the shell of a tortoise and strung with cow-gut. Apollo was so enchanted by the sound it made that he forgave me my transgressions. He kept the lyre and I was allowed to keep the cattle that, as the first act of my infant existence, I had stolen from him.

Outside Patrick's flat, a group of young men are leaning against the railings. They are not full-time thieves, muggers or confidence men. They are not full-time anything. They are young opportunists, always short of a few bob, and often fed up. Loud music blares from the rest of the house. One of the rent boys has found a sugar daddy, and they have invited Dionysus to help them with the celebrations.

The young men look up at the lighted windows and down into the basement. It is very far from being the kind of place that would attract the attention of thieves. For that reason, Patrick has no worries about leaving the flat unattended, with everything that he owns inside.

But one of these lads has a hunch.

A sort of inspiration.

Jessie is restless. She chews on her pen and wanders around in creative excitement. The poem is taking shape but she is not yet ready to start writing. So she moves from room to room, finding little tasks to occupy her hands while her mind works. She waters the plants and empties the waste-paper baskets. She clears the draining board and scrubs tannin stains out of the sink. All the while, the bones of the poem are gathering flesh.

Back in the office, still not quite ready, she finds herself at a standstill, gazing at the curtains. They are absolutely filthy. Still mentally working, she takes them down and brings them into the kitchen. As soon as she has turned on the washing machine she finds the opening line. Back in her study, beside the naked window, the poem begins to meet the page. Within minutes Jessie is totally absorbed and loses all track of time.

Patrick leaves the pub at closing time and parts company with the young couple that he met there and spent the evening with. As he walks back across town, a fine drizzle is falling which reminds him of soft days in the west of Ireland. He has had no word of his father since his mother died eight years ago. He has made absolutely sure that he will not get it, either. There is not one among his four brothers and sisters who knows where he is. He never misses them, seldom even thinks about them. But there are times when he misses the gentle landscapes of his youth, where none of the edges are sharp.

He can hear the boys' stereo from the end of the street. Despite its volume he has never minded it. He prefers it to the silence, and the sensation of being alone in the house.

Half-way down the steps to the basement, Patrick stops. His door is standing open. Absurdly, he looks at the key in his hand, as though its presence there might prove that he is imagining things, and that his door is safely locked, the way he left it. Inside the flat, in the shadows beyond the light cast from the lamp-post behind him, a white plastic bag moves in the breeze. Patrick's knees go weak. He is struck by the hideous impression that the bag is being moved by the breath of some monstrous beast which is waiting in there amid the wreckage of his life.

He backs up the steps and looks around at the empty street, then up at the brightly lit window above. There is nowhere else for him to go.

It is Paul who answers the door, but it's a moment before Patrick recognises him. He has whitened his hair with peroxide and gelled it into spikes with black tips. And he's wearing a tank-top that is so short it might almost be a bra.

'Patrick,' he says. 'Are you coming in?'

'No, thanks. Someone has broken into my flat. I was wondering if you heard anything.'

'Are you kidding?'

Corrie appears behind Paul. 'Whassup?'

'Some bastard's done Patrick's flat.'

'They take anything?'

'I don't know,' says Patrick. 'It's too dark. I'm afraid they might still be in there.'

'Want us to come with you?'

The fear of what lies below has made Patrick vulnerable. His heart is threatened by their solidarity. As far as he can see he has done nothing to deserve it. He has always thought of the boys as being deficient in some way, as pansies, male bimbos. He takes a deep, protective breath. 'Have you got a torch?' he says.

Corrie calls over his shoulder, 'Leo?'

A third face appears in the hall, another new one to Patrick. The boy is probably around the same age as the other two, but while their eyes are guarded and wise, his are young and full of expectancy.

'Yeah?'

'You got a torch?'

'I got a candle.'

Patrick shudders at the idea of creeping into the darkness below with a candle, a dim flame, creating more shadows than it can cure. 'No,' he says, 'we need a torch.'

'Ask a copper,' says Leo and disappears back into the music.

'We could make one,' says Corrie.

'What with?'

'Rags. Petrol.'

'God, no,' says Patrick. 'You'd set the whole place on fire.'

'So what?' says Corrie. Paul laughs. Patrick is abruptly alone again and afraid. He can see by the size of their pupils that the boys are high. How does he know that it wasn't they that broke into his room?

Paul puts a gentle hand on his shoulder. 'Come on,' he says, and leads the way down the front steps and towards the basement. Corrie follows, Patrick behind him, breathless with fear. At the door, Paul lights his Zippo. He holds it above his head like an Olympic flame as he treads softly into the flat. In the middle of the living room he stops and waits for Patrick to come forward. The thieves have found his alcoves. Everything they didn't want has been scattered around the floor. Books, clothes, crockery, and a pile of unsaleable photographs have been thrown out and trampled, all mixed up with the prints that had been left out to dry for tomorrow. And something else has been strewn around, too.

'My god,' says Corrie. 'Look at all the bottles. You're a bit of a dipso, aren't you?'

'Could be the branch,' says Paul. 'Sometimes they just want to know who you are and what you're up to. Looking for bombs and incriminating letters.'

It gives Patrick a moment of hope. Paul gives him light as he searches the alcoves and sorts through the mess on the floor. But there's no doubt about it. The radio is gone, and so are his two cameras.

He moves into the other room with Paul just behind him, still lighting his way.

'It's like the tomb of Tutankhamun, this place,' says Corrie.

Patrick whirls on him. 'Jesus! Everything I own is gone and you're laughing!'

Corrie giggles. Paul shushes him. There is a strong smell of chemicals. The developing trays are still sitting in a line on the worktop but the boxes of paper have been opened and dumped on the floor, exposed now and useless. They have taken the enlarger, the timer, and the two tanks for developing films.

Patrick stands motionless, too stunned to think.

'Is it bad?' says Paul.

Patrick nods. 'The ridiculous thing is that the stuff is practically worthless, you know? To anyone else, that is. They won't get anything for it second hand. But I'm . . .'

'You're what?' says Paul. 'Washed up? Finished? No, you're not. No one's ever finished till they're dead.'

Patrick notices that the safelight is still there, still intact. He switches it on and it works. Paul closes the Zippo. 'Come and have a cup of tea,' he says. 'Might even find you a snort if you're lucky.'

The tea is tempting, and so is the snort. But Patrick is afraid. He's afraid of everything just now, including Paul's kindness and his tendency to stand too close. The truth is that Paul has no interest in Patrick other than a comradely sympathy. He has no interest in men at all, except for the ones who pay. Given the choice, he might as well prove to be straight as gay but he doesn't know. He got into the game before he was old enough to find out, and his sexuality has been firmly harnessed to it ever since. It is the stock of his trade, the product he sells, that's all.

'I think I'll maybe try and tidy up a bit,' says Patrick. 'Thanks all the same.'

But as soon as Paul and Corrie are gone, Patrick knows that he can't stay. The demon is still there, despite the red light, leering at him from the damp air, mocking his destitution. It is driving him on again.

Chapter Nine

When Apollo and I had finished with our various deals, he brought me to Mount Olympus to meet my father. When Zeus heard all that had happened, he warned me that I must respect the rights of property and refrain from telling lies. I charmed him, though, despite himself.

'You seem to be a very ingenious, little god,' he said.

'Then make me your herald, father,' I said, 'and I will never tell lies, though I can't promise always to tell the whole truth.'

Zeus agreed, and gave me a herald's staff with white ribbons and a pair of golden sandals with wings, which enabled me to move at great speed between the worlds.

His brother, Hades, also appointed me his herald, to summon the dying and to escort their souls to meet him, in the underworld.

∽

Jessie has come to the end of the poem and is well pleased. She opens the top drawer of her desk and slides the two pages into the folder along with the other poems. Tomorrow she will look at it again before she makes her final revisions and types it.

Despite the fervent energy which produced it, it is not a good poem. It is a maudlin and overstuffed account of the nostalgic memories which came to her while she was sorting through her parents' possessions. In years to come the poem will embarrass her, but just now she is satisfied and pleasantly tired. It comes as a shock, therefore, when she realises that she has still to do the work on the Bailey book. She swears and enters into a debate with herself in the kitchen as she waits for the kettle to boil. It's not imperative that she finish the work tonight, but she has promised herself that she will. So she puts away the cocoa and reaches for the coffee instead.

It's going to be a long night.

Patrick is walking blindly, aimlessly, through the rain-drenched streets of King's Cross. In the end, he left the flat hurriedly. Beneath the boys' continuing party the door is still wide open.

There was nothing, not a single thing that he wanted to bring with him. Not a snapshot, not a book with a fond inscription, not even a pebble from some well-remembered beach to put substance into his empty pocket. Let them have it all, the bastards, whatever is left.

There are friends in the area, people he drinks with and has even gone home with on occasion, to share a bottle or a couple of joints. But for the last few years he has not been inclined to drop in on people for coffee or to share his meals or theirs. The area has a high turnover. Squatters come and go. As he walks towards the station, Patrick can think of several welcoming faces. There are people he could stay with, who might even lend him money and help him get back on his feet again. But he knows them only from the pubs, and the pubs are all closed. He doesn't know where any of them live.

Dionysus is furious. What is happening here has nothing to do with him and he doesn't like it at all. He is on the alert, suspicious, and very, very dangerous.

Patrick is walking because there is nothing left for him to do. If he has a destination in mind it is a vague one and lies somewhere beneath the silence of deep, dark water.

I must guide his footsteps carefully now and make no mistakes. And not purely for the sake of the errand I am on. Hera wants him safely delivered, it's true. But so do I.

There are those who are aware, from time to time, of the barely perceptible presence of my guidance. Patrick isn't one of them. He hears, but he doesn't listen. He has no awareness of the fact that he is crossing busy roads without looking and walking through dangerous streets without harm.

What he sees are the small, everyday wounds of the inner city, blown by his fearful mind into unspeakable horrors. With visions like these, who needs hallucinations? The bag lady, bending forward, toppling into a vacant doorway. Two prostitutes, eyeing him with contempt as he passes. A small patch of fresh blood on the pavement, widening in the rain. An ageing drunk, unshaven and ragged, sleeping it off beneath the fading pornography outside the derelict cinema.

'My god,' says Corrie, 'look at all the bottles.'

Patrick gets out of it, cuts across the King's Cross Road in front of the station and takes the dark street which leads up past the old gasworks and towards Camden Town. He walks quickly, away from the increasing pressure behind him.

'You're a bit of a dipso, aren't you?'

He walks so fast that the wet flagstones blur beneath his feet but he counts them anyway. It saves him from having to count the friends and lovers he has lost, the noses he has broken, the years in King's Cross, the bottles.

Old Hera has really nobbled this one. Poor sod. There is strong pressure on me to throw the wretched soul under a passing car and put him out of his misery, but on this occasion I resist it. Even though Patrick mightn't agree himself, Paul was right. He isn't finished yet.

But it takes longer than you'd expect for him to get from King's Cross to Jessie's house. There are a few trouble spots that I have to be sure he avoids. Like the massive drugs raid that is going on in a block of flats which lies directly across his route. If Patrick walked into a street full of cops in his present condition, he would certainly panic and draw attention to himself. And there's the juggernaut that took an ill-advised short-cut and mangled a car and its occupants. Patrick has photographed that kind of thing in the past but if he came across it now it would put a premature end to whatever sanity remains to him. And then there's another, even more dangerous obstacle. To get him across this one will take a bit of time. I put him into a holding pattern while I get that organised. It's no problem. He has no awareness that he passes the same shops and doorways three times.

'How's it going?'

'What?' says Patrick, given the go-ahead now, back on course.

'Nice evening.'

'I suppose it is.'

The man beside him is a stranger as far as Patrick is concerned, but he says, 'Didn't I meet you a week or two ago in the Goat?'

'It's possible.'

Anything is possible.

'Joe Mooney,' the man continues, 'and you are . . .?'

'Tired,' says Patrick, 'and on my way to bed.'

'Good for you,' says Joe. 'Smoke?'

Patrick hesitates, but accepts. Joe hands him his lighter. It is a seventy-five-quid job but the effect is lost on Patrick, who lights his cigarette without looking at it.

'One of those days, eh?' Joe goes on.

'Yes, I suppose you could say that.'

'Me too. Do you ever look at the horses?'

'Which horses would they be?'

'The horses,' says Joe. 'You know, the horses.'

'No,' says Patrick. He has never had the slightest interest in horses of any kind. His father never kept them, and his only association with them is plump ladies riding through Hyde Park.

'That's how I make my living,' says Joe.

Patrick looks at him sideways. However he makes his living, he seems to be doing well enough.

'I have contacts in the game, you see,' he says. 'You can't beat the system without that. Ever hear of a horse called Coldstream?'

'No,' says Patrick. He is beginning to get irritated with this man. He doesn't remember what he was thinking about before he came along but whatever it was is trying to reclaim his attention.

'He's the best 'chaser alive today,' says Joe. 'Jenny Pitman trains him. Did you ever hear of Lunar Music?'

Patrick sighs. 'No,' he says.

'He's the second-best 'chaser alive,' says Joe, 'and he's set to run against Coldstream the day after tomorrow at Hereford.'

'Is that right?'

'That's what everyone is thinking, anyway. But I have it from my cousin who works in Jenny Pitman's yard that Coldstream has a bit of heat in a hind leg. There's no way she'll run him.'

Dionysus is tugging hard at Patrick's mind. He has something to tell him. Patrick has a feeling that there's something he wants to remember and he wishes this stupid little man would go away and take his horses with him. He says nothing.

But Joe continues. 'So, the story is that he'll more than likely be pulled out of the race before tomorrow's declaration. But no one knows that yet. So there's still pretty good odds on Lunar Music, you see?'

Patrick is looking at Joe now with suspicion but Joe reads the expression as one of interest. 'So the trick is,' he says, 'to get in to the bookie's before they get the news that the horse is being withdrawn. But I've got a little problem.'

'What is your little problem?' says Patrick.

'My bank is across the other side of town. I'll never get there in time. So I have to find a way to get some cash together at short notice.'

Patrick stops and Joe stops too. He realises that he has picked the wrong man this time. It's a rare mistake. He can normally tell them a mile off. But the look of raw violence in this fellow's eyes is something he has never encountered before.

'All right,' he says. 'It's all right. I just thought you might have liked a bit of the action. I'll get a loan off my dad, that's all. There's no need to get upset about it.'

He backs off to a safe distance, then turns and walks back the way they have come. Patrick watches for a few moments, then goes on. It would take a better man than Joe Mooney to make a fool out of him.

So he thinks. It was tricky, but it worked. Patrick has been guided so perfectly over the canal that he doesn't even know he has crossed it. The rest should be plain sailing.

Jessie is so tired that the words are beginning to slide around the page in front of her. Full stops and commas are barely distinguishable from each other. She has a suspicion that she may not be doing a great job, but an innate stubbornness will not allow her to give in.

Patrick has no idea where he's going or why. His mind is racing in panic-stricken circles, trying to make sense of itself. He is soaked to the skin, but not cold at all. In fact, the only thing he can take any comfort in is being soaked to the skin. He hasn't been as uncompromisingly wet as this since he was a child.

In Ireland. He stops and looks around him, struck with the dazzling certainty that if he ceased to believe in all this brick and concrete it would dissolve. The hard edges would soften, and give way to the meadows and drumlins that have to be there underneath. But instead he sees, in an unlikely, office-bright light being cast from a downstairs window, his hat in the back of a car.

Patrick is overwhelmed by relief. It makes sense of everything. No wonder he was walking. What else would he be doing but looking for his hat? It is the one thing in the world that he loves.

There is only one problem. The door of the car is locked.

Jessie catches a movement out of the corner of her eye and looks out to see a shadowy figure trying to break into her car. She goes into the hall, switches on the outside light and opens the front door.

The man doesn't seem to have noticed. He is trying to open the back door now.

'Oy!' says Jessie.

Patrick swings round, startled, and throws up a hand to shield his eyes from the bright light that shines out from behind her.

'Patrick!'

He cannot remember her name.

But I can.

'Jessie.'

'What on earth are you doing?'

He gestures to the car. 'My hat.'

'But why didn't you knock?'

Now he has a new certainty about why he is here. There is nowhere else in the world that he could possibly be. Like a chastised child, full of contrition, he walks up the short flight of steps. He is cold, now, and hungry, and very, very wet.

'Sorry,' he says.

As Jessie closes the door behind them, a twist in the wind blows rain into her face.

It is, perhaps, the disgust of Dionysus as he watches Patrick disappear into the house of the enemy. But he can afford to give Patrick some rein, as much rein as he likes, in fact. He has plenty of other fish to fry while he waits to see what will happen.

Patrick sinks into an armchair, soaking Jessie's velvet jacket which is lying across it. Now that she has her wanderer blown in from the storm, she's not sure that she wants him.

He leans back in the chair and gazes at the ceiling. He is psychologically limp, defeated, exhausted. He doesn't even want a drink. All he knows is that for the moment at least, he is safe.

Jessie watches him. Even like that, soaking wet and gaping at the ceiling, he is well worth looking at. The feeling spurs her into action. She lights the fire, puts on the kettle, then goes upstairs to get towels and something for him to change into. She moves quickly, but not too quickly. She hasn't lost sight of her dignity.

Dignity is one of the qualities that are part of mortal inheritance. Honesty and integrity are among the others. There aren't very many, though. Most of the properties that mortals take pride in do not belong to themselves at all. They belong to the gods.

Jessie believes, despite her setbacks, that she has the ability to attract the attention of men and the power to make them desire her. And men do desire her. She has taken good care of herself. She also has an underlying kindness, so that men do not generally feel threatened by her. She is a listener to male woes and a flatterer of male egos. But these various qualities are not hers. They are lent to her by Hera and by Aphrodite, and they can withdraw their loans whenever they want to. If it comes to the crunch, Jessie will find that she has no bargaining power whatsoever.

She checks her face in the bathroom mirror as she's getting out the towels. She is a bit dishevelled from her hours in front of the desk but the new excitement is showing. Her eyes are bright and her colour is good. All perfectly satisfactory.

But Patrick, she soon realises, is not in any condition to notice. When she offers him a towel he just leans forward and holds it over his face until she takes it away from him and dries his hair with it. She has managed to find a tracksuit bottom, a collarless shirt and a baggy sweater which will fit him, but she practically has to shake him before he gets the idea and changes into them. He does it in front of the fire, shameless as a child, while Jessie occupies herself carefully with the tea.

When she comes back he is wearing her clothes and sitting down again on the wet velvet jacket. She rescues it this time, but it is unlikely that it will ever recover.

The first sacrifice.

Patrick leans back in the chair while Jessie takes his wet clothes and leaves them on the floor in front of the washing machine. Then she pours out the tea.

Rain rattles the window at Patrick's back. Outside this house there is a storm and he has been in it for years without ever knowing. Jessie hands him tea, offers sugar, sits down with her own in the chair opposite. He stares at the mug in between his knees. It is warming his hands.

After a while Jessie gets up and kneels on the floor beside

him. She puts a light hand on his shoulderblade and rubs, gently. 'Maybe you'd better tell me what's happening?'

Patrick nods but finds that he can't. He doesn't know. His walls are becoming fractured.

The kindness of women.

Something gives within. In a gesture that feels like a long overdue surrender, he drops his head on to her shoulder.

Chapter Ten

Dionysus does not take kindly to opposition in any form. The first time he wandered across the world, consumed by madness, determined to prove his divinity, he was resisted by the King of Damascus, on the banks of the Euphrates. Dionysus flayed him alive and continued on his way.

∞

Jessie decides to keep some of the nicer pieces of furniture from her mother's house just in case she ever does get that cottage in Wales. The idea has been ticking over gently in the back of her mind, but she approaches it carefully. It is still fearful enough, and capable of scaring her off. It has, however, occurred to her that she will be able to do her editing work almost as well from Wales as from Camden. And with the distractions of city life removed, she couldn't fail to find time for her own writing. Now that the house is sold, there is nothing bar the technicalities to get in her way. All she needs is courage.

Gregory has got the use of a lock-up garage that belongs to

a friend of his in Highgate and has arranged to take the day off work to help Jessie with the furniture. She picks him up at his house at 9.30, and they set off for the U-Haul depot to collect a van.

'Guess what the wind blew in last night?' says Jessie.

Gregory fastens his seat belt and settles down to enjoy the drive. 'What?'

'Guess.'

He doesn't need to. It is written all over her face. 'Not that fellow with the hat?'

'Without the hat, actually,' says Jessie, 'but the same fellow.'

Gregory punches the ceiling of the car. 'Zowee!'

It is still raining, but not so heavily as it was. Jessie turns the wipers down to intermittent. 'Not quite,' she says.

'No?'

'No. 'Fraid not.'

'Oh dear.'

'Oh dear is a bit closer to the mark.'

'Oh dear, oh dear.'

There are signs of a major tail-back ahead. Jessie makes a quick decision and takes evasive action. She swings into a side street and accelerates away between lines of parked cars. 'He spent half the night telling me his sorrows.'

'And the other half?'

'Sleeping, I hope. I put him to bed.'

Gregory lights a cigarette and Jessie opens the window a couple of inches. 'He's obviously in some sort of awful mess,' she says. 'I'm not sure I'm quite happy about leaving him with the run of the house. What do you think?'

'I don't know,' says Gregory, 'I haven't met him. But it doesn't sound too bad to me. Did he cry?'

'No. Why?'

'I was just wondering. I like it when they cry.'

'Gregory!'

'Sorry,' says Gregory. But as Jessie pulls the car up at a traffic light, they exchange a conspiratorial wink.

They take their time with the furniture. By midday they have loaded most of what Jessie wants into the van, but now she is facing some difficult decisions. It was easy enough the first time round to put aside the bits and pieces that she was sure she had no use for, but there are borderline things now, things she doesn't really know whether she likes or not, and things she doesn't like but which have sentimental value. Jessie wanders indecisively around for a while, picking things up and putting them down again, then she sits down in an armchair beside the empty hearth in the drawing-room.

'I need a break,' she says.

Gregory is examining a Chinese watercolour which lies on top of a pile of pictures in the middle of the room. 'You ought to keep this,' he says. 'It's lovely.'

'Do you want it?'

'No. I don't want anything. But you should keep it.'

'I don't know what to keep at this stage. I'd like to keep everything. It's getting ridiculous. I can't think straight at all. I keep wondering what Patrick is up to.'

'Not jealous already?'

'Don't be glib, Gregory. I hardly know this guy. He could be suicidal, you know? Or crazy. He could be burning the place down right now. He could be loading all my stuff into a van.'

'That would be ironic, wouldn't it? Some con trick, too.'

'You're not taking this seriously at all, are you?'

'Sorry. But what can we do? Do you want to go back and check on him?'

'What? Right back into London and out again? In the van?'

Gregory shrugs. 'Phone him, then.'

Jessie brightens. 'Why didn't I think of that?' she says.

The phone in the house has been disconnected, and they walk half a mile towards the centre of Bromley before they find a public one. Jessie sorts out change and goes in. Gregory squeezes in beside her. 'It's raining,' he says.

Patrick sits bolt upright in bed, his head full of vague and disturbing images. He has no idea where he is.

The bell is strident and alarming. A siren which wakes him from a dream of sirens. He jumps out of bed and finds that he is wearing clothes he doesn't recognise. It is a moment of profound terror.

But the bell, he comes to understand, is a phone and demands an answer. As he searches through the house for the handset, he dimly remembers the surroundings.

'He must have gone,' says Jessie. She is haunted by an image of the house, empty and ransacked, its front door standing open.

'Maybe he's asleep?' says Gregory, just as the line opens.

'Hello?'

'Hello, Patrick.'

'Who's that?'

'It's Jessie! How many other people have your number?'

There is a silence on the other end. Gregory's ear is pressed against Jessie's. He frowns and raises one eyebrow.

'Patrick?'

'Yes. Sorry. I've only just woken up. I'm just getting my bearings.'

'Are you all right?'

'Yes. Yes, I'm fine.'

'I shouldn't have woken you. Sorry about that.'

'No, it's all right. I should have been up.'

'You probably needed the sleep.'

'What time is it, anyway?'

'Quarter past one. I just phoned to see what your plans are.'

There is another silence.

'It doesn't make any difference to me,' says Jessie. 'But I was just going to do some shopping. If you're staying, I'll count you in for dinner.'

At the other end of the line, Patrick is engaged in a struggle. This is what women do. This is what they always do, right from the start. They organise you, regiment you, tie you down.

Jessie herself is a little surprised by her white lie. She hadn't intended it. It slipped out, somehow. Despite her resolution that she never would, she is already beginning to make the same mistakes all over again.

'I'm not sure, yet,' says Patrick. 'I'm not really awake.'

'It doesn't matter. I can play it by ear. But you're welcome to stay if you want to.'

'Thanks. I suppose I will, then, probably.'

Gregory winks. Jessie winks back and goes on: 'It's just that if you do go out, you won't be able to get back in. I don't have a spare key in the house.'

'Right. I don't suppose I'll need to go out.'

'As long as you wouldn't go out and leave the door open or anything like that.'

'No, I wouldn't do that. Of course not.'

'OK. I suppose I'll be back around five, then. Somewhere around then.'

'Great.' Patrick's voice is more assured. 'See you, then.'

'See you.'

Patrick puts down the phone. For the moment at least, it seems as though he is in if he wants to be.

And as he wanders round the empty house, he knows that he does want to be. Whatever the cost, he doesn't want to be out on his own again. Not for a while.

'What do you think?' says Jessie, as she and Gregory walk further into Bromley to find a place for lunch.

'He doesn't sound very Irish. Are you sure he's Irish?'

'Certain.'

'He sounds dishy, though.'

'We've established that he's dishy, Greg. But is he *compos mentis*?'

'No one's *compos mentis* when they get woken by the phone. But he sounded much better towards the end.'

'He did, didn't he?'

'Yes. But I'd say that you'd want to tread carefully, you know?'

'Why?'

'Well, you said it yourself the other night. He's definitely cagey.'

Patrick's shoes have been stuffed with newspaper and left in front of the fire to dry out. His coat is on a hanger in the kitchen and the rest of his clothes are waiting to be taken out of the washing machine.

There is muesli and milk on the kitchen table, bread beside the toaster, tea and coffee beside the electric kettle. On top of the kettle is a note, repeating what Jessie had said on the phone about not leaving the door open. He stares at the note for a moment, then screws it up angrily and throws it into the bin.

The only thing wrong with breakfast is the muesli. Hamster food. It gives him stomach cramps. He searches the cupboards for cornflakes instead, and in the one above the fridge he encounters the bottle of whiskey. It is half empty, half full. Patrick stands and looks at it for a long time. Wobbling.

'My god,' says Corrie. 'My god.'

'Cornflakes,' says Patrick, closing the door and trying the next.

It is six o'clock before Jessie pulls up the car outside Gregory's door. The rain has stopped.

'You're very mean, you know,' he says.

'Why?'

'Well, if anyone deserves dinner, it's me.'

'Oh, come on,' says Jessie. 'You know how it is!'

'Course I do,' he says. 'I'm just envious, that's all.'

'You're more optimistic than I am, then.'

'Of course. I always am.' He leans across and gives her a kiss on the cheek, then gets out of the car. The Chinese watercolour is under his arm.

'Thanks for your help,' says Jessie.

'You're welcome. And have a ball, you hear?'

'I'll try.'

'But don't forget the rest of us, will you?'

'I won't,' says Jessie. But Gregory is out of her mind before she reaches the end of the street.

The house has an air of emptiness as she hangs up her jacket in the hall. As she crosses the living room the only sound is the rustle of the plastic bags full of groceries that she is carrying. Patrick's shoes are gone.

The kitchen is spotless, everything put away. On the airing cupboard door, the hanger which held Patrick's coat is empty. So is the washing machine.

'Shit!'

She turns to put the bags on the table and, through the window behind it, she sees all Patrick's clothes hanging on the line. He is beyond them, kneeling on the ground between the tiny, overgrown lawn and the jungly flowerbeds.

Jessie remembers her dignity and walks, doesn't run, out to meet him. He stands up, trowel in hand, all smiles.

'Hi,' he says. 'Good day?'

'Yes. Quite successful on the whole.'

'I was just straightening up these things.' He points to the terracotta tiles which border the flowerbeds. They have been askew since before Jessie moved into the house. He has already done one whole side of the garden and half of another. 'I started to do some weeding, but I wasn't really sure what are weeds and what aren't.'

Jessie laughs. 'I'm not, either.'

'I just came out to hang up my clothes. It's really beautiful out here.'

He has had a wonderful afternoon. All his life he has hated gardens. Too many of his boyhood days were spent in back-breaking labour, bent over the family vegetable patch. But something has happened to Patrick. He has closed the door of the drinks cupboard.

And he is up for grabs, floating free for a while and fair game for any of the gods. Demeter, goddess of the earth, ancient and solid and fragrant, has got to him first.

'Do you know that you've got potatoes?' says Patrick.

'What?' Potatoes is one thing that Jessie hasn't got and has forgotten to buy.

'Look.' He leads her over into the furthest corner of the garden. The ground still rises there slightly where she once, ill-advisedly, built a compost heap. It is more than two years since she abandoned it because it brought rats. Since then she has done nothing in the garden, dreading what she might find if she started poking around in the undergrowth.

Patrick points out three or four wilted stems which stand among the sparse nettles and docks. Jessie has seen fields of potatoes growing with lush, green foliage. She wonders briefly if Patrick is quite safe.

But the soil around one of the stems has already been loosened. He pushes it aside to reveal a cluster of small but perfect potatoes, brown eggs in a black nest.

'How did they get there?' says Jessie, bending down beside him.

'Did you never grow them?'

'No. Never.'

He handles the potatoes gently, shaking the last of the soil away. 'You must have thrown out some old ones then. These guys are volunteers. They can keep going for years sometimes.'

'How do you know all this?'

'My dad used to grow a few vegetables.' Patrick pauses, then goes on. 'Actually, my mother did, mainly. I used to help a bit.' He begins to gather the potatoes. 'Shall I cook some?'

'Are they all right, do you think?'

'Yes, of course. What could be wrong with them?'

'I don't know.'

'They should be eaten soon, anyway. Before the frost gets them.'

There are nine potatoes under the stem but three of them are no bigger than marbles. They bring them all, anyway, and drop them into the sink.

'What shall I do to go with them?'

'Are you serious?' says Jessie. 'Are you really going to cook?'

'Can I? Would you mind?'

'No. I'd be delighted.' Together they unpack the shopping. There is hake, broccoli, salad, a crusty stick of French bread and a bottle of wine.

'Shall I open it?' says Jessie.

'No,' says Patrick. 'Not for me, anyway.'

It is not the first time that Patrick has come off the drink. He has done it before for a week, for a month, for three months at a time. Since he was never sufficiently introspective to differentiate between the usual state of liverish irritation and the less usual state of withdrawal anxiety, he never found it much of a problem. Walls that can keep out the pain of the past can keep out the pain of the present as well.

Just now, as he moves round the kitchen, he is happy, glad to have something useful to do. As he cooks, remembering techniques long since fallen into disuse, his hands are quite steady. This is because the tremor which is beginning to afflict him has been banished to much, much deeper regions of his being.

Jessie, meanwhile, has returned to her office and the Bailey manuscript. She can't believe what she has come home to. He gardens, he cooks, he hangs out his own clothes and he clears up after himself. It is too good to be true. And what is even better is that her mind switches easily away from him and into her work. By dinner-time she has run through another two chapters and is in the home straight. In the kitchen, Patrick has laid the table and is making dill sauce to go with the fish.

As they sit down to eat, he says: 'I hope I'm not being too much of an intrusion.'

'No, not at all.'

'The weird thing is that I didn't really intend to come here. There are plenty of people around who would have given me a bed for the night. I wasn't looking for one, though. I was just walking. I suppose I must have been in a state of shock.'

Jessie gets up and brings salt and pepper to the table. 'You certainly seemed to be when you arrived,' she says. 'I thought you were having some kind of breakdown.'

Patrick sucks air through his teeth. 'Was I that bad? I'm sorry about that. I feel a bit of a fool.'

'Well don't. You don't need to.'

They fall silent, eating. The fish is perfect and the potatoes are better than any she ever bought in town, but Jessie barely notices. Her mind is hovering around the question that must inevitably be asked, but she finds that it is almost impossible to ask it. The answer is much more important than it ought to be.

Patrick is enjoying the food enormously. It is the best meal he has had in years and he is making the most of it. If he is not worried by the question that Jessie isn't asking, it's because he has developed a phenomenal ability to devote himself to the present moment at times like this. His philosophy, in so far as he has one, is that it is small matters which deserve attention. Left to themselves, the big ones will go away. And if they won't, then he will.

When at last the silence becomes insufferable, Jessie's resistance breaks down.

'So what are you going to do now?'

Patrick is startled back into a larger reality and it shows. It gives Jessie her second glimpse of his fragility. As he covers it with a nonchalant shrug of his shoulders, it occurs to him that he might say 'Wash up', but he doesn't. Instead he says: 'I'm not sure. In some ways it may not be such a bad thing, if you know what I mean. I was in a bit of a rut where I was. Sometimes you need a bit of a shake-up to make you move on.'

'Yes,' says Jessie, a little dubiously. She is not as adept at dealing with shake-ups as Patrick.

He begins to clear away the plates. Jessie has bought strawberry tarts from the little French bakery in Bromley. She puts on the kettle, wondering if she is being foolish or if he is being evasive. She has the impression that they are somehow circling around each other.

Now that the question has been asked, Patrick too is aware of some danger in the air. He has never looked too closely at his ambivalent attitude to women. It lies in the Pandora's box of confusing things which he prefers not to think about.

But from where I'm standing it is perfectly simple. Hera has made repeated attempts to lure him away from Dionysus. And he, up until the last failure, has been most willing to be lured. Being mortal and unaware that he was already spoken for, he has always been completely unable to understand Hera's fury when she failed, on each occasion, to claim him. Dionysus won't protect Patrick from the psychological battering that she inflicts. Why should he? It serves Patrick right for not admitting who is boss and binds him ever more tightly into his service. So Patrick, confused, hurt, retreating, puts it all down to the capricious nature of women.

*

He will never ask Jessie if he can stay. Never. He will wait for as long as his pride will allow for her to ask him and then, if necessary, he will walk out into the midnight streets.

'Shall I make some coffee?' he says.

The phone rings and Jessie answers it. It is Lydia, wondering what has happened to 'Life Drawing'.

'I've done most of it,' says Jessie, 'and I've made an awful lot of changes. I'm not sure I shouldn't give Frances a ring.'

'Don't.'

'But I'm being pretty drastic, you know?'

'Be drastic,' says Lydia. 'It's only suggestions. Frances knows that. But speed it up a bit, will you? I've got Jennifer's new thing coming out and we want it for the Christmas market.'

'That'll be tight.'

'You can do it. Who was it that answered the phone earlier on?'

'What?'

'I phoned this afternoon. A man answered. Said you were out.'

Jessie glances towards the kitchen. 'That was Patrick,' she says. 'Just a friend.'

'Ah.'

'Goodbye, Lydia.'

'Goodbye.'

The little game they were playing seems to have lost its importance as Jessie returns to the table. Patrick is pouring coffee. 'I forgot to tell you there was a phone call earlier,' he says. 'A woman. She didn't leave a message.'

'That was her. It doesn't make any difference.' Jessie puts milk in her coffee. 'Do you mind if I make myself scarce? I've got to get on with some work.'

'No, go ahead.'

'You're welcome to that bed for the time being, if you want it. While you sort yourself out.'

His relief shows in his face. 'Thanks.'

And Jessie's does, too. 'Especially if you cook like that,' she says.

PART TWO

APHRODITE

Chapter Eleven

Having proved his divinity throughout Boeotia and the Aegean Islands, Dionysus boarded a ship bound for Naxos. The Tyrrhenian sailors on board were enchanted by the youth's effeminate beauty and decided to steer for Asia and sell him as a slave. When Dionysus rumbled them, he caused a great vine of ivy to entwine itself around the mast, then turned himself into a lion. The pirates, confused and terrified, threw themselves overboard and into the sea, where they turned into dolphins.

Patrick sleeps long and dreamlessly. When he wakes, it takes him a minute or two to get his bearings, then he remembers and stretches luxuriously. Even with the curtains drawn this room with its pale blue walls and white woodwork is brighter than the one in King's Cross ever was. For a long while he lies without moving, just savouring the bright comfort of his new life. He hopes that Jessie hasn't gone out. He has promised himself that he will make pancakes for her breakfast.

With a slight reluctance he takes off Jessie's grandad shirt and puts on his own clothes. It is a return to his old identity, and yet not quite, because the clothes smell completely different from the way they always did when they came back from the launderette. They smell of expensive washing powder and fresh air, and of Jessie's house, snug and warm. As he buttons his shirt he opens the curtains and looks out. It has rained again during the night and the garden is gleaming and fresh. The results of yesterday's labours are visible, the beginning of new order.

Patrick hums a tune as he straightens the bed and picks up the clothes he slept in. He has the new leaf feeling that he sometimes got as a child when he made the decision that he was going to be helpful around the place and avoid his mother's disapproval. He goes into the bathroom and runs hot water into the hand-basin, enjoying the novelty of it and of Jessie's musky soap slickly turning between his hands. But when he looks up and encounters himself in the mirror, his sense of well-being evaporates. It is a familiar feeling, learnt way back in those chaotic childhood days. No matter how hard he tried, he was never quite good enough.

Patrick hasn't seen himself in a properly lit mirror for nearly six years. He would see no reason to complain about those years, but every one of them has taken its toll. They show in his skin, his eyes, the grey hairs shoving through the black. Even his stubble is greying. He stares at his reflection until the details begin to become magnified and the image threatens to melt into some Daliesque monstrosity, then he looks away and blanks out his vision with soap and water.

But washing his face makes no difference to the way it looks. Afterwards, he sits on the edge of the bath and stares at his hands. Even they have grown old. His spirit sinks down until, despite himself, it reaches the place where the pain lies. He must be crazy to think that he can just change, just take up a new life in a place like this with a woman like Jessie. As he washes, he realises that he has nothing except the clothes he stands up in, not even a toothbrush. It has all been a dream, a childish fantasy. There is nothing for him to do except to go back where he belongs, to King's Cross.

Downstairs there is no sign of Jessie. The clock says 2.30. Patrick isn't sure whether to believe it or not. There is bread beside the toaster, coffee and tea beside the kettle. He looks round, hoping to find a note, something which would recognise his existence and make him feel welcome, but there is none. So he makes toast, butters it and brings it out into the garden. The smell of the broken earth where he lifted the potatoes reaches him and he breathes deeply, hungrily. Beside him, Jessie's bird table leans precariously over the tangled grass of the lawn. Patrick straightens it and heels in the hole at its base, then leaves a few crusts on the top, a little offering for Demeter as he takes his leave of her. He would have liked to finish straightening out those tiles. The brief spell of work he did here has changed something for him. He wonders now if he might be able to get the money together to go back to Ireland and rent or even buy some small place in the West. From time to time he reads the *London Irish Weekly* so he knows that it's still possible to find small farms going cheap.

The sun is beginning to break through the clouds as Patrick leaves the garden behind him and goes through the house to the hall. His black hat hangs on a peg above his coat and as he puts it on he has a sense of returning to a bleaker sort of reality, like an actor changing his bright costume for street clothes. He makes a mental search in case he has forgotten anything, then opens the front door. Jessie is on the doorstep, fumbling about in her pocket for her keys. She has a plastic bag in her hand with a newspaper sticking out of the top.

'Hello,' she says. 'Where are you going?'

Patrick is acutely aware of the stubbled face he saw earlier in the mirror, but there is no way of hiding it from her.

'King's Cross,' he says.

'Why?'

He shrugs. 'I left all my stuff there, Jessie. I don't even have a razor blade.'

'Hang on a minute,' she says.

He waits on the doorstep, looking up to avoid looking out at the angular nature of the street and its houses. The sky is surprisingly clear and blue. It occurs to him that he could stop in at the *Irish Weekly* office and find out where Ray is. Ray would certainly give him a hand to get set up again, or if not, then to find something else. Except for that twenty quid. He can't face Ray without that. He is just wondering whether he would have the neck to borrow it from Jessie when she comes back and stuffs a crumpled bundle of carrier bags into his hand.

'And I got a key cut for you,' she says, dropping it into his other hand. Her fingers brush his as she does so.

'I might not be here when you get back,' she goes on. 'I have some business in town.'

Her face is open, fresh, almost eager. As he looks into her eyes it is not gratitude he feels, but the first, welcome stirrings of desire.

The door of the basement flat is still ajar, the plastic bag still wedged underneath it, still breathing. It seems likely that no one has been there, but even so, even in the bright daylight, Patrick feels the familiar dread.

There is no sound from the boys above. Patrick has a vision of them lying around the flat, their bodies open, murdered by some madman for their sins. He creeps through the door, every nerve on standby. He isn't sure whether he has more to fear from the gloom within or from the dark shadow that he has begun to perceive at his back. But when he turns round, the street is empty apart from the anonymity of passing cars and buses. He edges forward. Nothing has been touched since he was last here. The floor is still strewn with his possessions.

As he crosses to the window he is struck by the strong smell of dampness in the room and wonders how it can have built up so strongly in less than two days. He pulls the grey cloth back from the window, hooks the torn edges into the bent nails that tore them. The bottom of the cloth is heavy with damp and flecked with pale mildew. Wherever he can see the cotton meeting the floor it is the same. How could he have lived here for so long without noticing? The place is a dungeon, a doss-hole.

Yet the face that he saw in the mirror this morning belongs here, surely?

A shiver runs down Patrick's spine. He begins to gather his clothes from the floor and stuff them into Jessie's plastic bags. Then he picks through the rest of the mess and gathers his toothbrush, his razor and blades and shaving brush. There are one or two books here that he has enjoyed and he wonders if Jessie might like to read them. But when he picks them up, he realises that they, too, are contaminated, thickened and crinkled by damp. They smell musty and old. He puts his nose into one of the bags of clothes. The smell is there as well. Everything. How long has it been there? How long has he been carrying it round with him like a leper's bell? Did Jessie smell it, too? In the art class? In the pub? Did she smell the gutter and see the old tramp in the lines of his face and take pity on him? What does he know of her, after all? She has given him a bed and a good feed like a mongrel fetched in from the street. Women do that kind of thing. It makes them feel good. But they turn round and throw it all back at you in the end. Tear you to pieces.

The tremor is spreading slowly outwards. It is reaching his thighs and his shoulders. The room is taking on a presence of its own.

Patrick steps backwards, kicks a bottle and sends it skidding across the cracked lino. 'My god,' says Corrie. The tremor has reached his arms and his calves. He turns and walks quickly out of the flat.

At the top of the steps, he pauses and looks up and down the street. From the front room of the boys' flat comes a shriek which sends a shock-wave through Patrick's innards, but it is followed by young laughter, and then more of it. Patrick puts his hand into his pocket. There are two keys in there, two possibilities. The pubs are closed until six and he may well have to wander the streets until long after that before he can be sure of finding one of his drinking buddies in one of them. By then the streets will be dark, and as full of horrors as they were two nights ago. And Ray is lost, receding behind the spectre of a twenty pound note to join other faces from the past. Patrick takes the two keys out of his pocket. They appear to be identical. There is only one way to find out which is which. He leaves the bags at the top of the steps and goes down. The first key fits. The jamb side of the lock has been torn away from the wood by the thieves, but it doesn't matter. Someone can fix that if they want to. He pulls the door shut against an unexpected, contrary wind, and leaves the key where it is.

Patrick cooks again. Afterwards, Jessie brings her work in and sits with it in front of the fire. Patrick stretches out on the couch against the opposite wall and leans on his elbow, reading a novel. The nervous shake has long since left his limbs, but it is oscillating deep down at a very high frequency and he is restless, unable to concentrate.

He sighs and turns over another page. Jessie glances across at him. She is wondering whether or not to take herself back to the office. Her concentration, too, is slightly impaired but she at least knows what is causing it. It is Patrick's presence. Even with his face slackened in repose he is one of the best-looking men she has ever seen.

Can this possibly be the same Patrick who was pole-axed by the sight of himself in the mirror this morning? Beauty is, indeed, in the eye of the beholder. But who, you might ask, has put it there?

Jessie turns back to her work, pencilling in correct punctuation, suggesting alternative words, weeding out spelling mistakes. Frances Bailey has a few favourites which she uses over and over again.

Patrick's eyes slide from the book and come to rest upon the soft, rusty downpour of Jessie's loosened hair. He imagines the feel of it between his fingers and the nape of her neck concealed beneath. His breathing begins to thicken and he turns away and on to his back to avoid temptation, but he is comforted by the knowledge that it is not desire which has been lost in his life, merely the occasion for its arousal.

Jessie feels Patrick's eyes upon her and hears his sigh as he turns over. Quietly, she collects her papers into a pile and goes back to her study, away from temptation. She has no intention of rushing things.

Hera has lost him before by coming on too strong, too soon.

Chapter Twelve

The Romans changed all our names, and tried to change our natures, too. They succeeded in changing their perception of us, perhaps, but not what we are.

Cupid is an example. I am another. They called me Mercury and, knowing me to be responsible for trade, set me up as guardian of their market-places. But I wasn't to be so easily manipulated, and they could never understand why their markets were so often filled with travellers and tricksters, minstrels and thieves.

And they made the same mistakes with Dionysus, learning nothing from the old stories. They called him Bacchus, portrayed him as a benign and amiable character, and refused to take him seriously at all. That kind of attitude can be guaranteed to cause trouble. Dionysus took offence and set out once again to prove his authority. The Roman senate prohibited the celebration of the Bacchanalian rites. The rest is history.

∞

Patrick spends most of the next day in the garden. Jessie is delighted to see the place getting straightened out and has given him permission to do whatever he likes.

Hera has no problem with Demeter, none whatsoever. Demeter's nature is placid; she gets on with pretty much everyone apart from Technossus. She and Hera have always been willing to share. Their interests are hardly ever in conflict.

As Jessie stands outside her parents' house and watches the auctioneer drive away, she remembers the moon as it appeared to her in her dream. It was ancient and austere; it seemed to make love to her somehow without touching her at all, and left her utterly drained, as though the orgasm it sucked from her was life itself, or the light that it cast across the sky when it left her. She thinks about Patrick and the growing feelings she has for him, and wonders if the dream has any relevance to their situation. For the light that she perceives in him seems to come from a distance. It is reserved, unreachable, guarded somehow, but whether it is guarded by something threatened or threatening, something fearful or fearsome, Jessie can't decide. She walks out of the gate and snaps the padlock closed, her heart as bleak and cold as the empty house behind her. It is all over now, too late to change her mind about any of the things that are still in there. In less than two weeks time, they will all go under the hammer. She has made up her mind that she won't be there when that happens. The whole business makes her feel sick.

Patrick finishes straightening out all the tiles. Afterwards he harvests the rest of the potatoes and puts them in the vegetable rack in the kitchen. They bring the smell of the earth in with them and he catches it from time to time as he drinks tea. A short break was all that he intended, but a strange lethargy descends upon him as he sits there. His spirit becomes heavy, and his body, too, and he somehow can't see the sense in getting up again and returning to work. What, after all, is the point?

One drink from that whiskey bottle would give him the impetus. Just one. Why the hell not? 'My god,' says Corrie, but the little faggot can go and fuck himself. There were bottles in that basement from years back. Patrick just forgot about taking out the rubbish, that's all. He doesn't have a drink problem. It was just a way of passing the time while he was stuck in that dingy hole. Things are different here.

But what would Jessie say? She wouldn't say anything, probably, but what would she think?

Patrick, although he doesn't know it, has already come to associate Jessie with the powers of the mother goddess she serves. He associates her powers with all women. And he is not wrong. All the deities exist as potentialities in all mortals. If Patrick convinces himself that Hera is around, he will undoubtedly find her, wherever he goes. She will be constellated by his expectations, even in the most unlikely of people. There is always evidence available for whatever you might choose to believe.

Jessie would think nothing of Patrick helping himself to her drink. She would be pleased, in fact, at least for the moment. It would be a sign that he is making himself at home, which is what she wants him to do.

But he does not yet feel at home. He is trapped in a terrible conflict, and he needs help.

*

There is a knock at the door. Patrick wrenches himself from the chair and goes to answer it. On the step is a young boy, very blond, very neatly dressed. In his hand is a plastic bucket with a large sticker on the side.

'We're collecting for the disabled,' he says.

Behind him, at the bottom of the steps, is a man in a wheelchair with a blanket tucked around his legs. Patrick still has, somewhere, the few bob he had in his pocket when he arrived. But there is something familiar about the man in the wheelchair.

It is Joe Mooney. And Joe Mooney has recognised him as well. He is reversing the wheelchair away from Jessie's house as nonchalantly as he can. Patrick laughs. 'I see you have another little problem,' he calls.

Joe salutes and wheels himself along towards the next house. Patrick, still laughing, returns to the kitchen and goes straight out into the garden.

The sun comes out again from behind one of the mooching clouds. Patrick weeds the hummock of old compost, tracing the yellow nettle roots right down to their capillaries and breaking the deep, stubborn grip of the docks. The compost is crumbly and black. As he dredges through it, hunting out the last of the roots, the trowel strikes persistently on some kind of stone underneath. Patrick digs at the sides of the heap and discovers the regular edges of flagstones. The trowel is too small and there isn't a spade, so Patrick borrows the little coal shovel from beside the fireplace in Jessie's office. It's not ideal but he works slowly and methodically, throwing the compost out on to the tangle of weeds that was once the lawn, feeling like an archaeologist as he reveals the flagstones, one by one. In the middle of the heap, the shovel strikes something else made of stone, this time lying above the level of the ground. He has just finished uncovering it when Jessie arrives home.

'You heathen!' he says, when she comes out to see what he's doing.

'Why am I a heathen?'

'Throwing your sloppy old peelings and tea-leaves on top of this beautiful thing.'

'What beautiful thing? What is it?'

'It's a sundial,' says Patrick. 'Look.'

He points to the end of the stout column of stone which lies on its side in a bed of compost. Jessie bends down as he shows her the green brass triangle set into the stone, and the inlaid circle of figures.

'Isn't it lovely?' says Jessie. 'I didn't know what it was. There were weeds growing all over it. I thought it was some kind of phallic symbol or something.'

Patrick looks at her out of the corner of his eye. 'I see,' he says. 'You have something against phalluses, have you?'

Jessie laughs, just a little too loud.

She goes back into the house and cooks while he carries on with the excavation. He comes across the base of the sundial next, and clears it with great excitement. Then he washes them both and sits on the upturned bucket, wondering if there is any way of putting it back together again. It is made of sandstone and has snapped quite cleanly at the point where the column once met the base.

'That corner of the garden must have been a suntrap,' he says to Jessie when he comes back in. 'You could put a table and chair out there.'

He is drying his hands on a tea towel to Jessie's consternation, but she lets it pass and is rather proud of herself for doing so. 'Trouble is,' she says, 'I never seem to get time to sit around and relax. Not in the daytime, anyway.'

'You could bring your work out there. And I could wait on you with pots of tea and cucumber sandwiches with the crusts cut off. It would be good for you to get out into the fresh air.'

'That's all very well,' says Jessie, 'but there isn't any fresh air in London.'

Patrick is a little wounded by her lack of enthusiasm. The excitement he has felt throughout the afternoon has been enhanced by the sense that he was sharing, that he was unearthing treasure which could belong to them both.

He cannot quite give himself over to the pleasure of the meal. His system is still making adjustments to the change of circumstances and he is a little edgy. Jessie senses his mood and accepts it, giving him the space he needs to settle and relax. The confrontation that he fears is avoided but as the two of them are clearing the table he misses his grip on the clay fruit bowl and it shatters across the kitchen floor. For a moment they both stand frozen, staring at an apple which rolls smoothly across the lino and comes to rest beneath the table. Then Jessie lets out her breath. She loved that bowl. It was made for her by a friend who has since died. There was an inscription on the bottom.

Patrick stands in a state of shock. The pieces lie where they landed, like a frozen frame of the action which put them there. Patrick is not so far away from such an explosive moment himself.

Jessie senses it. 'Thank god for that,' she says. 'I've been wondering how to get rid of that old thing. I was beginning to think it was indestructible.'

She bends and begins to gather the pieces, concealing the

base with the writing on. Patrick picks up the fruit and puts it on the table. He is getting into debt again.

Jessie decides to work in the study for the evening. She knows that Patrick is suffering some kind of distress but he is withdrawn and unapproachable and she doesn't know how to help him. As he finishes the washing up and wrings out the dishcloth he is in a state of panic about the prospect of the evening ahead. The book he has been reading does not have the power to hold his attention. His mind keeps trying to re-route itself along the old, comfortable paths but continually comes up against the same, unbreachable barrier. He has no money.

As Jessie leaves the room with her coffee, he says: 'I don't suppose you have a TV hidden away somewhere?'

'I have, as a matter of fact,' she says. 'It's in my bedroom.'

Patrick had a TV for a while in King's Cross but the reception there was never good and in the end he sold it for thirty quid during a rare drought. But now, remember, he is available for any of the gods who can get their bid in. And TV is an ideal distraction for him. Its presence eliminates the tendency which is inherent in most people to think about themselves and their lives, and that is exactly what Patrick wants just now.

It is the first time he has been in Jessie's bedroom and he enters it cautiously, more than a little fearful. It is the shrine of the goddess, decked out in the sensuous colours Jessie loves, deep menstrual reds and soft pinks. The air is fragrant with the essential oils that she sometimes burns when she's feeling wound up and insomnious. But Patrick is very aware that they mask the more primitive smell that will always, washed or unwashed, perfumed or not, accompany women.

He turns on the light and then the TV. It's on top of a tall chest of drawers, which is suggestive of the position it occupies in Jessie's life. She considers it to be an ugly but necessary tool to be kept out of the way and used only in cases of emergency. Patrick flicks through the channels. There are just the basic four, no cable. He settles on a documentary about the prison system that has just started. The only chair in the room is piled high with clothes so he sits, a little apprehensively, on the edge of the bed.

But he is not comfortable. He cannot get rid of the awareness of Jessie's presence, if not in the room then immediately outside it and about to come in. He feels, he realises, a little like a prisoner himself, awaiting sentence. He watches the images on the screen but his ears are not yet tuned in to the sound. He is listening for Jessie's footsteps on the stairs.

The office is directly beneath Jessie's bedroom. She listens for a while to Patrick's footsteps overhead, wondering if he is having a snoop. She is on edge about him being there, even though she can't think of anything that she wouldn't want him to see. She hasn't kept a diary for several years and she has learnt not to be ashamed of feminine necessities like tampons and contraceptives. None the less, her bedroom is her own private space and no one has been in there except herself since John left.

After a while she relaxes and turns to her work but she is tired from the general upheavals of the week, and can't give it the attention it requires. Above her, Patrick crosses the room again and switches the channel, then turns up the volume. Jessie grits her teeth and puts her hands over her ears for a moment. Sharing the house is going to take some getting used to.

*

Patrick has found a good film. Gradually he relaxes and leans back on the bed, propping himself up with his arms, but it doesn't remain comfortable for long. He listens for a while to the silence in the rest of the house, then lies down on the bed, his shoulders against the headrest, his elbows on the pillows. During the advertisements he relaxes still further and as he does so he notices one of Jessie's hairs on the pink pillowcase. He picks it up and runs it through his fingers, amazed at its length.

The movie returns. Patrick watches it and begins, absently, to wind Jessie's hair around his middle finger. When he reaches the end of it he looks down to see the effect. It is like a fine, silken thread. He hunts on the pillow and finds another hair, and another. And on the dressing table is a hairbrush with still more.

He watches the movie with half his attention. By the next set of advertisements he has a copper band around his finger, softly gleaming in the muted pink light of the room.

The door handle clicks like a gunshot. Patrick jumps and sits up, swinging his feet off the bed. With his back towards the door, he rubs surreptitiously at the hair on his finger but it has no elasticity. It won't slide off.

'I just brought you some cocoa,' says Jessie. He turns and smiles. She has, he notices, brought hers as well. He stands up, acutely embarrassed, and slips his hand into his pocket. Jessie crosses the room and hands him a cup. He takes a step back as he accepts it. Jessie pretends not to notice his behaviour. The TV rescues them both from the awkwardness of the situation.

'That's *Dog Day Afternoon*, isn't it?' says Jessie.

'Yes, I think so.'

'It's one of my favourite films.'

Patrick smiles stiffly and raises the cup of cocoa, slopping it slightly. 'I think I'll take this off to bed.'

'Really? Don't you want to watch the end of it?'

'No,' says Patrick, 'I've seen it before.' It is one of his rare, desperation-driven lies.

'I'll leave you alone if you like,' says Jessie. 'I'm not quite finished downstairs.'

'No, no. It's not that at all. I'm quite tired, really. That's all.' He heads for the door, giving Jessie a wide berth. She is strongly tempted to ask him what he has in his pocket, but she lets it go. 'Goodnight, then.'

'Goodnight.'

Patrick crosses the hallway to his room and closes the door behind him. He sits on the edge of the bed and puts the cocoa down on the floor, hissing in exasperation as he slops it again, over the pale carpet. His hands are trembling slightly and he interlinks his fingers and bends them until they crack. The room no longer feels like the haven it was in the morning. He has done it again. Made an almighty fool of himself. He cracks his fingers again, then makes another attempt to get rid of the band of hair. It is infuriatingly tenacious. He rubs at it, trying to work it off over the end of his finger but it will not go. By now the ends have become entangled so he has no chance of finding them and unwinding the damn thing. For a moment he stares at his quivering hand in perplexity. What if it never came off? What if he were condemned to wear it for the rest of his life?

In sudden revulsion he stands up and shakes his hand, as though the ring had a life of its own and might give up and drop off. The trembling is beginning to spread inwards, up his arms and towards his heart. With an effort of will, Patrick sits down and slowly, with painstaking care, slides the hair up his finger and off the end. Then he opens the window and throws it out.

In Jessie's bedroom the TV is still on but she isn't watching it. She is looking at herself in the full-length mirror, slightly despondently. It's rare for her to put on weight but her sedentary life tends to pool what she has around her hips and thighs. Even so, despite her best efforts she cannot convince herself that the image which confronts her is ugly. Nor has she been the slightest bit pushy. She knows that Patrick's weird behaviour is his problem but it's unsettling, and as long as he's in her house it's her problem, too. As she turns away from the mirror, Jessie decides that it's time to get Gregory's advice.

Chapter Thirteen

One day, the wise goddess Athene found Aphrodite working quietly on a loom. Athene complained; it was an infringement on her area of patronage. Aphrodite acquiesced, and has never worked since. She has one divine duty and one only. That is to make love.

∞

Gregory has plans for the weekend so Jessie invites him to come on Monday, even though she suspects that Patrick may be gone by then. But Patrick shows no signs of leaving. He alternates between periods of determined, almost frenzied activity and spells of depressive silence. Several times Jessie comes into a room and finds him just getting up from a chair, about to embark upon something. On each occasion, she has the impression that her entry has disturbed him from some long episode of immobility.

She is right. It is the immobility of conflict, the same conflict which besieged him that day in the kitchen when he brought in the potatoes and sat down for tea. It doesn't always express itself so clearly to him as it did then but it is essentially the same condition.

Jessie has a suspicion that he might be hiding from something, perhaps even on the run. But the last thing she wants to do is to start grilling him and run the risk of scaring him off. So she leaves him alone, and tries harder than she has ever done before not to impose her will on anything that happens in the house.

They are both, in a sense, engaged in the same struggle. Each of them recognises, however dimly, the forces which have led to the downfall of their relationships in the past, and each of them is trying to avoid repeating the old pattern. And meanwhile, something else is happening here. Jessie and Patrick are sliding steadily towards another of the Olympian deities who is waiting in the wings.

On Monday, there is a friendly squabble about who is going to cook. Jessie doesn't enjoy cooking for herself, but she loves to make a fuss of her friends. But Patrick insists, and she gives in. She is beginning to understand how badly he needs to have something to do.

Jessie lays the table, complete with candles, and opens a bottle of wine. Patrick throws a slosh into the stroganoff he's cooking but declines to take a glass when Gregory arrives. Instead, to fill in the post-introductory lull, he takes Gregory out to the garden to look at the sundial.

The garden has already changed beyond recognition. Patrick has weeded out everything that looked small and insignificant from the flowerbeds and spread the compost evenly among them. He has cleared the flags and scrubbed them clean. Earlier in the day he took the garden shears and trimmed back the buddleia and laburnum which were leaning out over the windows of the conservatory and blocking out the light. The shears are still propped against the wall of the house. Tomorrow he plans to start on the lawn.

Jessie stays outside the back door and watches, giving Gregory space to follow his researches. As she stands with her glass in her hand, she catches a glimpse of something odd which draws her attention away from the men. She bends down to look more closely. On the coping stone of the low wall which surrounds the laburnum tree is a little twist of her hair, glinting in the light thrown out from the conservatory. The starlings have taken Patrick's crusts from the bird table, but it is autumn now and none of the birds is collecting anything else. No one has use for Jessie's hair.

She stares at it in bewilderment. It is not one of the tangles that she pulls from the plughole of the sink from time to time, nor is it the fluffy cleanings from a hairbrush. It is a carefully fabricated circlet. Something that someone has made.

It gives Jessie the creeps, reminds her of some kind of voodoo charm. She remembers Patrick's strange behaviour of the other night and wonders if the two things are somehow connected. She has heard that there are occult fellowships gaining strength here and there around the country, and it occurs to her once again that she really knows nothing at all about this man who has moved so abruptly into her life. On the other side of the garden, Gregory and Patrick are looking down at the fallen sundial in a purposeful sort of way, discussing the possibilities of putting it up again. The daylight is almost gone, but she can still just about see them as they bend down together and heave the short pillar upright, then make a few adjustments and step back. It stands on the broken base, held secure for the moment by its own weight. The two men congratulate each other, and Patrick calls over to Jessie to come and see, but as he does so she becomes aware that she is only wearing a light blouse, and the evening is growing cold.

'Well done,' she calls, then turns and goes back into the house.

Patrick follows her in. 'Is everything all right?'

'Yes. I'm a bit cold, that's all. I'll keep an eye on the pots.'

'They'll be OK for another few minutes. Why don't you come and help us?'

'You don't really need me, do you?'

'I suppose not.' Patrick goes into the conservatory and sorts out a few lengths from the old timber that Jessie saved when the staircase had to be replaced a year ago. He takes them outside, but before he can cross the garden to where Gregory is waiting, he, too, catches sight of the ring of Jessie's hair. He had put it out of his mind so successfully that its reappearance comes as a profound shock, and he stands paralysed, staring.

'Got some?' Gregory calls.

Patrick looks up. 'Yes.' But still he can't bring himself to move. In his mind the resurrected sundial has become imbued with the same ominous and primitive menace as the tiny band of hair, and he has no desire to step out of the light towards it. He is on the point of returning to the house and telling Jessie that he will have that glass of wine, after all, when Gregory begins to walk towards him. In desperation, Patrick picks up the circlet and throws it towards the branches of the laburnum.

'What was that?' says Gregory, stepping into the light.

'Cockroach,' says Patrick.

*

Some perceive the gods as being outside themselves, others as being within. Patrick's life is haunted by shadows, insubstantial but threatening forces in the world around him. His tendency is to mistrust people and he is continually suspicious of their motives with regard to him. He has a preference for being with a crowd of people, where the talk is bound to steer clear of the personal and remain among the wider issues with which he is comfortable. Gregory likes to party as well, but for another reason. As far as communication is concerned, he, like Jessie, prefers one to one. What fascinates both of them is what makes people tick, what draws them together and pushes them apart, what they feel, and not what they think. They are both inclined to look towards their own conflicts and motivations more than those of others, whereas Patrick cannot, for fear of what he will find. By the time he and Gregory have finished propping up the sundial, they are getting on well. But when they sit down to eat, the conversation is a little less successful. In normal circumstances, Jessie would have found the evening boring, but she is too enchanted by Patrick to take much notice of what he is saying. Gregory does his best, but he finds photography boring, and Irish history, and motorbikes. In an attempt to bring the subject round to more acceptable territory, he says, 'And have you read *Zen and the Art of Motorcycle Maintenance?*'

'I haven't,' says Patrick. 'I never took much interest in maintenance. Always got someone else to look after that side of things.'

'Ah,' says Gregory, 'I see.'

Later that evening Jessie and Gregory go down to the local for a pint. Patrick decides to stay and watch television instead of joining them. Gregory is surprised, and is about to press him when he catches the urgent negative in Jessie's eyes. It suits her fine.

'What do you think?' she says, as Gregory brings the glasses over to their table. It is Monday night, and the pub is almost empty.

'He's a good cook,' says Gregory. He has not, in fact, found Patrick very interesting.

'Is he gay?' she says.

Gregory puts down his pint and sighs. 'One of the problems with straight people,' he says, 'is that they think that anyone who's gay is constantly on the lookout and automatically fancies anyone else who is gay.'

'One of the problems with gay people,' says Jessie, 'is that they are always making generalisations about how straight people think.' She takes a few sips of her pint, then says, 'Anyway, you are always on the lookout.'

'So are you! It doesn't mean you fancy every straight man you see, does it?'

'You don't fancy him, then?'

'No.' He doesn't, at all. In fact he can't understand what Jessie is so worked up about.

'But did he fancy you?'

'No.' Gregory takes another swig from his pint, timing his moment. The beer mat is stuck to the bottom of the glass. He puts it down carefully and wipes his lips. 'He fancies you, though.'

Jessie had intended to mention the circlet of hair she found. She had intended to describe Patrick's strange behaviour and ask Gregory what he thought about it. But all that is forgotten now.

*

The door has been opened for Aphrodite.

'Does he?' says Jessie. She is so accustomed to concealing such feelings that she is attempting to hide them now even from Gregory. But he isn't taken in. He digs her with his elbow and she breaks into a satisfied grin. 'How do you know?'

'It's obvious. You can't ask me how I know. I just do. I could see it.'

'Are you sure?'

'Positive. I'd say he's mad about you. Just a bit scared, that's all.'

It's a handy cop-out that one, often used by women as an explanation of why relationships fail to materialise, or fail to mature, or fail to last. It's a misconception, though. There are exceptional cases, but in general men are bigger, stronger, and much more disposed towards aggression than women are. How could they possibly be afraid of them?

What they do often fear, with some justification, is the lurking and dimly perceptible presence of the immortals, waiting their chance to move in. In such cases women, too, are often scared.

Gregory is vaguely aware that he may be egging Jessie on into something he shouldn't. There is something about Patrick that makes him uneasy, but he can't put a finger on it. And the more he thinks about it, the more uneasy he becomes. There is a silence while Gregory ponders and Jessie fantasises.

Into the silence walks James, with Corrie on his arm. Gregory forgets Patrick instantly. He would forget Jessie, too, if she wasn't sitting beside him. He and James have known each other for years. They have never been lovers and it's unlikely that they ever will. James is into an entirely different scene. But there is, none the less, a great deal of open affection between them. Gregory nurses a private hope that he and James might end up their days together, if James survives.

But it won't be for a while. James is currently very much in love with young Corrie. He met him at a party one night and drove him home. James has been in an emotional bind ever since. He will not pay Corrie to sleep with him. He has never paid anyone to sleep with him. But he wants to get Corrie away from the game and into a serious relationship.

Corrie exploits the situation magnificently. He has never had it so good. James takes him out, buys him clothes and meals and drinks, and always gives him money at the end of the day. He has no problem about giving Corrie money as long as he doesn't sleep with him. He still hasn't slept with him. Corrie is learning the arts of the geisha. He has James wrapped around his little finger.

Gregory calls them and they come over. Corrie is fidgety, so James sends him to the bar for a round of drinks. Jessie opts out. She has never liked James. She thinks that he teases Gregory and makes a fool of him, and Gregory can't persuade her otherwise. She finishes her pint and stands up.

'You going?' says James. 'I hope it isn't on account of us.'

'No,' says Jessie, 'I was just going anyway.' She turns to Gregory. 'Any last bit of advice?'

Gregory winks and says, 'Go for it.' Then as Jessie is half-way out of the door, he remembers the unease that he still hasn't been able to identify. He calls out the first thing that comes into his mind, across the whole length of the pub. 'Whatever you do, use a condom!'

*

Jessie laughs as she walks away down the street. Gregory has been on at her for years about the dangers of sex without condoms. She knows that he's right, and a slight shiver runs through her as she considers the risk she's about to take. But apart from the basic ungainliness of the things and the embarrassment they cause, Jessie will never forget the experience which put her off condoms for life.

She blames them for the break-up with Alec. They were living in Kentish Town in a small but comfortable flat. Jessie had been away for the weekend with her parents. Her father was just beginning to show signs of the dementia that was to make the last year of his life a torment and put the whole family under stress. It was the first time that either of her parents had given any indication that they might some day weaken and die and Jessie was alarmed, and anxious to share her feelings with Alec. But when she arrived home, Alec wasn't in a position to be receptive to her distress. He was sitting very much at ease in the kitchen, drinking vodka and smoking a joint. And he had company.

It wasn't that such circumstances were uncommon in their life. They had many friends, male and female, and Suzie was often around. But not, as far as Jessie knew, when she wasn't there.

She joined them, and Suzie soon left. That might have been the end of it, except that when Jessie went into the bedroom to unpack her bag, her eye was drawn to the bedside table where Alec kept, among other things, the condoms.

The drawer was lying open. Jessie went and looked into it. Alec's driving licence was there, and his passport and the spare set of keys to his mother's house. Everything was there that was always there, including the condom packet. Open.

It was always open and so was the drawer. The only thing

that wasn't open before was the gateway to Jessie's suspicions. Horrified, she sat down on the side of the bed. She remembered buying the packet at the chemist's a fortnight ago. She remembered, she believed, how many times she and Alec had made love since.

Never count condoms. Better to count paving stones, lovers you have lost, or even noses you have broken. Count costs, if you must, count calories, and if you are suspicious, count your change. But never, never, count condoms.

Anything can happen. There's always the one that falls down the edge of the bed, or the one that gets twisted and thrown away, or the one that might be left in a pocket on the off-chance of a quick one before dinner. But Jessie counted. Nothing was said. There were no scenes and no accusations, but within weeks of the occurrence, Alec was out. He'd had enough, he said, of Jessie's carping criticism and her jealous, suspicious behaviour.

It was the first time that Aphrodite abandoned the scene in favour of Hera. But just now there is a reversal.

Patrick is still watching the television as Jessie climbs the stairs and goes into the bathroom. She keeps her hair dry while she showers and afterwards takes it out of its plaits. When she has finished she brushes her teeth, fits her dutch cap and ties up the cord of her dressing-gown. She has never before in her life been so bent on seduction.

Patrick sits up as Jessie comes into the room.

'What are you watching?' she says, as she crosses to the dressing-table.

'A thriller, I think.' Sometimes Patrick follows the plot of what he is watching and sometimes he doesn't. Sometimes his mind goes off hunting around in itself, throwing up little startled birds of thought which drift warily back towards the coloured screen and disappear.

Jessie begins to brush her hair. 'Is it good?'

'Not really.'

'Maybe there's something else on? I wouldn't mind watching something myself, tonight.'

Her hair has become a broad sheet which glistens and lifts at the ends with each sweep of the brush. Patrick watches, TV forgotten, as she puts down the brush and ties her hair loosely with a thin scarf of Indian cotton. His heart fills with terror as a familiar feeling, ancient and universal as time itself, rises up and threatens to take control of him. As Jessie turns towards him he stands up to leave, convinced, as he has been throughout his life, that such feelings originate outside himself and that the best way to escape them is to run. But Jessie passes by him and reaches up to flick through the channels. '*Miami Vice*?' she says. He doesn't reply, and when she turns round, his eyes are on her and not on the television. 'Do you like *Miami Vice*?'

Patrick's escape route is blocked. Since the feeling that he is experiencing is not his own, it must belong to her. The woman in front of him, like so many women before her, has become, for him, a goddess.

And Patrick can therefore absolve himself of all responsibility. He lets go; offers himself into her hands.

'I don't think I've tried it,' he says, 'but I probably would. I like most kinds of vice.'

Jessie laughs. 'It's great to have company,' she says, stepping backwards away from the television. She pauses, close to him. 'I'm glad you're here.'

She reaches out to touch his arm, in what could still be taken as a friendly gesture if necessary. But it isn't. Patrick turns to her and slides his hand beneath that soft haven of hair where it so longs to go.

And Aphrodite claims them. Within her divine auspices, they will share, for a while, that blissful sense of union that comes upon lovers and remains for as long as they worship, without question, her power.

Lying beside Jessie in the semi-darkness of her room, Patrick knows that he wants this to work more than he has ever wanted anything before. And Jessie, her head on his shoulder, swears a solemn vow to herself that she will not be jealous, or critical, or possessive.

Me? It suits me down to the ground. I get on great with Aphrodite. We have a son, you know. Or a daughter, depending on which way you look at it. Hermaphroditus. Neither, actually. Both. Two in one. Aphrodite and I get on just fine.

That night, when she does eventually sleep, Jessie has a strange dream. In it, a weird-looking man with secateurs in his hand is climbing a pear tree. He winks at Jessie as he climbs down, then clambers into her lap. By this time he is shrinking and becoming an infant, but the only things that don't recede in proportion are his genitals. They are the largest and most grotesque organs she has ever seen.

When she wakes, Jessie tries to make sense of the dream. She wonders if it means that she hates men and wants to castrate them. It worries her more than a little. She doesn't tell

Patrick, and it's just as well. He wouldn't have understood it, either.

Hardly anyone really understands the language of the messages I send.

Chapter Fourteen

In the presence of Aphrodite, all other gods lose their authority. Who would stand against her? Where would any of them be without her, after all? She may not be mistress of creation, but she is mistress of procreation, and without that, there would be neither mortal upon earth nor immortal in the heavens.

Besides, everyone knows that she never stays around for too long.

∽

Aphrodite has given Jessie and Patrick the strength they need to resist their former patrons, but it still isn't easy. Patrick would go to the ends of the earth for Jessie, but he still doesn't know how to begin dealing with himself. He is often withdrawn and moody, often restless, often anxious and tense. Occasionally he blows a fuse, throwing down some uncooperative tool or plaything and storming out in disgust. But he always takes pains to direct his anger away from Jessie, and to hide from her the worst depths of his depression.

These are confined to the times when she is out of the house, or occupied with her work in the office, so she never sees him like that, staring for hours on end at one spot on the floor, his mind in monotony, churning the shallows. Whenever she returns her presence pulls him out and spurs him into activity of some kind or another, back in the here and now.

There are times at night, too, when he lies beside her, aware of her warmth and her comfort but alone none the less and unable to sleep. At those times he longs to wake her and ask her for help, but he doesn't. He wouldn't know what to say. He doesn't know himself what it is that plagues him and threatens to pull him down into some awful abyss every time he sinks towards sleep. And he is afraid that she would not know, any more than he does, what he can do to escape it.

Jessie is more aware of his pain than she lets on. The temptation to organise him is strong, to get him up and get him going and cheer his life along. She could do it, she knows. But she won't. She has made that mistake before.

The life drawing classes which brought them together have been forgotten. They have served their purpose, after all. Patrick blames his previous state of existence on the seductive nature of the London pub scene, so they don't go drinking together. But they fill spare evenings with trips to the theatre or the cinema, or walks in the park or along the embankment, all those things that lovers do. And on days when Jessie isn't overloaded with work, they stay in bed for much of the day and, unknowingly, worship Aphrodite.

Jessie is so charged with new vitality that she sometimes worries that she might be burning herself out. Patrick spends a lot of his time sleeping, but she is awake early each morning, no matter what time she got to sleep the previous night. She is delighted by the turn of events in her life, but it has all happened so abruptly that she finds herself unable to quite trust it and lives with the fear that it will end as suddenly as it began, and leave her once again washed up on the shore of someone else's life. With that in mind, she makes concerted efforts to keep her work in order and give it as much time, if not more, than she did before Patrick came on the scene. Her mind is re-energised and constantly active; she works hard at trying to understand Patrick, analysing his behaviour and moods according to whichever of her favourite philosophies of life seems to fit them best at any given time, and now and then she meets with Gregory to discuss her different theories. And, as always happens when she encounters new love, her thoughts become dramatic and poetic. Occasionally she writes down a few lines of a poem or an idea for a story that she intends to return to, but time is too short and too precious, and Patrick's presence is too demanding for her to find the time and the peace that she needs to put work into her writing. Nevertheless, she lives in the belief that she will have it some day, and that all that is happening now is as it is meant to be in order for that to come about.

To overcome the problem of money, Jessie leaves a jar in the kitchen labelled PETTY CASH, and both of them draw from it for the household shopping. It pleases Jessie that Patrick doesn't seem to find it embarrassing. She has no problem about being the breadwinner in the team, and he seems to have no problem with being the housekeeper. Within weeks they have settled into an easy, if unconventional partnership.

But for all that there has, as yet, been no contract made. There has been no ceremony, no exchange of vows, and no test of the solidity of the relationship. They have slid into being a couple, and could, as far as Jessie is concerned, slide out again just as easily. She has no intention of marrying

Patrick, or of trying to coerce him into any kind of obligation to her. But she would prefer it if their relationship were on a slightly firmer footing.

Aphrodite has still not been put to the test. But she soon will be.

Probate on Jessie's mother's estate is finalised on a Tuesday. The following Monday morning, the money from the Bromley house comes through. Jessie hasn't really believed in it until it arrives, just like that, a huge, fat cheque in the post. Maxine's share will have to come out of it, and some estate duties, taxes and solicitors' fees. But what is left is quite a considerable amount.

Patrick is still asleep. Jessie sits at the kitchen table for a long time, looking at the cheque, then gets out a pen and a notebook and does a rough estimate on the figures. Then she sits for another long time, looking at the papers in front of her while her mind slowly comes around to what it could mean to her life. Finally she gets up and puts on the kettle to make coffee for Patrick, but after a minute or two she turns it off again and goes into the living room. The Tarot cards are in their usual place, on the shelf. She takes them down a little self-consciously, because the one time she suggested to Patrick that she might read them for him he launched into a bitter attack on esoteric mumbo-jumbo and the hippie mentality that embraces it. Even though he calmed down later and made a restitutional speech about people being free to believe whatever they want to, she was sufficiently disturbed by his derision to have steered clear of the subject since then.

But now she needs advice. She listens for a moment before kneeling down on the rug. The house is silent. The cards seem to make a tremendous noise as she shuffles them, and she is struck by the absurd feeling that she is doing something illicit, even treacherous. She stops, angry at the sense of her freedom being restricted in her own house, and it is as though the anger clears the way for the arrival of a calm and determined spirit. Jessie forgets about Patrick's existence, and deals the cards. She deals them without thinking, this time; a full spread of thirteen cards, each position representing a different aspect of her life. Immediately she wishes that she hadn't. She can't remember which place means what, and her book doesn't have this layout. So she is faced with a jumble of bright images and the key she has for deciphering them doesn't quite fit. She groans in confusion and is tempted to pick them all up and start again, but she doesn't.

That much she does know about me. I will usually answer once, but never twice.

The Fool is there again and has somehow or other reversed itself, even though Jessie is sure she put it back the right way up last time. The two of cups is also there, quite central. Otherwise all the cards are different. The only swords to be seen are the four and the seven, and they both represent temporary truce or retreat. There are, however, other cards which augur ill. She manages, somehow, to delude herself into turning The Fool round again, but she can do nothing to avoid the menacing presence of the Moon. It sits at the bottom of the reading, signifying madness and despair, in the one position of which Jessie is quite sure: events yet to come.

She runs her eyes around the rest of the reading, hopeful of goodies, and she finds them. The three of cups is there as well as the two, promising a new nest, and the nine of pentacles, solid and comfortable, a welcome harbour in a storm. It's enough. She sweeps the cards into a pile and replaces them in the pack, comforting herself with scepticism. Patrick is surely right about all that stuff. It's a waste of time. She goes back into the kitchen and makes the coffee, her hands going through the actions mechanically while her heart wavers with indecision. Then she lays it out carefully on a tray and takes it upstairs.

Patrick sits up sleepily as he feels her weight on the edge of the bed. He runs a gentle hand down her arm. 'Coming back to bed?'

'No. I brought you some coffee. Are you awake?'

He yawns. 'Depends.'

'On what?'

'On what you want me to do.'

Jessie sighs and lies down beside him on top of the covers. 'Something's wrong,' he says. 'What's wrong?'

'Nothing's wrong. I just wanted to ask you something.'

Patrick is wide awake now, and Jessie can hear the anxiety in his voice. 'What do you want to ask me?'

Jessie screws up her courage. 'I don't suppose you'd fancy living in a cottage in Wales?'

Patrick relaxes back on to the pillow and slowly lets out his breath. 'Say that again?' he says.

'I've got the money from my mother's house. I always had this idea that if I could afford it, I'd like to live in the country, in the mountains preferably. What do you think?'

Patrick stares at the ceiling, doing his best to ward off the sense of excitement which is trying to get a grip on him. He has learnt that the best way to avoid disappointment is to expect nothing, either from himself or from others. But if this were real, it could be the final break he needs, to get away from the vacuum of the inner city. The place doesn't matter. It is his dream of Ireland, of hills and hollows, gentle contours, land to be worked.

'Are you joking?' he says.

'No. I haven't decided yet. It's just an idea.'

'It's a good one,' says Patrick. 'A bloody marvellous one.' He sits up and reaches for his coffee, then changes his mind and runs his hand through the soft richness of Jessie's hair.

And as the day goes on he allows a new optimism to take root. While Jessie is at work in her office, he goes out into the garden and clears the leaves off the rough lawn which he has created with the hedging shears. It doesn't take long, and afterwards he looks around for something else to do. But the garden is small and easily kept. He has already tidied up everything he can. The autumn sunshine is weak, but the sky is clear and it is too pleasant out there to waste. He is afraid that if he goes inside again he will fall into the despondency that has become all too familiar over the last weeks.

Despite the windless air, a few leaves fall even as he stands there, and he picks them up one by one and brings them to the dustbin that Jessie has bought for compost. On his way back, he stops to look at the sundial. It has lost the menacing quality he perceived on the night of the dinner with Gregory. A few days after that, he took away the temporary props, set stout supports into holes that he chiselled in the base, and lashed them to the column with tarred rope. The job satisfied him more than anything else he has done since he came, and he sees the sundial now as the focal point of the garden. As he stands there looking at it he knows, suddenly, how he will spend the afternoon. Inspired, happy, he goes into the house and borrows Jessie's pencils.

PART THREE

*D*IONYSUS

Chapter Fifteen

There are twelve seats on Olympus, and many times that number of candidates for them. Since there are no elections as such, most of the posts are decided by sheer force of influence, and despite the constant arguments that go on, changes are rare. They do happen, however. When Dionysus came along, for example, Hestia resigned in his favour. More recently Ploutos, the god of wealth, has deposed Hephaestus, the smith god, patron of crafts and skilled trades. There's a bit of a row going on about that. Being blind, Ploutos got himself hitched up to a dreadful spectre by the name of Poverty, and wherever he goes, she drags along at his heels. There have been many attempts to separate them, but none have been successful, and the argument continues, about whether they are occupying two seats or one.

And new gods are born every day. Most of them get little more than a sniff of power, but occasionally one comes along whose rise is meteoric. The Church was one of those, and I came within an inch of losing my seat to her, before she began to disintegrate from internal pressure. More recently we have seen the arrival of Technossus. His mother, Athene, goddess of reason and patron of science and mathematics, has long had a close relationship with Ares, the god of war. Throughout history she has aided him in the development of engines and armaments, but it wasn't until the early part of this century that he finally persuaded her to get into bed with him. Everyone up here was amazed, since Athene had been chaste since time began. But we had seen nothing, yet. Technossus grew so fast that he reached maturity in next to no time, whereupon Athene jumped into his bed. The result of their incestuous union was Telecom, the young god of information, and there is no doubt that he has inherited his father's rapid growth.

Gods die, too, though it is rare. The first to go was Pan. Dear old Pan. Everyone loved him. I can see him still, that sprightly old goat-footed chap with his bushy beard and his set of sweet pipes, dancing among the nymphs and satyrs, greening the world around him, creating bucolic bliss.

We were, all of us, mortified to learn of his death, and it was I, of course, who got stuck with the job of breaking the news to the world of mortals. I was so bereft that I lost all my love of the ambiguous, and bawled out the news in plain language to the first mortal I encountered, a fisherman heading for Italy by way of the Island of Paxi.

'Thamus,' I yelled, 'are you there? When you reach Palodes, you must spread the news that the great god Pan is dead!'

And he did. Pan is dead, but not forgotten. His template remains in the human soul, and people still search for him among the few areas of the world that have not yet been claimed by Demeter or Technossus or Ploutos. None find him.

But Dionysus can do a fair imitation. He uses certain substances to help him, chief of which is found in an innocuous-looking little mushroom called *psilocybe*. Its effect, however, is fleeting and leaves its users as sensually inept as before, but with a longing for Pan which is greater than ever.

Only children really know how to experience life with Pan, and then only before their parents have managed to remove their ability to see ghosts. Only children can lie in Pan's arms and laugh as the grass licks their faces, then return later, find the same blades of grass, and lick them back. Only children can hear the real sound of Pan's pipes in the trees. My pipes were a fraud. My pipes make music. Pan's made the world come to life.

And for all that, for all the power that he had, he was never seen on Olympus, but lived his life on earth, in Arcadia, among mortals. That is why they loved him, love him still above all of us.

That was the problem, I suppose. He was simply too good to be true.

Everyone remembers Pan. Not everyone knows that he is dead.

It is late April and the builders have finally finished their work and gone. Patrick is out on the land, turning over sods with a spade. Behind him is a low, two-storey house, freshly white-washed. It is old and the walls, built with whatever stone was available, bulge here and there. The slated roof has a substantial sag, but it is there because the huge beams which support it were put in unseasoned, and warped as they dried. There are no leaks. And there are remarkably few sharp edges.

At one end of the house, a small, lean-to dairy used to stand,

and beside it, with a separate door, was a privy, which consisted of a wooden box with a hole in it. Anything that went through that hole fell into the stream which dives straight down the grassy crag at the back of the house and runs underneath the yard. Jessie and Patrick loved that privy. It was one of the things that originally drew them both so strongly to the house. But the surveyor declared the whole lean-to unsound, and in the course of discussions about how to rebuild, it became transformed into a studio for Patrick. It stands now the full height of the house, with large windows looking out over the valley and glass panels in the roof giving light from the back.

Patrick was intimately involved with its design. It has a new floor of irregular flags, waste from the derelict quarry on the other side of the crag. It has an open fireplace which backs against the house and shares the main chimney. As the masons were rebuilding the stone walls, Patrick persuaded them to leave a few stones out of the inner course, so he has a number of niches, like little shrines, where he can keep his materials. He doesn't want shelves or drawers in there. He hasn't even decided yet what kind of a surface he wants to work on. The space is wide and bright and totally free of clutter.

And it has succeeded, as Jessie hoped, in taking Patrick's mind away from the issue of the television. When she first mentioned that she didn't intend to bring it with them when they moved, he stared at her in disbelief. 'But what will we do in the evenings?'

'Loads of things. It's going to be summer soon. You can work in your studio, for one thing.'

'What, twenty-four hours a day? I'll have to wind down now and then, you know.'

'But we'll be in the country. We'll be out working in the garden or walking, or calling in on people.'

'Calling in on who?'

'We're going to meet people, aren't we? Get to know the neighbours?'

'And what about winter? It gets dark at four o'clock in the winter.'

'But there's hundreds of things to do. What did people do before they had TV?'

'I haven't the faintest idea. Drank a lot, probably.'

Jessie laughed. 'We can do loads of things, Patrick. It isn't going to be like London. We can have people in for dinner or sit by the fire and read.'

'Oh, great.'

'Well, what do you want? You could take up some kind of hobby if you really need something to do.'

'Like what? Knitting? I can just see it.'

Jessie was surprised by the strength of his resistance. She hadn't encountered anything like it in him before. 'I don't know,' she said. 'What do you want me to say? We could do things together. Play chess, maybe, or Scrabble.'

'Scrabble!' Patrick stood up, a look of horror on his face. 'What are you trying to turn me into?'

He left the room, banging the door behind him and racing up the stairs. He would have slammed out of the house if it hadn't been dark. The night streets still reminded him of the time when he had really believed that the meaning of existence was a black hat on the back seat of a car.

When Jessie felt that things had been quiet for long enough, she made her way up to their room, but found it empty. Patrick was lying in bed in the spare room with the light out, pretending to be asleep. Jessie went in and sat on the edge of the bed.

'Compromise?'

'What?'

'Leave it here with Gregory until the end of the summer. Then we can talk about it again.'

Patrick turned on to his back, but said nothing. After a while, Jessie sighed and stood up. She had already backed down further than she wanted to. As she moved towards the door, he said, 'September.'

Jessie stopped and turned back to him, miming intense deliberation. 'End of September,' she said.

The door of the house stands open. Before it is a narrow yard, and below that a bare meadow sweeps down for about three hundred yards until it meets a deep gorge cut by a wide, swift stream which runs down from the nearby mountains. Patrick, however, can see neither the mountains nor the trees that line the gorge. The hillside is muffled by cloud.

He bends down and examines the soil he has uncovered. The mist condenses in his hair, drips down his cheeks and gathers around his upper lip. He licks the sweet drops, drinks them, missing nothing.

'Jessie!' He waits for a moment, still poking at the soil, then walks up towards the house and calls her again. For the last few weeks he has been swelled by a boisterous enthusiasm which has made him seem larger than before, and more confident.

Jessie comes to the doorstep.

'Will you come and have a look?' says Patrick. He waits while she slips on a raincoat, then they walk together across the yard and down the steep bank which drops into the field.

'I don't think this is it, but it might do.' Patrick has spent several hours over the last few days searching for the site of the vegetable patch which he is convinced must have been somewhere close to the house. Their holding consists of six acres of land, divided into two small fields which lie beyond the outbuildings and the long meadow below the house. The land at the back is rocky hillside where the thin soil supports nothing but heather and tough grass, and they passed over the option of buying it.

The old garden was, in fact, outside their land. It used to lie at the edge of the heathery moor on the other side of the road which runs down the hill beside the meadow, and it was as black and rich in peat as the bog gardens of Patrick's childhood. But it is lost now, beneath the young plantation of spruce which stretches for an unbroken mile to the foot of the mountains. Within a few years, the trees will hide the mountains from the house.

'What do you think?'

'It looks all right to me,' says Jessie. The overturned sods look to her like any overturned sods.

'The soil's good enough,' says Patrick, 'but the stones are going to be a bit of a problem.' He picks some out to show her, small ones, shaley and sharp. The earth is full of them.

'It could have been further on down,' he says, straightening up, 'but I can't dig up the whole meadow. In any case, this would be a good place, wouldn't it?'

'I suppose so.'

'Better if it's not too far away from the house. Specially when the children are small.'

Jessie brushes aside the imaginary children with a laugh. But Patrick, she knows, means it. He has never wanted children before, but now he does. His lost child is on his mind more and more, and he feels that if he has another, or several others, it might somehow atone for his desertion. He equates childlessness with middle-class boredom, and large, rowdy families with vitality and excitement. Besides that, he is tired of being an only child. He wants someone to play with.

Jessie has always believed that she would want children, too, given the right circumstances. It seems to her now that the circumstances have never been righter, nor could they be, but something within her is holding back. She has seen the changes that children have brought about in the lives of a number of her friends. Some of them have even become lost to her on account of their increased responsibilities. She is afraid, too, that now she is forty, something might go wrong. She hasn't forgotten the pear tree dream. But more than anything else, she fears that the arrival of a baby would make it more difficult than ever for her to get down to her writing.

She turns back towards the house which, even at that short distance, is vague in the thick mountain mist. When Patrick called her, she was in the process of sorting out her papers and putting them into a new filing cabinet. Her computer is already set up, and her small library of reference books and dictionaries, but she contradicts Patrick every time he refers to the room where they are as her office. For she is fully determined now to get down to some writing. The room is her study.

'Well?' says Patrick.

'Well what?'

'Shall I start the garden here or not?'

'Yes. If you want to.'

'You don't really care much about it, do you?'

She steps back to his side. 'I do,' she says, 'but I suppose I see it as your department.'

He looks slightly downcast. 'I always had the idea that we might work on it together. Some of the time at least.'

Jessie looks at the stony soil and considers. 'I don't really know anything about it,' she says, 'but I'll help you sometimes if you tell me what to do. I'd like to.'

He nods and slips an arm around her shoulder. She turns towards him for the full embrace, and for a while they are as still and as peaceful as the mist.

Patrick opens more new ground every day, sifting out the stones through a gravel sieve and scattering them on the muddiest bits of the yard. He cannot believe the pleasure he takes from the feel of the earth between his fingers, the soft, warm clouds that wrap themselves around him as he works. For the first time in his life, he is beginning to feel at home.

'Jessie!'

Jessie sighs and puts down the manuscript she is reading. She is always just that little bit behind, always just about to catch up, put everything else aside and start on her own writing.

'I'm working!' she calls back. Patrick is hanging up his jacket in the hall outside her study. He puts his head around the door. 'I'm not going to disturb you. I just wanted to tell you that I met Piers Ploughman on the road with his tractor and he says he'll bring us a load of manure.'

'I wish you wouldn't call him Piers Ploughman.'

'Why not?'

'Well, for one thing, it's not his name. And for another he's probably never seen a plough in his life. There's not much ploughing done around here, is there?'

'I suppose not,' says Patrick. 'But whatever his name is, he's going to bring us a trailer load when he gets round to cleaning out the lambing pens.'

'Sounds good.'

'He says it's organic, apart from the straw.'

'Apart from the straw?' says Jessie. 'But what else is there in a lambing pen that could be anything else but organic?'

'Shit, I suppose.'

'How can shit be organic or not organic? That's ridiculous.'

'What are you complaining about?' says Patrick, 'We're getting it for nothing after all.'

'I'm not complaining,' says Jessie, relinquishing at last her hopeful hold on the manuscript. 'I'm just trying to work out how he thinks it's organic.'

'Does it matter that much?' says Patrick, picking up the manuscript and leafing through it, losing Jessie's page.

'Not to me,' she says. 'You're the one who's into all this organics, not me.'

'Don't you want to be organic, then?'

'Of course I do.'

Patrick lets out a dramatic sigh. 'I can hardly tell him to keep it now, can I?'

'Don't worry about it. I'm sure it'll be wonderful manure. Wonderful shit.'

Patrick drops the papers back on to her desk. 'Coffee?'

'Only if I'm allowed to drink it in here, on my own, in peace.'

'Oh, all right,' he says, sulkily, then kisses her gently on top of the head. As he goes out he starts into a quiet burlesque of himself. 'Women! I'll never understand them. Now they want you, now they don't. "Leave me alone, Patrick," she says, Yes'm, yes'm . . .'

Jessie listens until he gets beyond earshot, into the kitchen. She loves him more every day.

And why not? Patrick is happy. He has never, as far as he

knows, been happier in his life. The year moves on. The potatoes have sent up the thick, lush growth that Jessie recognises,
and they are already eating their own lettuce and radishes.
Food never tasted so good.

Patrick is deeply indebted to Jessie, but this time he is
determined to get it right. He will grow all their food and
cook wonderful meals with it. And he will expand, one way
or another, into the market-place, begin to help with the
finances. Within a year or two he hopes to pay her back by
earning the living while she gets on with her writing. He is so
enthralled by the unexpected turn his life has taken that he is
almost tempted to dwell on the circumstances that caused it.
But not quite.

He does, though, in some ways, explore it through his art.
He settled in the end for an architect's drawing board, and it
stands now at an angle to the large front window, catching
two kinds of light and allowing him to keep an eye on his
crops as he works. He has the feeling that everything he has
done before now has been constricted, as though he has
always been drawing on small pieces of paper, and just in the
corners. Now he wants to be expansive, to move around and
use the whole length of his arms. He tries not to know what
he is going to draw, and sometimes the results are surprising.
Strange figures emerge, their outlines angular or balloonish or
inverted. Sometimes the mountains appear, or the crag
behind the house, or fern-like carrot leaves, or the free fall of
Jessie's hair. As soon as he knows what he is drawing, he
moves in on the detail. And in detail, he excels.

But there are times when what begins to manifest itself on
the page produces a sense of apprehension. At those times,
Patrick tries to change the emerging lines into something else
which never quite works. He is as much afraid to draw from

the darkness in his life as he is to look into it. And until he learns, he will never produce his best.

But there is plenty of time. Patrick is still pulling out of the struggle for survival that followed his departure from King's Cross. And he has already come a long, long way. He has allowed Jessie as far into his life as he is able to go himself, and everything he tells her meets with the same understanding and forgiveness. The more secure and content Patrick becomes, the more the causes for regret diminish and he can allow himself, selectively, to admit more memories. He has told Jessie about the woman who taught him to cook and to appreciate good wine and good coffee, and he thinks of her now with affection more often than scorn. He has told Jessie as well about his days as a motorcycle messenger in London, and the succession of women that he lived with during that time. If he hasn't told her yet about the child, by now seven or eight years old, that he has never seen, it is because he has not yet come far enough to be able to face the circumstances which led to that particular upheaval. There is still a long way to go.

Jessie listens to his stories without jealousy. In some ways they are comforting. The fewer mysteries there are in Patrick's life, the more willing she becomes to trust him. She knows that he has come through some sort of crisis and is emerging not only intact, but more delightful all the time. If she is not threatened by the facts of Patrick's polygamous past, it is because she believes that he has at last found what he has been looking for all his life. She believes that she is it.

And in a sense she is right. Patrick has found what he is looking for, even if he didn't know what it was before he found it, even if he still does not quite know what it is. He is about as far away from Dionysus as he has ever been in his adult life. But Jessie doesn't know that. Patrick has never talked to her about drink. If he doesn't drink now it's because he doesn't feel like it. She has no reason to suspect that things have ever been different. It's an understandable mistake, and one that is of no consequence. The mistake she is making that is a lot more serious is to believe that the power which keeps Patrick beside her belongs to herself.

Chapter Sixteen

Zeus, the enormous, overbearing father of us all, keeps the rest of us in line up on Mount Olympus. He is the hurler of thunderbolts from the blue, bearer of power which is without association, unrefined and blatant, never quite comprehensible.

There was a conspiracy once, to depose him. It was led by Hera, who was infuriated by his infidelities. All the Olympians except Hestia, the gentle goddess of the hearth, got together and knotted him up beyond reach of his thunderbolt, leaving him helpless. There was, naturally enough, a lot of discussion about who would succeed him, and this was overheard by a sea-nymph called Thetis. She foresaw a civil war developing on Olympus and sent for Briareus, who untied all Zeus' knots at once with his hundred hands.

Zeus cut up rough. He chained Hera up in the sky with anvils hanging from her ankles and wouldn't let her down until all the Olympians had vowed never to rebel any more. We did, all twelve of us. But one of the gods had not yet taken his seat among the ruling twelve. He has it now, though, on the right hand of Zeus, and butter wouldn't melt in his mouth. His name is Dionysus.

∽

The mountains are grazed throughout the summer so their grassy slopes are bare all year round. The faces that the nearest ones show to Jessie and Patrick's house are angular and grim with slides of scree. On the other side they drop away more gently, and it is from there that most of the tourists who visit the area climb them. But the stonier routes are not as forbidding as they look. By August, Jessie has climbed the four that lie within walking distance of the house. Three of them she climbed with Gregory during the week that he spent with them in July.

It wasn't that Gregory had any particular interest in climbing mountains, but he wanted time with Jessie to discuss the recent events in his life, and there was never enough time to do it during Patrick's brief absences from the house. So they walked and climbed together, and Jessie led the way while Gregory talked, so engrossed in his problems that he barely noticed the beauty of the surroundings. He was envious of Jessie's blissful set-up. He had been having problems with James, which began when some strange character moved into the basement flat of Corrie's house and started getting aggressive about the boys playing music at irregular hours. They ignored him, partly because they were there first and partly because it is their automatic reaction to any form of irritant. But one day the man accosted James as he left the house and, after plastering him with abuse, broke down and wept, saying that the flat was the only home he had and that the boys were making fun of him and trying to drive him insane.

James wasn't sure that they needed to. He became worried for Corrie's safety and made an all-out attempt to get him to move out of King's Cross and in with him. But Corrie made light of James's fears, and although he never actually refused, it became clear at last that he had no intention of changing his address or his lifestyle.

James had been torn away from his previous social circle by his passion for Corrie. He was welcomed back, but something else had changed. James had had enough of circles. He was ready to settle down. All this and more he told to Gregory over several evenings in Jessie's house in Camden, and Gregory listened and comforted and realised after some time that his feelings for James were far stronger than he had admitted to himself. Deluded by Aphrodite, Gregory came to believe that James was spending so much time with him because he loved him, too. The fact that he talked almost incessantly about Corrie did not succeed in dispelling the illusion because he also talked about how much he wanted, for the first time in his life, a stable relationship. One night, rather drunk, Gregory suggested that James might like to move in with him. He has been rather drunk ever since.

After he had gone, Jessie persuaded Patrick to go up the fourth of the mountains with her, but it was the first and last that they climbed together. Because although he enjoys walking as well, and loves the increased sense of fitness that the hills have brought, Patrick prefers to walk with a purpose. He doesn't drive and shows no desire to learn, so he often walks down to the nearest village for the newspaper or the milk, and on a fine day he sometimes takes the longer but more interesting quarry route. He cannot see any sense at all in climbing mountains just for the sake of it.

So lately, when Jessie walks along the shaley track through

the young forestry, she does it alone. She usually doesn't go as far as the top of the mountains, but likes to wander among their craggy shoulders and find the secret places, the little grassy bays and sheltery overhangs where she can sit and drink tea and allow her imagination to wander in peace.

But it doesn't often go very far. Jessie has plenty of excuses for not having started on her writing. There are still bits and pieces to be done on the house, small improvements, perfections. She has invested a certain amount of time in going round to meet their neighbours, and the neighbours, most of them, have called by in their turn. The editing still has to be done, and Patrick, in good form, is marginally more demanding of her attention than he was when he was more withdrawn. She believes that she is not writing because she still doesn't quite have time. But Jessie is not writing because she doesn't have any ideas. Satisfaction, rich and thick as comb honey, has completely clogged her creative faculties.

As she climbs away from the valley, Jessie startles the lean mountain sheep and they bound away from her, nimble as goats, pausing only to call for their lambs. The day started out grey and cool, but during the last hour the sun has burned away the mist and taken sole possession of the sky. Jessie has stripped off her cagoule and sweater and tied them round her waist, but even so the heat and the weight of her knapsack are grinding her towards a halt. She sets her aim on a smooth grassy hollow where she has rested before, but when she arrives she finds that it is already occupied. A ewe is sleeping there, her twin lambs sprawled around her feet, panting in their unshorn coats. Jessie watches them for a while, uncertain whether or not she wants to disturb them, but the ewe somehow senses her presence and wakes, and hustles her little ones over the edge of the depression and out of sight.

Jessie drops her knapsack on to the flattened grass where they were lying and checks the ground carefully for droppings. The warmth and the sweet smell of the sheep is still there in the grass and she lies down on her stomach and breathes it in for a while before sitting up and unpacking her lunch. There is something else in the knapsack as well, that she had almost forgotten: the Tarot cards, wrapped in their blemished silk. Jessie pours tea from a flask and eats a sandwich of Patrick's home-made soda bread, looking out over the moor to where the house, with its white walls, is clearly visible. The sight of it, and the knowledge that Patrick is there, fills her with pleasure. It ought to be enough, all this, but somehow life is never perfect. In the morning, over breakfast, Patrick brought up the issue of children again.

Jessie finishes her sandwich and pours more tea, then unwraps the cards and lays them on the grass. The colours seem gaudy against the tired green of the mountainside, and Jessie is reminded of the guilt she felt the last time she read them, in the house in London.

One card. One card only: yes or no. She cuts the pack; lets it fall open where it will. Five of swords. Attack. Peril. Her heart sinks. She feels that fate is against her, somehow, and that it is all unfair. The cards should be different; they should tell different stories, just as her life should. Where are the happy endings?

She resigns herself, sighs, wraps the cards up again. In truth she is all too willing to believe that entering into pregnancy and childbirth at this stage of her life is a perilous undertaking, and is somewhat relieved to know that the cards have advised her not to go into it. She had intended to discuss the matter with Gregory when he was there, but he had been too wrapped up in his own problems to offer much attention to hers. For the moment, like it or not, the cards are her only confidants, and she puts them away carefully before resuming her lunch. The tea is still hot, and she drinks it slowly, looking out over the landscape again. Outside the whitewashed house, she can just make out the figure of a man crossing the yard.

Patrick is still opening new ground, but for next year now. They won't be anything like self-sufficient in vegetables this year, but what they have planted is flourishing. Beneath the ground, wireworms are mining a few carrots and a single cut-worm has caused the mysterious collapse of several heads of lettuce, but on the whole, the vegetables are growing as boldly as they can at such an altitude.

A week after her walk in the mountains, Jessie joins Patrick in the garden to help with the weeding. Behind them in the yard a few brown pullets and a young cock are cautiously exploring their first taste of freedom. Jessie bought them a few days ago from a dealer near Ffestiniog who raised them by the thousand in covered yards. They have spent those few days in the old hen house, making the place their home. So far, they have not acquired confidence. So far, they have not discovered the garden.

The sun is high and the mountains are in haze. Jessie and Patrick are working in T-shirts. From the valley below, surprisingly clear in the still air, comes the sound of a motorbike starting up.

'Hello?' says Patrick. 'The leather mob has arrived.'

'What?' says Jessie.

'That's a heavy bike,' he says; 'an old one I'd say.'

The sound of the bike gets softer for a while as it runs

behind the contours of the land. Then it is there again, climbing sweetly up the steep roads towards them. Patrick straightens up to try and get a glimpse of it passing, but to his surprise it appears around the wall beside the bridge at the bottom of their meadow, heading up their track.

Now Jessie straightens up, too.

'Who is it?' says Patrick. Jessie shrugs.

The rider steers the bike carefully through the ruts and bumps of the track, so slowly that each spark in the cylinder is distinguishable from the next.

'It's Dafydd!' says Patrick. 'What's he playing at now?'

He no longer calls Dafydd Piers Ploughman. Dafydd owns the land at the back of the house and has grazing rights for sheep on the mountain beyond the forestry. Jessie and Patrick have given him the use of the sheep pens behind their outbuildings and have helped him once or twice with gathering and sorting sheep. During the shearing, Patrick went down to Dafydd's farm in the valley and spent two days catching the ewes and marking them after they were shorn. Both he and Jessie have become good friends with Dafydd, and he seldom visits the neighbouring land without calling in for a cup of tea.

'What are you up to?' says Patrick as Dafydd pulls into the yard and switches off the engine. 'You never told me you had a bike.'

Dafydd takes off the helmet. 'It's a new one,' he says. 'Reconditioned.'

'I can see that,' says Patrick, hunkering down and examining the engine, the gearbox, the brand new tyres. 'Single cylinder,' he says, worshipfully.

'Want a spin?' says Dafydd.

'Can I?' says Patrick, eager as a child.

Dafydd hands him the helmet, and he starts the bike and

turns it, then eases it gently back down the track. Jessie and Dafydd watch him out of sight, then exchange a conspiratorial smile.

Patrick turns away from the bridge and drives up the steep, narrow road which lies between their boundary wall and the edge of the forestry. At the top, there is a long, level stretch where the road passes the craft-workers' cottage and crosses the lap of the mountains before descending again into the next valley. He changes gear, and rolling his wrist gently, respectfully, opens up the throttle.

A few minutes later, turning back in through the gate, Patrick has decided that he will never own another motorbike. The drive has exhilarated him, but it has also reminded him of his messenger days, his narrow escapes, his complete inability to resist the temptation of speed. His life has changed, settled. He loves the quiet pace of it now and the chance to appreciate the surroundings that only walking can give.

His face is flushed as he hands the helmet back to Dafydd. Dafydd puts it on the wall.

'Tea?' says Jessie.

'No, ta,' says Dafydd. 'I'd better be getting back.'

'Can I give you a lift?'

'No. I left the Land Rover and trailer at Cae Coed. It's only five minutes down across the Black Ram.' He moves towards the gate at the other end of the yard.

'Thanks,' says Jessie.

'Hold on a minute,' says Patrick. 'What about your bike?'

'It's not my bike,' says Dafydd, 'it's yours.'

'Happy birthday,' says Jessie.

Patrick stares at her, dumbstruck. She grins with glee, interpreting his slack-jawed expression as one of astonished delight.

In fact, it is thinly disguised horror. His mind has gone into a tailspin, assailed by so many implications that he can barely grasp the slightest of them. With a supreme effort, he succeeds.

'How did you know it was my birthday?'

Dafydd has disappeared beyond the sheep pens. Jessie moves over and slips her arms round Patrick's waist. 'You told me,' she says. 'Ages ago.'

He dimly remembers something like that from the early days of careful divulgence. He drops his head on to Jessie's shoulder and draws her close. For a long time they stay in that gentle embrace, but Patrick's attention is a long way from it. Another womb has been prematurely split open.

Jessie is the driver, the one who makes the decisions. She is not aware that she makes the decisions, but she does. She and Patrick talk about everything, down to the smallest detail, but it is more in the nature of mutual affirmation than discussion. Jessie makes suggestions, Patrick complies. Or Patrick makes suggestions and Jessie agrees. He adds to her plans, her proposals and her shopping lists, but they remain essentially hers. As do the car, the property and the money. She offered when they first moved to open a joint account in both names, but Patrick declined. He has never had a bank account in his life. Instead a drawer in the Welsh dresser has replaced the jar in the Camden kitchen.

Jessie has learnt her lesson from the condoms, and keeps no account of the cash. She seldom uses it herself, preferring to use plastic money when she can, but she keeps enough of an eye on it to be sure that it's always topped up. She wants to be sure that Patrick never has to ask her for money.

To that end she anticipates as many of his needs as she can, and quite often buys things on the off-chance. He has paper and pencils and charcoal to last for the next six months, and pastels and paints that he hasn't yet opened. There are books that he reads and books that he will never read on the shelves in their bedroom. And she is always buying him clothes. She has moved him up gradually from the black trousers and plain cotton shirts that he came with, to denims for the garden and comfortable, well-tailored jeans for the evenings. She buys him warm-coloured shirts in brushed cotton and silk and loose, round-necked jumpers with subtle designs. He wears them all willingly, happy to please her. She panders to his vanity, and the better he feels, the better he does, in fact, look.

Only once did Jessie overstep the mark. She came home with a beautiful shirt that she bought in a sale because she couldn't resist it. It is white, with a blunt collar and open neck. The sleeves are wide and loose, but pulled in at the cuff like something a Cossack might wear.

Patrick stared at it, aghast. 'That's not a shirt,' he said, 'it's a blouse!'

So Jessie wears it now, instead. She never thinks twice about what she is spending these days, even though it is far more than she is earning. She justifies it all as investment in their new home. But the money which remains from the sale of the Bromley house is dwindling fast. It is still subsidising the mortgage on the Camden house where Gregory is living for a nominal rent, caretaking until she can find a buyer.

The money in the drawer of the Welsh dresser, however, dwindles very slowly. Apart from the newspapers and provisions he buys in the village, there is no need for Patrick to spend money. All his needs are met.

But now there is this motorbike. He is no longer confined to the security of dependence. He has his own mobility, and somehow that obliges him to move back out into the world and encounter it again. The bike is more than a birthday present. It is a symbol of responsibility. And worse.

Patrick sighs and straightens up. 'Thanks, Jessie. You shouldn't have.'

She kisses him lightly and leads him inside. From the cupboard where it is hidden, she produces his birthday cake and a card. It is the funniest one she could find, and Patrick laughs as well as he can. But it's a poor attempt. Within, he has already seen, lies the trap.

The only document that Patrick has owned in the UK is a driving licence, which he got for showing his Irish one. Since the day he left art college, he has called himself Patrick Robinson. The name on the licence, before he burned it, was Robert Fitzpatrick.

Patrick has never signed on the dole, never been hospitalised, never taken on work that required a social security number. The motorbike he rode in his messenger days belonged to a friend who had lost his nerve. On the one occasion that Patrick was pulled in by the cops for speeding, he gave his friend's name and got off with a warning. He does not have a criminal record. What he has is no record at all.

And he wants it that way. Jessie, he is sure, would have no problem with his change of name. She would laugh, it would be just another idiosyncrasy to be proud of. It is not Jessie that Patrick is worried about.

It is Zeus; the vague and unpredictable manifestation of authority.

Patrick stares at the change of ownership form in his hand. It is a simple form, but even the few details it requires are more than he is willing to divulge. He will never be registered, listed or numbered. He will never be identified, systemised or data-coded. He refuses, point blank, to be counted.

Along with the form there are three blank cheques, all with Jessie's signature. One is for the tax, one for the insurance, and one for the replacement of his lost driving licence. She is pleased with herself. She has thought of everything.

But Patrick is falling prey to a rising fury. Jessie is still glowing with pride and vicarious pleasure. He gives her the best smile he can and goes back out to the yard. She follows him and stands at the door watching as he goes over to the bike and looks at it. After a while, he takes the helmet from the wall, and Jessie thinks he is going to go for another ride. But after a moment of hesitation, he pushes the bike across the yard, into the cow-shed and out of his mind.

Chapter Seventeen

Hippolytus was a priest in the temple of Artemis, a pure-minded man and celibate. He was also, unfortunately, extremely beautiful.

Aphrodite, the goddess of desire, was vexed. She was not vexed by his purity of mind, nor by his beauty, but by his virginity. She cannot abide it when mortals fail to succumb to her power. So she set her cap at Hippolytus, using the young Queen Phaedra as her mortal vessel.

Poor Phaedra, infatuated, mesmerised, possessed in fact, pined into sickness for love of Hippolytus. Unfortunately, by one of those wonderful Greek ironies, Hippolytus was her son-in-law, which made him pretty strictly out of bounds to her. She would have wasted herself into an early grave rather than give in to Aphrodite's scheme were it not for the kind-hearted interference of her maid.

Be warned. With the best will in the world, it doesn't do to interfere in people's lives. The worse mess someone is in, the more certain you can be that they are under the strong influence of one or another of the gods. At best you will cause the kind of trouble that Phaedra's maid did. At worst you will get yourself mangled in the middle, blasted by the meeting of two opposing forces. It's better, on the whole, to stay out of it.

But the maid, believing herself to be acting in the best interests of all concerned, went and told Hippolytus. He blew his top, in public, too, pouring such scorn over the female of the species that no one could have been left in any doubt about his feelings in the matter. Least of all poor Phaedra. She had no choice left but to put an end to herself. For all her effort in withstanding Aphrodite's influence and for all it had cost her, the goddess still won the final hand.

We generally do.

Infuriated by the stubbornness of Hippolytus, Aphrodite induced Phaedra to write a suicide note claiming that Hippolytus had violated her.

He had, in a sense, with his outrageous condemnation of her and all of her gender, but psychological violence has never succeeded in attracting the same kind of retribution from the authorities as plain, old-fashioned rape. The king responded accordingly, and with a bit of help from Poseidon, contrived to do away with his son.

There was, of course, a great deal of posthumous remorse and exoneration, but the death of Hippolytus has neither been forgotten nor forgiven. Artemis lost a beloved devotee and is well aware of whose fault it was. 'I'll wait till she loves a mortal next time,' she said, 'and with this hand, with these unerring arrows, I'll punish him.'

∞

The bike is still in the cow-shed a week later when Jessie drives into Bangor to meet Lydia at the station. The roads are wet with recent rain, but the dense cloud has begun to break up and the sun is shining through the gaps. The tourist season hasn't yet come to an end and the popular resorts are snarled up with traffic so the journey takes a lot longer than Jessie expected. When she pulls up outside the station, Lydia is waiting, sitting on her bag and reading a novel.

'Glad you could make it,' says Jessie as Lydia throws her bag into the back and drops into the passenger seat. 'I half expected you to get overrun with work and call it off.'

'No,' says Lydia, 'I won't give this up in a hurry. But I have to go back on Thursday.'

'Thursday! But that only gives you two days!'

'Better than nothing.'

Jessie stops at the farm supply shop on the edge of town and loads up the back of the car with fenceposts and chicken wire.

'What are they for?' says Lydia.

Jessie finds a gap in the traffic and accelerates out on to the road. 'The hens. We have to keep them out of the garden. They're scratching up all the seedlings.'

'Hens,' says Lydia. 'I find it hard to picture you in that setting, you know? The country life, out in the yard at dawn with your apron on and your bucket in your hand.'

'I wouldn't bother then, if I were you. It's nothing like that.'

'I didn't really think it was. But what are you going to do with the wire? Fence in the hens or the garden?'

Jessie shrugs. 'We're not sure, yet.'

Lydia watches the scenery as they leave the outskirts of the town behind them. The mountains loom above them on either side, bleak but strangely beautiful. There has been another heavy shower, but the sun is blazing so strongly now that Jessie has to shield her eyes against the glare from the road, and the landscape all around them is steaming. Trekkers in brightly coloured cagoules and sturdy boots are moving in small groups along the well-worn mountain paths.

'You'll be delighted to hear that there's a new Frances Bailey on the way,' says Lydia.

'Hmm,' says Jessie, 'delighted.'

'It sounds good, from the synopsis.'

'They always do.'

'You don't have a serious problem about it, do you?'

'No,' says Jessie, changing down into third. A few cars ahead of them she can just see the back of a caravan which sways slightly after each bend. 'Actually, it's great, the way it's going here. If I'd realised how easy it was going to be, I'd have done it years ago.'

'Doing any writing of your own?'

Jessie shakes her head, her buoyant mood deflating slightly at the uncomfortable reminder. 'I will, though, soon.'

'I'll be looking forward to seeing it, then,' says Lydia, returning her attention to the scenery. To Jessie's relief, the car with the caravan pulls in at the viewing point at the top of the next pass and the traffic begins to move more freely.

They drive in silence down the side of the mountain and into a narrow, wooded valley where anglers in faded waxed jackets replace the multi-coloured climbers. Then Lydia says, 'And how's the kept man getting along?'

Jessie has prepared herself for this. 'Useful,' she says. 'Possibly more so than most kept women.'

Lydia laughs.

She softens a little towards Patrick after that. During the last months that he and Jessie were in London she avoided him assiduously, but now she is pleasantly surprised by the difference between her preconceptions and reality. The house is full of the smells of cooking and the table in the old kitchen is laid. There is a large bunch of wild flowers in the middle of it, and another one in the spare room where she is to sleep. When Lydia admires them, Jessie shrugs. 'I didn't pick them,' she says.

Patrick is in good form. He has successfully avoided thinking any more about the motorbike on the old assumption that if left alone, the problem will work itself out. He has confined the chickens to barracks and spent a satisfying week in the neighbouring fields and woods, cutting gorse and fallen branches of oak and ash for firewood.

'I'd like to do something physical,' Lydia says as they sit down to a late lunch. Patrick has cooked the first baby carrots and a few of their own new potatoes as a treat.

'Don't worry about that,' says Jessie, 'I've every intention of getting you up the mountains. You may wish you'd kept your mouth shut.'

'I'm on for the mountains all right,' says Lydia, 'but I meant something more manual. Like making hay or throwing sheep around or something like that. Maybe I could help you build your chicken coop?'

'What chicken coop?' says Patrick.

'Aren't you building a chicken coop?'

'Are we?' says Patrick to Jessie.

'I got the wire,' says Jessie. 'Isn't that what we're going to do with it?'

'Is it?' says Patrick. 'We couldn't do that to them, could we? Now that they've learnt how to walk?'

'Don't listen to him, Lydia. They always knew how to walk.'

'Yes. But not very far.'

'How far do they have to be able to walk to lay free range eggs?' says Lydia.

'At least to the village and back, I'd have thought,' says Patrick.

'So we'd better put the wire around the garden, then?' says Jessie.

Lydia helps herself to more fish. 'Can I help you with that, then? Bang in staples and things?'

'Damn,' says Jessie.

'What?'

'I forgot the staples.'

She goes to get them after lunch, from the hardware shop in the nearby town. While she is gone, Patrick and Lydia start to knock in posts. Lydia is extremely impressed by the garden, but she says nothing about it to Patrick. She has repudiated the feminine habit of boosting male egos to such a degree that she can no longer praise men for anything. She and Patrick are coming to like each other none the less, and they work well together.

'What kind of stock will you keep?' she asks him.

'Yes, that's the next decision, I suppose,' he says. 'I fancy goats myself, but the farmers maintain that they knock down the walls.'

'What about Jessie? What does she want?'

'Jessie . . .' he hesitates, then decides that it's safe. 'Jessie lives in her head most of the time. I think that if I came home with a camel she wouldn't really notice.'

Lydia nods ruefully, and laughs.

When Jessie comes back, the three of them work together on the fence until they run out of posts and pack in for the day.

Patrick, to his surprise, feels much less excluded from Jessie by Lydia's presence than he did by Gregory's. He lights a small fire in the old kitchen that evening, and stays up to chat much longer than he ever did when Gregory was around. Even so, he decides not to go along with them the following morning when they set off up the mountain, and walks down instead to buy the papers and pay a call on Dafydd.

The day is similar to the one before: bright sun interspersed by dark cloud and showers.

'This is the life,' says Lydia, as she kicks through puddles in the wellingtons she borrowed from Jessie.

'Really?' says Jessie. 'Would you fancy it?'

'I don't know,' says Lydia. They cross the wooden stile at the end of the plantation and begin to climb across the sheep-shaved heath beneath the line of rugged peaks. Jessie considers herself fitter than she has been for years, but Lydia is matching her step for step, despite her sedentary lifestyle. It takes them under two hours to reach the first summit, and as they rest at the top, Lydia looks across at the others.

'Shall we take in another one?' she says.

'Maybe,' says Jessie. 'Would you really live like this, if you could?'

'Like what?'

'Well, like we do. Here in the mountains.'

'If I could, perhaps, I'd live in the mountains. But not like you do. I'd never go for that cosy turtle-dove set-up.'

'I don't understand what you have against men,' says Jessie, unpacking the flask and sandwiches.

'I don't have anything against men,' says Lydia, 'but I have a lot against women who set aside their own lives on account of them.'

Jessie's abdomen lurches with a sudden discomfort. 'Go on,' she says.

Lydia reaches for the jam-jar of milk and unscrews the lid.

'Well, there are a lot of women who don't feel complete unless they're involved in a relationship. Why should they feel like that?'

'Conditioning, I suppose.' Jessie pours tea into two plastic cups and Lydia adds milk.

'Perhaps; perhaps not. But you'll find that a lot of those same women are just as helpless inside a relationship as they were before they were in one.'

'I don't know what you mean,' says Jessie, unwrapping sandwiches.

Lydia looks up as the sun disappears behind an untidy cloud. 'I think we're going to get wet again,' she says.

'We'll soon dry out once we get moving. But tell me more about these helpless women, will you?'

Lydia sighs and accepts a sandwich. 'You know the syndrome,' she says. 'Women who can't get on with their lives because they need a relationship and then when they have one they can't get on with their lives because they put all their emotional energy into the relationship.'

'But what's wrong with that, if it's what people want to do?'

'There's nothing wrong with it if it's what people want to do. But quite often it isn't. Or at least, it isn't what people say they want to do.'

Jessie takes a bite out of her sandwich and looks down at the mountain on the opposite side from the house. There are voices down there, a party of climbers out of sight behind a fold in the mountain's rocky shoulder. Lydia follows her gaze. 'Sounds like we've got company,' she says.

But Jessie doesn't want to change the subject. Lydia's words have made her angry. 'Are you talking about me?' she says. 'Are you talking about my writing?'

Lydia looks down at the ground between her feet. 'I don't know, Jessie,' she says. 'You tell me.'

The two of them cook together that evening, both working hard to cement a companionship that has become uneasy. Jessie had intended to ask Lydia's advice on the matter of children, but once again she finds it impossible. On that issue, she is entirely on her own.

Patrick was working in his studio when they returned from their walk. Dafydd, on hearing that he was in company with two women, invited them all to join him for a shepherd's pie and a pint in the village, but Patrick declined. He had been working on a study of the new cockerel and carries on with it now, experimenting with some chalk pastels that Jessie bought.

When Lydia comes to call him for dinner he becomes a little tense. No one apart from Jessie has ever set foot in his studio.

'Do you mind if I look?' says Lydia, leaning into the studio and peering around. He hesitates, but in the end he agrees. She has given him no reason to mistrust her.

He fiddles restlessly with the pastels as she walks around, studying the pictures on the walls, going through a pile on the floor. She takes her time. She is part of the scene in London and gets invited to a lot of openings. She believes that she knows something about art.

'Have you shown them to anyone yet?' she says.

'No,' says Patrick. 'Only Jessie. She seems to like them.'

'Ah, but Jessie's into literature,' says Lydia. 'She doesn't know anything about art.'

She returns to the drawings. Patrick stands benumbed, staring out of the window, seeing nothing.

It was intended to be a compliment. Lydia really does think that Patrick should ask someone who knows what they're doing to look at his work. She had no intention whatsoever of injuring him.

But Artemis did. She has not forgotten, will never forget, the death of Hippolytus. Her arrow is unerring, and it hits Patrick where it hurts most.

'What's that one?' says Lydia, looking over his shoulder at the drawing on the board. 'Ah, the cock. He's a nice character, isn't he? I always thought that they were more aggressive.'

'Are you two coming, or what?' says Jessie, at the door.

'Coming,' says Lydia, leading the way out of the studio. Patrick still stands glued to the floor, rolling the crayons between his fingers.

Jessie crosses the room and stands beside him. 'Is something wrong?'

'No. Why?'

'I don't know. You just look a bit sulky.' She reaches up and runs her fingers through his hair but the gesture seems degrading and possessive to him. Patrick bottles a rising anger.

'Are you coming in to dinner?' says Jessie.

'Yes,' he says, as sweetly as he can. 'When I'm ready.'

Jessie goes ahead into the house and as she comes in, Lydia tells her how much she likes Patrick's drawings. She doesn't mind boosting Jessie's ego.

Not now, anyway.

There is a roar from the yard as Patrick starts up the bike. He has already passed the front door by the time Jessie gets to it, and he doesn't look back.

*

I hadn't anticipated this. Artemis is the supreme huntress, stealthy and patient as a cat. I am as much taken by surprise as Patrick is.

I could avert him, of course. I could arrange the most spectacular crash, send him flying through the air for fifty feet and land him, winded but unscathed, on a grassy bank. But there would have to be an awful lot at stake to make me cross Artemis, and I'm not convinced that Patrick is worth it.

Better to wait, keep an eye on things. There may be another opportunity.

When Patrick steps into the village pub he is almost overwhelmed by a sudden onset of panic. The small bar at the front is smoky and full of strangers and the familiar, musical mumble of voices is disturbing even before it fades and trickles to a halt. Every eye turns towards him. Patrick looks down, takes a deep breath, and digs his hand in among the loose change in his pocket. It is too late to turn back.

'Good man, Patrick,' says a familiar voice, and when Patrick looks up he sees Dafydd on his feet, reaching for a spare stool. Patrick crosses the bar to Dafydd's table, letting out his breath. The curious eyes that still follow him have lost their power.

'Have you met Mel?' says Dafydd, nodding towards his companion.

'No.' Patrick reaches across the table and accepts the offered hand, slightly disconcerted by the firm grip and the intense grey eyes above it.

'What are you having?' says Dafydd. Patrick only intends to have one drink. He has, in any case, only a couple of pounds in his pocket and not enough for a round. 'I'll get it,' he says.

'No you won't,' says Dafydd. 'I owe you two days' shearing and after tomorrow I'll owe you a day's gathering as well.'

'Really?'

'Yes. I'll be bringing down the ewes and lambs from your mountain. Are you busy?'

'No. I'd love to.'

'Good. So what are you having?'

'Guinness, I suppose.'

But when Dafydd returns from the bar and sets the cool, dark pint down on the table, the feeling of panic returns to Patrick and almost overwhelms him. He shifts his weight on the stool and looks around. There are still a few faces turned towards him but they are not as unfamiliar as he had first thought. Dai Evans, the postman is there, and two of the local farmers who had been helping Dafydd with the shearing.

'Good to see you down here,' says Dafydd. 'A man needs a pint now and then.'

'Yes,' says Patrick, 'of course he does.'

As he reaches out for the glass, his hand is a little unsteady. An image of Jessie comes into his mind, her face sour and full of recrimination, and in response to it comes the old spirit of anger and resentment. He drinks from the pint, long and freely, and within minutes the conflicting feelings are replaced by a warm and liberating sensation of coming home.

'Patrick's living up in Garreg Uchaf,' says Dafydd.

'The high rock,' says Mel, 'up in the clouds.' His eyes seem softer to Patrick now. He no longer has any doubt that he is among friends, and as he empties his glass and sets it back down on the table, he is at a loss to understand why he has been depriving himself of a pint or two for all this time. It makes absolutely no sense to him at all

Chapter Eighteen

Demeter, goddess of cornfields, crops, the fertile earth, is engaged in a fearful struggle against Technossus, and she needs all the recruits she can get if she is to hold out against him. He has already excluded her from most of Britain, Europe and America and is making strong inroads into the so-called under-developed nations, ousting small farmers and sharecroppers and replacing them with huge plantations which cannot be farmed without large machinery. But she is not defeated yet. Not quite. She is even making a small comeback in the indus-trialised nations where a dribble of people are leaving the cities and following the dream of self-sufficiency and healthy living. Not all of these succeed, but it may be just enough. She just might, with a bit of luck, hold on to her seat.

∞

It is midnight when Patrick comes in. Jessie is in bed, reading. 'Where on earth did you disappear to?' she says.

He sighs deeply as he sits down on his side of the bed and begins to unlace his shoes. He is a little unsteady.

'I just thought you and Lydia might like a chance to talk. I had a few pints with Dafydd.'

'But you might have told me.'

Patrick sighs. 'Might I?'

'You left without dinner.'

'Oh yes, dinner.' Patrick giggles. 'I forgot about dinner.' His laces seem to have tied themselves into impossible knots, and he gives up on them and kicks his shoes extravagantly across to the other side of the room. He is feeling absolutely marvellous.

Jessie grits her teeth and looks up at the ceiling as Patrick, struggling with his jeans, topples sideways. 'Whoops!' He rights himself and pulls his shirt over his head. A button flies off, bounces once and lands in one of his shoes.

'Bingo!' he says. 'Did you see that? Tiddlywinks!'

Jessie fights down a rising irritation as he pulls back the covers and slips in beside her, naked except for his socks.

'What room is Lydia in?' he says.

'The spare room, of course. Where she was yesterday.'

'Ah, yes,' says Patrick. 'Not in the nursery.'

The nursery is the third room upstairs which opens off theirs. They use it for storage. Jessie calls it the box room.

'Why should she be in there?' she says.

'She shouldn't,' says Patrick. 'She should be in the spare room.'

Jessie laughs and puts down her book.

'Because then,' says Patrick, 'she won't hear you scream.'

He dives on to her with a roar, and she is so shocked that she does almost scream. But he is just tickling, and nuzzling her neck, and then he is kissing her with a tender intensity.

There is a quality in that kiss that has been absent in their relationship before now. In the beginning there was the inevitable unease that unfamiliarity brings, but by now the sexual side of their lives has become relaxed and open. They have played all the usual lovers' games, taking it in turns to be dominant and submissive, and they have settled into each other like symbiotic plants.

Jessie has observed Patrick closely. When they make love he is attentive and considerate. He adjusts to the needs of her body more carefully than any man she has ever known, but always with reserve, as though his desire arises in a way that is secondary to her own and in some way subject to it. He is a little too careful, as though some aspect of him were not involved at all but set apart and watching, as if through glass.

She tried in the early days to engross him, to persuade him to let go and allow his feelings to lead him, but he seemed unable to understand and there was a danger that he would take her well-intended words as criticism. In those days he was so besieged by insecurities that she couldn't risk crippling him still further, and she has come to accept that if some aspects of his character are still hidden from her, it is perhaps best that they should be.

Tonight, though, he is different. Jessie knows it's because he is drunk, but it makes him no less exciting.

Aphrodite has always been charmed by Dionysus.

Jessie is so much aroused, in fact, that she almost forgets about her cap.

'Patrick, hold it,' she says into his ear.

He stops, and for a moment he is quite still. Then he looks into her face, bemused. 'Hold what?'

They giggle together like teenagers. 'Give it to me,' says Patrick. 'I'll hold anything, any time, honest.'

Jessie, still laughing, fumbles in the drawer of the locker beside the bed. Patrick rolls away and sighs. 'The barrier method,' he says. 'The almighty god Latex, defender against the parasitic scourge of children. Defender of middle-class order and peace of mind. All praise.'

Jessie finds the diaphragm and squirts cream on to it from a tube.

'Pesticides, herbicides, spermicides,' Patrick goes on, 'fratricide, matricide, infanticide. Protect us, almighty rubber, against the seething masses of the unborn.'

'Shall I put it in or shan't I?' says Jessie.

'You shan't,' says Patrick. 'Thou shalt not defend the ultimate virginity, the violation of the womb by . . . What are they called?'

'Nihilists,' says Jessie. 'Shall I or shan't I?'

'What are the options?'

'Goodnight or good morning.'

He sits up and looks blearily at the clock. 'Good morning, please,' he says.

Jessie slips in the cap and slides into his outstretched arms. But it's pretty much back to square one. The chasm has still not been bridged.

It takes two to bridge one, though. It might be thought that Aphrodite, being the goddess of procreation, would be slighted by the advent of contraception. But not so. She is, first and foremost, the goddess of desire, and she has discovered that contraception offers her the chance to prolong her involvement with most mortals. Pregnancies and crying babies are more often than not the occasion for her departure from the scene. Motherhood is Hera's department. Contraception gives Aphrodite more opportunities on earth than ever before.

And Jessie is doing her utmost, in more ways than one, to resist the return of Hera.

Dafydd arrives early and Jessie brings him into the kitchen where she and Lydia are having breakfast.

'He'll be down in a minute,' she says. 'Will you have a cup of coffee while you're waiting?'

'I may as well,' says Dafydd. 'I'd say he'll be a bit the worse for wear.'

'Where are you going?' says Lydia.

'Gathering. I'm going to bring the wether lambs down to the valley for fattening.'

'And where will you be gathering?'

Dafydd gestures towards the gable end of the house, above the fireplace. 'The mountain.'

Lydia groans in exasperation. 'God. I'd love to help.'

Patrick groans, too, as he comes through the door and looks at the plate of scrambled eggs on toast that Jessie has put out for him. He reaches groggily for Lydia's coffee cup. Jessie hands him his own.

'Two cups,' he says. 'If that doesn't wake me up, nothing will.'

'I wish I could come with you,' says Lydia, gently reclaiming her coffee. 'I wonder if I could get out of this meeting tonight?'

'Why don't you?' says Jessie. 'We could all go. Would we be any use, Dafydd?'

'Of course,' he says. 'The more the merrier.'

Patrick sits down and stares gloomily at the eggs. He puts a finger in one ear and shakes it furiously.

'Phone them,' says Jessie. 'Go on. You can have a meeting any time but you won't get another chance to do this for a while.'

Lydia looks at the clock on the mantelpiece and then back

to Jessie again. Patrick picks up his fork with some determination, then sighs and puts it down again. 'I don't suppose I could have a doggy bag,' he says.

'You can live without breakfast,' says Jessie. 'I've packed you some sandwiches. You'll survive.'

'Hugh Roberts and his lads are doing the eastern side,' says Dafydd, 'so we'll start right over at the village end. With any luck we should meet up with them somewhere around the middle and drive the whole lot down together.' He looks at his watch. Patrick pours himself more coffee. Lydia looks at the clock again, then clicks her tongue. 'No,' she says. 'It has to be business before pleasure. I'll have to go back.'

'That's a shame,' says Patrick.

'Yes,' says Dafydd, standing up and looking at his watch again. 'What about you, Jessie?'

'I'll have to take Lydia to the station.'

'Messed up everybody's day, haven't I?' says Lydia.

'Hardly,' says Patrick, swallowing his coffee and heading for the door. 'See you again some time?'

'Yes,' says Lydia. 'I hope so.'

The mist is still clinging to the peaks as Dafydd and Patrick set off, but it is drifting away and the day promises to be fine. As they walk together across the bridge and on to the grassy path that leads up towards the scree, Dafydd says, 'Phew! I thought for a minute there we were going to be stuck with the women.'

Patrick looks up and grins. Since they first met, he and Dafydd have been a little uncertain of each other. Now, after last night, they are friends.

The two dogs trot on ahead, all eagerness and lolling tongues. They are lean and strong, working dogs not pets.

They are symbolic of Dafydd's power. Patrick worships him a little. He is a modern farmer with a lot of sheep and a lot of machinery, yet he hasn't lost sight of the basics of life. It is land and not acres that he farms. He is enjoying the rich and fragrant morning as much as Patrick is.

As they start into the more serious gradients of the mountain, the sun begins to burn away the light morning mist. It is going to be a scorcher.

'Look at the day I'm going to miss,' says Lydia as Jessie drives down the bumpy track and out on to the road.

'Still not too late to change your mind,' says Jessie.

'Yes, it is. What will you do today?'

'I don't know.' Jessie has thought no further than getting Lydia to the station. She has been holding off the sinister feelings that are demanding her attention, but they close in on her now. Despite their love-making of the previous night, Jessie is beginning to feel that Patrick has somehow betrayed her. His departure was like a rebellion, but against what she doesn't know. She needs time and space to think about it.

'Does he often do that?' says Lydia.

'Do what?'

'Go off drinking like that.'

'How do you know he went off drinking?'

'I heard him come in, lurching all over the place.'

Jessie's blood runs cold. Lydia's face is turned away, gazing out at the hillside pastures running down towards the valley and Jessie has no desire to ask her whether she heard anything else. She can think of no way in which Lydia could possibly be responsible for the turmoil she has been thrown into, yet it seems that she is somehow gloating, as though the events of the previous night have proved her right, yet again.

'Did you have a row or something?'

Jessie slows the car at the junction with the main road and turns left, towards Bangor. 'We never have rows,' she says.

'That's great,' says Lydia, glancing at her watch. 'Good for you.'

When Patrick comes home he is tired, dishevelled and smelling of sheep. Dafydd has gone with a trailer of lambs and has left the rest in with Hugh Roberts's in the sheepfolds on the other side of the bridge until he can collect them in the morning. The ewes and ewe lambs have gone back to the mountain until winter.

'How did you get on?' says Jessie, as Patrick settles gingerly into a chair and begins to take off his boots.

'I think, on the whole,' he says, 'the other two dogs were rather more use.' He embarks on a brilliant imitation of Dafydd. 'Round the back, Patrick. No, round the BACK! The other side!'

Jessie laughs and ruffles his hair, then bends down to help him with his boots.

'I think they're rusted on,' he says.

'Do you want a bath, or do you want to eat first?'

'Food. Lots of it. Dafydd says he'll give us a couple of lambs for the freezer.'

'What freezer?' says Jessie.

'Haven't we got a freezer? What's that thing in the feed shed?'

'That's ancient. They used to put the goose into it to hatch.'

'Did they? How do you know?'

Jessie opens the oven and gets out stew and baked potatoes. 'I don't know how I know. Dafydd told me, I suppose.'

'When were you talking to Dafydd?'

'What do you mean, when was I talking to Dafydd? You're not going to start getting precious about Dafydd, are you?'

'No, of course not. I just wondered, that's all.' He swings his chair round to the table and makes an extravagant lunge at the stew. Jessie threatens him with the ladle and he swipes at it like a bear. She collapses into a chair, and drops her head on to the table, helpless with mirth.

Patrick is a little more restless than usual that evening, and can find nothing fruitful to do with his time. After his bath he wanders from room to room, wondering whether he was right to decline Dafydd's second offer of shepherd's pie in the pub, but in the end he decides that he's just tired, and brings a book in to read beside the fire.

Jessie is mulling over her old notebooks again. She looks up as Patrick comes in. 'Feeling better?'

'Better than what?'

'I don't know. Better for the bath.'

'Yes, I suppose I am. Can't beat a good soak.'

Jessie puts down her notebook and goes out to the new kitchen to put on the kettle. 'Tea or Horlicks?' she calls.

'Tea, if you're making it.'

Jessie comes back in and sits on the edge of her seat while she waits for the kettle. 'I've been doing a bit of thinking,' she says.

'Oh?'

'Yes. It was something Lydia said. About my writing.'

'What writing?'

'Well, that's the point, isn't it? What writing?'

Patrick closes his book, a little wearily. 'Go on.'

'Well, Lydia has this theory that women get too dependent

on relationships and that's why they don't make anything of their own lives.'

'You've made more of your life than I have,' says Patrick, dropping the book and looking around the room. 'I mean, all this is your life, isn't it? It's not mine.'

There is a hint of bitterness in his voice as he says it, and it takes Jessie by surprise. 'I wouldn't see it like that,' she says. 'After all…'

'After all, what?'

'I don't know. At least you're out there in the studio, getting things together. But I'm not doing anything apart from fuddling along through other people's manuscripts. I'm not doing anything creative or original. And there's no point in moaning and saying that I don't have time. I have to make time, somehow. Otherwise I'll be looking back at my life in ten years' time and wondering what happened to it, you know?'

Patrick buries his face in his hands and sighs. He puts the sudden reappearance of depression down to tiredness, and begins to think about his bed.

'I've just been looking through these,' Jessie goes on, 'and there's quite a few good ideas in them that I never worked out. I'm sure that if I just get organised I can start putting some time into it. I'd be a lot happier with life if I did.'

Patrick looks up, and his face has a scornful expression which takes Jessie by surprise. 'Are you not happy, then?' he says.

'It's not that,' she says. 'I am happy. I mean, I'm happy here, with you. But that thing about the writing . . .' she looks across at him, but he is looking down at the hearthrug. 'I thought you'd understand that, Patrick, with your drawing and everything. I thought we had that much in common.'

Patrick picks up the book and stands up. 'I'm just tired,' he says. 'I can't really see why it matters just now. Perhaps we can talk about it again.' The kettle comes to the boil and snaps itself off. 'I don't think I'll have that tea after all. It'll only keep me awake.'

'Horlicks, then.'

'No, thanks.'

'I could bring it up to you.'

For a moment he looks at her, suspicious of her generosity, unsure whether he wants it. Then he capitulates and nods. 'That would be nice,' he says.

That night Patrick dreams, and remembers the dream well enough to relate it to Jessie in the morning.

'I was in the London Underground, on the Circle Line. I think I was part of some kind of expedition or something. I had one of those little barrels round my neck like the Saint Bernards' wear.'

Jessie turns towards him sleepily and kisses his chest. 'Getting ambitious, eh? Plain old sheepdog isn't good enough for you?'

He laughs, relieved. In the dream, the collar had made him feel slightly humiliated. 'That must be it,' he says. 'Anyway, everyone on the train, the whole expedition, was heading for King's Cross. But there was one of those weird things that you get in dreams. The others were all facing me. I was the only one who had my back to the engine.'

Jessie gets up and puts on her dressing-gown. She is usually interested in dreams, but for some reason she doesn't want to hear this one. 'Bacon and egg?' she says.

A fine drizzle is falling. Patrick puts on a raincoat after breakfast and crosses the yard towards the garden. The hens are still locked in the hen-house, crooning mournfully like recaptured slaves, and from the other side of the bridge he can hear the wether lambs bawling for their mothers and sisters. The mountains are lost in mist again, but Patrick can just see the top of Dafydd's trailer down beside Hugh Roberts's sheep-fold. He is about to walk on down the track and give Dafydd a hand to load when he hears laughter from several voices down there. For a moment he stands undecided, suddenly isolated, then turns his attention to the fence. The new posts that Jessie picked up when she took Lydia to her train are leaning against the bank, waiting to be used. Patrick sighs and bounces on his bended knees a few times to ease the stiffness in his legs. Then he goes back to the house.

Jessie is sitting in the armchair in her study. It is too wet to walk and there is no urgency about the two manuscripts which are sitting on her desk beside the computer. She has decided to take the day off and see if she can do some writing.

It gives her a wonderful feeling. Everything is right with the world, and at last, she feels, she has come to that point of perfect equilibrium which presides over each new beginning. She has taken off her shoes and folded one leg underneath her in her favourite attitude. All her old notebooks and diaries are lying in a pile on the floor beside her, and she has nearly finished going through the first of them. She has noted down a few ideas, but at the moment she has forgotten them and is reading through an old litany of complaints against the world and smiling at the naivety of her former self.

'Jessie!'

He always does that. Always calls from the front door as if

he were just passing by and wondering if there is anybody home. She doesn't answer.

'Could you give me a hand?' he says, leaning round the door. She sighs and unfolds herself. 'Doing what?'

'Holding the posts. Or you can hammer if you like. It won't take long.'

Jessie doesn't fancy either of the jobs, or the rain. But she puts on her anorak and boots and comes out with him. The first few posts go in easily. Unlike Lydia, Jessie has no interest in hammering, so she holds and looks out at the landscapes around her. It is all, still, a little unreal. The grass in the meadow is long, ready for cutting. They have promised it to Dafydd for hay, but he was too busy with his own to cut it while the weather was fine, and he is waiting for another good spell. At the bottom of the meadow, low trees cling to the edge of the gorge and hide it from view. The craft-workers' car passes along the road. Jessie reckons that already she recognises about a third of the cars that pass. The area still hasn't been invaded by tourists.

A light wind blows the drizzle sideways for a minute. Now that she is out in it, Jessie doesn't mind it at all. It is the same water that flows down the crag at the back and that they use for drinking, so clean and soft that it almost has flavour.

They have already set posts to the edge of the ground that Patrick has cleared, but he wants to go further. His plan is to enclose about double that area, to give him work for the autumn and winter. At the highest end of the opened earth, a rock is visible, jutting out from the grass. Patrick has met its lower edge and has been excavating it carefully, trying to find out how big it is. Jessie holds a post between the rock and the bank, and Patrick hammers with the flat stone he is using. The post sinks down about six inches then stops, with a jar that hurts their hands and arms.

'Whoops!' he says. 'No go. Move it along a bit, will you?'

Jessie does. The rain is dripping into her eyes and down her neck. Patrick wallops the post again, and again it meets resistance. A third time they try, a third time they meet rock.

'Damn.' He pulls the post, a little roughly, from Jessie's hands and flings it to the ground. Then he fetches the crowbar from the bank and begins to probe the ground.

The rock he has encountered is more than a rock. It is a little toe belonging to the foot of the crag which stretches underneath the house and down into the meadow. For a long time, he spears the ground with the crowbar, his movements becoming more urgent and angry as he goes on.

Jessie watches, aware that the news isn't good. But she hasn't yet realised what Patrick is coming to understand.

At the lower end of the vegetable rows is the septic tank which they had to put in when they made the new bathroom upstairs. At the left-hand side is the stream, emerging from the pipe which carries it beneath the yard. On the other side of the stream is the wall of the outbuildings, which becomes, further down, the wall of the meadow.

Patrick has reached the end of his garden.

His breathing is rapid and shallow from anger and useless exertion. He looks across at Jessie who is standing with her hands in her pockets, off in her dream world, totally impractical. In sudden fury, he rams the crowbar so hard into the soil and the bedrock beneath that he jars every bone in his body. Then he turns and strides towards the house.

Jessie stays where she is for a while. Displays of emotion were never allowed during her upbringing, and she hasn't the faintest idea how to deal with them. The rain is soft and soothing against her skin. At the bottom of the meadow, the trees are quite still. The only movement in the landscape is a single crow crossing the sky in silence. Behind her, the front door opens and closes again.

'I'm off for the paper,' says Patrick.

Jessie changes, makes tea, and returns to her study. She picks up her notebook again, but her heart is no longer in it. Instead she chooses the easier of the two manuscripts and settles down to work.

Patrick is a little longer than usual down in the village, but he's in better form when he comes back. He makes coffee for Jessie and brings her a plateful of specialities, tiny sandwiches sticky with honey, and squares of chocolate and halva.

The rain has stopped, but he doesn't have any desire to go back to the fencing. Instead, he goes into his studio.

The cockerel is still on the drawing board. It is one of the few things he has drawn from life as opposed to from imagination, and it is not good. He knows it is not good as he looks at it now, and is acutely embarrassed that Lydia should have seen it. His use of colour is poor. The bird looks something like a dishevelled hawk, and he has completely missed the pride and brilliance that he had been trying to capture.

He looks at the piece for a long time. He doesn't want to put it on the wall. Nor does he want to put it on top of the other drawings which lie in a pile on top of two upturned orange boxes behind him. But he is afraid that if he puts it underneath the others, he will be tempted to look through them and discover that they are equally bad.

He wanders round for a while, tidying the alcoves, studiously avoiding the drawings on the walls. He sharpens a few pencils into the empty hearth and sweeps the shavings into a neat little pile in the centre. Then he returns to the cockerel. But there is no way to improve it. Nor, yet, does he want to destroy it. Instead he just leaves it, and returns to the house. It is the first time since they moved to Wales that he has thought about the TV.

Chapter Nineteen

There are those who suggest that Hestia, the old hearth goddess, is dead. She is not, though, not quite. She still has small areas of influence in outlying areas such as the Himalayas and the Andes but she will never reclaim her position in Western civilisation, at least as long as electricity continues to be generated and people sit around in front of their TVs. But even before all that, long before in fact, she had resigned her seat among the Twelve Great Ones on Mount Olympus.

She didn't mind resigning; she had always hated all the carping and bickering that went on among the family. And after all, someone had to make way for Dionysus.

∽

That evening, when Jessie finishes work and comes into the kitchen, she finds that the dinner is almost ready.

'Are we eating early?' she says.

'I thought so,' says Patrick. 'I was hungry. Besides, Dafydd says there's some music on in the Bell tonight.'

'Oh?' says Jessie. 'What kind of music?'

'I'm not sure.'

Jessie clears the table and gets out knives and forks.

'I met some nice people down there the other night,' Patrick goes on. 'It made me realise how isolated we are up here. We never seem to see anyone apart from Dafydd and those people who do the cave paintings.'

Jessie thumps him gently in the back. 'They're not cave paintings.'

'I think they are.'

'Well, whatever they are, they seem to be doing very well out of them.'

'Oh, indeed,' says Patrick, 'I can't deny that. They're in the right kind of business, no doubt about it. Ashtrays, coasters, wall plaques for the tourists who are fed up with looking at their migrating ducks. Maybe I should do something like that?'

'Don't be ridiculous.'

'Well, why not? I'm wasting my time drawing cockerels and stone walls and . . . bloody . . . mountain nymphs.'

Jessie moves round and stands in front of him. She puts a hand on his arm and tries to look into his eyes, but he is gazing fixedly into the peas which are bubbling under a stem of mint.

'Don't ever say that,' she says. 'Don't ever say you're wasting your time. Some of those drawings out there are brilliant, Patrick. You know that.'

'No, I don't,' he says. 'Nor do you, for that matter. What do you know about art?'

He is still gazing at the peas, which are taking it in turns to bounce to the surface. He gets the impression that they are trying to escape, and turns off the heat.

Jessie gives up trying to contact him, but she is disturbed by what he has said. She tries to remember what she was doing before it all arose.

'Plates,' he says, briskly. 'Salt and pepper.'

'Right!'

'Shall we go, then, tonight?'

'To the Bell?'

'To the Bell, to hear the resonations.'

'Is that what they're called?'

'Could be, couldn't it?' He laughs. The peas are subdued now, and he drains them.

After dinner, Jessie goes upstairs to change. She puts on the white shirt that she bought for Patrick, because she has realised that white suits her well, with the red hair. Since she got the shirt, she has bought herself one or two other things in white as well. It is a new departure.

Patrick comes into the bedroom as she is making up her face.

'Warpaint,' he says. 'You mean business, eh?'

'Just a bit of mascara,' says Jessie. 'Want some?'

'You what?'

'Why not?' she says. 'Men used to wear make-up. They wore it long before women did, in fact. I think men look brilliant in it. Just a bit, mind you. Nothing outrageous.'

'You've done that before, then, have you? Hung around with blokes who wear make-up?'

Jessie thinks about it, and realises that she hasn't. Nor is it something she has seen in photographs or films. She doesn't know where the image comes from, but she knows that she likes it. 'Do you think it's kinky?' she says.

Patrick shrugs and sits on the bed to change out of his

denims. 'Whatever you're into, I suppose,' he says. 'But it isn't my idea of fun.'

The evening is fine, so they decide to walk to the village across the Black Ram and down through the woods. As they close the door of the house, Jessie says, 'Have you got money?'

'No,' says Patrick. 'Haven't you?'

'No. Is there some in the drawer?'

'Should be.'

There is a moment of hesitation, then Patrick goes back into the house. As he is about to open the drawer of the dresser, he stops, and a wave of dread passes through him. It is not because the drawer might have no money in it, but because he is sure that it always will.

The area known as the Black Ram begins at the yard gate and stretches over the shoulder of the valley and some distance down the other side. It is about a hundred acres of scrubby land, all heather and bog, where once a rogue black ram caused havoc by breeding with the sheep that grazed there. Black sheep are popular now, but in those days they were a curse to farmers because the wool fetched less from the factories. The black ram, however, was not only never caught, he was never seen. The only evidence for his existence was the extraordinary number of black lambs that were produced by the landowner's ewes. There were rumours, though, that he stood four feet tall at the shoulder and could cover ninety ewes in a day.

There are tricky patches of bog on that land, but the way between them is clear and firm. Above the house called Cae Coed, the path forks and one branch leads down to the road, while the other takes the shorter, cross-country route to the village. There is about a mile in the difference.

Once past the Black Ram, the countryside changes to grassy hillsides with patches of bracken and gorse. Patrick and Jessie walk side by side, looking out at the view along the valley to the sea until the path narrows to cross the bank of the churning pool. Patrick stops and Jessie stops behind him. Together they stand and peer down into the black water.

Above it, the hillside is almost sheer, and cut in two by the stream which feeds the pool. The bank that the path runs along is narrow and straight, but otherwise the pool is circular.

'Dafydd says someone fell in there one night,' says Patrick. 'An Englishman on his way home from the pub. That was before they put the fence up.'

'It wouldn't surprise me,' says Jessie. 'It would be easy enough to do.'

'Yes. Looks lethal, doesn't it? Apparently there's a sort of sluice in the bank at the other side that they used to open when they were doing the churning. Then when they didn't use it any more, they left it open, but it keeps getting blocked and silting up again.'

Jessie wobbles the posts. Their hold on the ground is tenuous because there is no earth there for them to go into. Beneath the thin turf of the track is a stone wall.

'I don't think the fence would be much help if you were about to go in,' she says. 'I think you'd just bring it with you. What happened to the Englishman, anyway?'

'That was the weird thing,' says Patrick. 'He woke up in the morning on the opposite bank, dry as a bone.'

'He probably didn't fall in at all.'

'The story is that he remembers hitting the water but doesn't remember a thing after that. Dafydd's grandmother said that the place was a sort of stone circle before it was turned into a churning pool, and that the old god who was worshipped there threw the Englishman out because he didn't want people dragging the pool and disturbing him.'

'Maybe it's true,' says Jessie. 'It's a great story, anyway. I'll have to remember it.'

'Why?'

'Well, stuff like that could come in useful if I was writing something. You know, tales of the old folk.'

Patrick moves off again and Jessie follows him along the path.

'Are you going to write about the people around here?' he says.

'I don't know. I might do. I don't know what I'm going to write yet.'

Dafydd is already in the bar with Mel and they make room at their table for Patrick and Jessie. A few mop-headed youths are wandering in and out to the back room with drums and microphone stands.

Dafydd introduces Mel to Jessie, and he greets her with a wide but tight smile.

'Mel's a Welsh Nat,' says Dafydd, winking at Jessie. 'He can't stand the English.'

'Oh, good,' says Jessie. 'Nor can I.'

Patrick is pleased with her, proud to show her off. But when he returns with the round, he sits himself firmly between her and Dafydd. It is an unnecessary precaution. He has no reason at all to worry about Jessie's loyalty, and if he did, the danger would be Mel. He addresses himself mainly to Patrick, returning immediately to a conversation they were having two nights before about the Welsh language and the shoddy way it is taught in schools. Patrick learnt Irish as a boy and at one time spoke it fluently among the native speakers in Donegal, and although he couldn't care less about either language, the common ground makes him feel more at ease with Mel. But Mel, very slyly, is making eyes at Jessie.

He is governed just now by Ares, the god of war. Mel is a lot more militant than he lets on even to Dafydd. If he had his way, he would settle the English by taking up arms. But because he cannot, his pent-up energy is constantly under restraint and looking for outlets. Jessie knows nothing of what lies in Mel's soul, but Aphrodite does. And Aphrodite loves Ares.

Jessie finds that she is a little attracted to Mel, but also rather uncomfortable about the way he is being deceitful to Patrick. She turns her stool sideways to avoid catching his eye.

They drink two pints in the bar, then Mel buys a round to bring with them into the back. Jessie asks for a half, but he brings her a pint and winks as he hands it to her. She turns away as disdainfully as she can and looks around the room they are in. It is a large extension built out into the space where the car park used to be and so new that the plaster on the walls is still unpainted, still drying. Behind it the car park has moved into what used to be a field, and is big enough now to accommodate the increased tourist trade that the landlord anticipates. Over beside the rough, wooden stage, the members of the band are taking their time to get their equipment just perfect. This is the biggest gig they have done so far.

Along one wall a few tables have been set up. The pub regulars have already claimed most of these, but Dafydd manages to squeeze his little party in among some of his friends about half-way down. On the other side of the room, up at the end near the stage, is a large group of teenage girls, most of them giggling, most of them drinking shandy. At the back, a few boys are drifting in, standing with their glasses in their hands and refusing, manfully, to look at the girls.

The band finally gets organised and starts, quite stylishly, into a number which has no introduction. The vocalist is attractive and confident, but he's not a singer. He doesn't need to be. The band does nothing but rap, and all of it in Welsh.

Jessie finds it funny, and looks sideways to share her amusement with Patrick, but he is deeply engrossed in talking to Mel and she fails to catch his eye. She catches Mel's instead.

In spite of herself.

Jessie resists the tug in her lower abdomen that Mel's hungry look has produced. She turns back to her pint and watches the dancers instead.

There are already quite a few of them out there, all girls so far, jigging self-consciously to the music. The boys at the back are almost facing the wall in their determination not to be seen looking. Patrick and Mel are still involved in deep discussion. Dafydd, cut off from Jessie by the other two, is drawing pictures in a puddle of beer.

The band finishes the first number and starts straight into another. Now that Jessie has stopped trying to decipher the words, she becomes aware that the lads are quite good. The monotonous vocals blend in with the instruments smoothly and the rhythm is tight and hot. The girls who are dancing liven up. One or two of the bolder ones are beginning to drag in the boys, who cast off from the sides with apparent reluctance, handing their drinks to the ones who remain on shore.

But the boldest of the girls is ignoring with disdain the boys who are glancing surreptitiously in her direction. She has eyes for only one, and that is Patrick.

And why wouldn't she? Healthy and tanned, inwardly lit by his renewed acquaintance with Bacchus, he is a sight for sore eyes. There are other good-looking men in the room, but this girl has known them for most of her life. Patrick has the advantage of novelty. Egged on by her pals she is approaching Dafydd's table. She is not super-cool, not chewing gum or smoking a cigarette. She is not a siren. She is a maenad, a devotee of Dionysus.

'Hi Dafydd.'

'Hi, Bronwen.'

'Hi, Mel. How are things?'

'Pretty good.'

'That's good.'

Neither Dafydd nor Mel thinks of introducing Bronwen to the others. She is not particularly close to either of them, and certainly not coming to join them. Mel offers her a cigarette, which she declines. Her nerve begins to fail, but when she looks around she sees that her friends are watching.

'Is he yours?' she says to Jessie.

'What?'

Patrick is gazing slightly foolishly up at Bronwen. She is very good looking, and she knows it. Her shoulder-length hair is layered and curls gently inwards around her forehead and cheeks. If she wasn't good looking she wouldn't be where she is now.

'Is he yours?'

Jessie grasps her meaning. 'Oh, yes,' she says, and then, but a bit too late: 'You could say that.'

'Can I borrow him, just for a minute?'

Patrick is regaining consciousness and beginning to understand what's going on.

'Of course,' says Jessie. 'Help yourself.'

'Just hold on a minute,' says Patrick. 'I can't dance.'

'Of course you can,' says Jessie. She is delighted by the attention that Patrick has attracted. It reflects, very clearly, upon her.

'Come on,' says Bronwen.

Patrick is genuinely reticent, but he doesn't want to give Bronwen offence. He turns to Jessie rather helplessly. 'Must I?'

'Yes,' she says. 'Go on.'

He stands up awkwardly and follows Bronwen a couple of steps towards the floor. He is aware, suddenly, of his age among that flock of young things and is acutely self-conscious. He turns back to Jessie, but she shoves him gently away, like a bird pushing a fledgling out of the nest. Beside her, Mel expands quietly into the vacant space.

For a while, Patrick shuffles rather clumsily round after Bronwen, who has ignited into frenzied action. Then, slyly, the band changes key. Their drummer, who writes most of their riffs is, unknown to himself, one of Apollo's favourites; a musical genius. And one night, a few weeks ago, a mysterious sequence came floating into his room and hovered for a while around the foot of his bed. He was careful. He didn't jump up and make a grab at it, but waited quietly until it found a spot that it liked in one of his arrangements. Then he got up and played it, and now it is his for ever.

Not all the people in the room notice, but the sequence strikes one of those delicate nerves in Patrick's soul and suddenly he is in tune with the band and moving, moving to amaze himself and Jessie, watching from the wings. He is not

manic or suave or extravagant. He is not showing off. Jessie
and the rest are forgotten. Patrick has become part of something larger than himself out there on the dance floor.

Mel moves still closer. 'Do you dance at all?' he says.

Jessie hears him and means to reply, but she is too mesmerised by what she is watching. Patrick is beautiful. His
movements are rhythmically perfect, springy and graceful as
a kid goat. He no longer needs to follow Bronwen. They are
bound together by some inner understanding of why they are
there and dancing. They are involved in a rebellion of the
first order. Rebellion against inhibition.

Hats off to Dionysus! Where would humanity be without
him? Who else has the power to cure, even temporarily, the
mild form of autism which has reached epidemic proportions
in the Western world?

He is at his best at times like this, joining forces with his
brother Apollo, watching with a knowing eye the mortals
who are flinging themselves around his new extension,
utterly in thrall.

'Why not, then?' says Mel.

'What?' say Jessie.

He gestures with his head towards the dancers. 'Why
not?'

'Oh, all right, then.'

She stands up and Mel manoeuvres himself out from
behind the table. He places his hand lightly in the small of her
back as they go, and she represses a shudder. As they start to
dance, Patrick spots them and slides over, his face full of
excitement. Deftly, he slips off the band which is holding
Jessie's hair, and then he's gone again, into the crowd.

Jessie tries to keep sight of him, but Mel pulls her arm, demanding her attention. She relaxes and begins to dance.

But it won't help. Dionysus may well have got a hold on Patrick, but something will have to be salvaged from this. He's not having Jessie as well.

Within minutes of joining the dance, Jessie's head, to her horror, begins to spin. She makes her way unsteadily back to the table, where Dafydd gets up solicitously and takes her arm. 'Are you all right?' he says, with genuine concern in his voice. He helps her to sit down and scans the crowd.

Patrick is still dancing, but he has lost by now the extraordinary fluidity which possessed him earlier. He would, none the less, have danced the whole evening if he had been given the chance. He is having a ball.

Jessie holds her head in her hands and tries hard not to move.

'Got the spins, have you?' says Mel. 'Do you need to puke?'

Jessie doesn't answer. As long as she stays perfectly still she is fine, but even talking is risky. Dafydd rest a brotherly hand on her shoulder.

When the band comes to the end of the number, Patrick looks round and sees Jessie sitting with her head in her hands. As he begins to make his way out of the crowd, Bronwen says 'Thanks', and looks around for the next bit of fun.

The dancers are temporarily demagnetised and drift slowly away from the centre of the floor, but as soon as the band starts up, the direction reverses.

Patrick draws the hair back from Jessie's face like a curtain. 'What's up?'

'I think she's got the bends,' says Mel. 'Must be something to do with my dancing.'

Patrick leans down. 'Are you dizzy, Jessie? Come on, love, yes or no?'

'Yes,' says Jessie, and finds that speaking isn't so dangerous after all. 'Sorry about this.'

'That's OK. Maybe we should go outside for a while? Get some fresh air?'

Unwisely, Jessie nods. Patrick gathers their jackets, and as he does so, Dafydd hands him a chaser that he had bought for himself. Patrick smiles his appreciation and throws it back in one go. Then he takes Jessie by the waist and steers her out through the bar.

The cool air of the street outside is refreshing, but not much help. Jessie sits on the wall of the tiny yard at the front of the building. Patrick stands beside her, a little restless. After a while, he says, 'Any better?'

'Not really. But you go on in if you want to. I'll be fine if I just sit still for a while.'

'Would you rather go home? The walk might do you good.'

'Would you mind?'

'Not really. Not at all.'

But he does. It is against a strong resistance that he puts his arm around her and supports her across the road and up the steep path on the other side.

For a while Jessie makes progress by keeping her eyes shut and allowing Patrick to guide her. She has the feeling that something is pulling her inwards and down in a billowing, bucketing whirlpool. They make it up the hill and along the tree-lined path which runs between a few outlying houses, but when they reach the more open countryside beyond, Jessie gives in.

'I can't,' she says. 'I have to lie down.'

The ground is damp from the dew which is rising to meet the darkness, but it is solid. It doesn't move. Jessie lies on her back and sighs as the dizziness stills and is gone.

Patrick stands beside her, looking back along the path the way they have come. The band is still audible, but barely, just a rhythmical drone in the distance. Patrick submits and lies down beside Jessie on the grass. Gently, he strokes a stray wisp of hair from her face. 'Are you OK?' he says.

By the time the dizziness finally leaves her for good, Jessie's mind is surprisingly clear. It is she who leads the way along the narrow tracks in the darkness and warns Patrick of upcoming brambles or stones underfoot. When they get to the churning pool, she continues without changing pace, keeping close to the steep bank and well away from the fence. But Patrick drops back, stopped in his tracks by a sinister presence which teases and beckons from the dark water.

'Jessie!'

She is waiting for him on the other side. 'What's up?'

'I can't seem to see very well. I'm not sure where the fence is.'

She comes back for him, takes his hand, and guides him safely past.

Chapter Twenty

Dionysus, arriving in Thebes, brought the women away from their homes and out into the hills to join his revelry. The king, Pentheus, was incensed. He had Dionysus brought before him, and took him down into a murky cell beneath the palace. But Dionysus drove him mad, and when he tried to chain him down there in the darkness, he shackled a bull instead.

Repression never did, never will succeed, where Dionysus is concerned.

∞

On the days that Patrick doesn't go down to the village pub, he takes a glass or two of whiskey, or opens a bottle of wine to go with the evening meal. He sees no reason not to. Jessie replaces the bottles and the money in the drawer of the dresser. She, too, sees no reason not to.

But Patrick has disturbing dreams. In one of them he is being pulled backwards and away down the meadow by some creature that has caught him from behind. Jessie is sitting at the front of the house reading through a huge sheaf of papers, and he calls out to her to help him but she doesn't hear. In another dream he is out on a boat crossing the sea, when the crew members suddenly start running away from him. He laughs and asks them what they're doing, but they leap from the deck and turn into dolphins which disappear beneath the waves. When he returns to the tent where he is living with Jessie, the zip is stuck and he can't get in.

I'm doing my best.

Patrick is, too. He tends to sleep more, and his forward momentum has stopped, but he keeps the things close round him in good order and is rarely idle. On an October day that is clear but cold, he stands in the yard and looks down towards the gulley below. There is little wind in the yard, but down there a strange eddy is swirling the rusted leaves of the trees high into the air and twisting them across the road towards the forestry. Patrick watches for a while, wondering how he might go about drawing what he sees, until a passing tractor breaks his concentration and brings him back to the present.

The fence around the garden was never finished, and the two rolls of wire peel back from the last posts they reached, so it looks as if something has blasted its way out. The hens, meanwhile, have fallen into a depression. Their little hen-house is too small even for institutionalised birds to live in, and they have started to stand in a miserable huddle and refuse to eat. Patrick goes to the feed shed and gathers some tools. As a temporary measure, he rigs up a wire across the middle of the yard. Jessie keeps her car in the parking space on the other side of the house, and Dafydd can turn the tractor or the Land Rover in the meadow.

But Patrick has forgotten Dai Evans. He has barely finished tying up the wire when the red post van comes crawling up the track, and he has to take it down again so that Dai can turn in the yard. The chickens scatter in all directions, and two of them head straight for the garden.

When Jessie comes to the door she sees Patrick in the garden waving a couple of letters after the two chickens, who are racing away down the meadow.

'Anything for me?'

'It's all for you,' says Patrick. 'Help me get these biddies back in, will you?'

Together they round up the terrified birds and drive them back into the yard. Patrick puts the wire back until he can think of something better.

'No sign of your log book yet?' says Jessie.

'No.' Patrick has had one letter since they moved into the house, and that was from Gregory, who sent him photographs of the sundial.

'I wonder what's happened to it?' says Jessie. 'Maybe you should drop a line to Swansea and see if you can hurry them up.'

'Why should I want to hurry them up?'

'No reason, I suppose. I just thought you might like to get the bike on the road. Officially, I mean.'

For the bike is on the road. Patrick takes it every time he goes down to the pub and leaves it concealed in the trees outside the village. If he didn't do that he would have to walk the four miles back along the road. He will never pass the churning pool by night again.

They have reached the door of the house. Jessie has one eye

on the letters in her hand. There is one from Lydia. 'It might have fallen down the back of a desk or something,' she goes on.

'What might?'

'The log book.'

'Ah. The log book again.'

'There'd be no harm in finding out.'

'Will you bloody well shut up about it?'

'What?' says Jessie. 'What have I said?'

'You sound like somebody's mother, going on about things. It's my bike, all right? It's my problem.'

'I only said . . .'

'You're only nagging me! If you're so worried about the bike, why don't you get on it and take it back where you got it from?'

Jessie shakes her head in disbelief. 'What's wrong? I don't know what's got into you lately.'

'Nothing has bloody well got into me!' He is shouting now, causing the chickens to pause in their delighted scratchings and look around them in confusion. 'I just can't stand being managed, that's all!'

What has got into him? And what has come over her? Round and round and round. With the return of Dionysus comes the return of Hera. Or was she there all along, lurking in the background, just as he was? One thing is certain, and that is that wherever one of these two is to be found, the other will be found also. If Hera is not already present, Dionysus will produce her. If she becomes too strong in any given situation, he will appear to thwart her. In the muddled architecture of the average human psyche, these two exist in uneasy relationship to each other, that which seeks to control and that which refuses to be controlled. All over the country, all over the world, there are women playing Hera to their men's Dionysus. There are men playing Hera, too, and women taking up with Dionysus. The gods everywhere are involved in struggle against each other. But there is no struggle more bitter than this one.

Patrick strides into the house and straight up the stairs to the bedroom. Jessie follows, more slowly, and wanders around the kitchen in bewilderment. She tidies things that don't need to be tidied and tries to remember what she was planning to do for the day. What bothers her most is not what Patrick has said, but the look of contempt that was in his face as he said it. It is happening again, the old nightmare, despite all her efforts.

She makes coffee and brings it up to him as a peace offering. He is lying on the bed, reading a book about permaculture.

'Ah,' he says, 'I was just about to come down and make some.' He sits up and takes the cup. 'Thanks.'

Jessie sits beside him and traces her fingers along the veins of his hand. 'Let's not fight,' she says.

He sighs and strokes her back. 'Forget about it,' he says. 'I'll probably go down to the village in a minute to get the paper. Anything we need?'

'No I don't think so. Milk, perhaps.' She gets up to go and hovers for a moment at the door, as if expecting something more. Patrick smiles, affectionately.

'I'm sorry,' says Jessie.

Throughout the day, the mist is intermittent. Several times, Jessie decides to go out for a walk, but each time she gets to the door she changes her mind. The mountains, whenever they come into view, seem hunched and hostile. For a while she sits in the study and looks again at old notebooks, but they start to bring up uncomfortable memories, so she goes into the kitchen and lights the fire. But as she puts the match to the firelighters, she realises that she is only doing it because she wants the house to be warm and welcoming for Patrick's return. She is making absolutely no use of the space that his absence has given her. With a determination that is almost angry, she goes back to the office and switches on the computer. She has decided to start writing, right now, right here. It doesn't matter if she has no ideas, no characters, no plot. What matters is to do it and to do it often; every day if possible. Once the time has been given to it and the habit formed, the rest will come of its own accord.

Jessie's blood is up, and the first words are beginning to form in her mind. But she is not as ready as she thinks she is. When she sits down at the computer, it sends up an unfamiliar message. She stares at it, trying to make sense of its language, then goes through her routine of cures for improbable situations. None of them works. She tries to phone Gregory, who has always been her consultant on technical matters, but he is out of the office. With a sinking heart, Jessie sits back in her chair and looks out of the window. The mist that still surrounds the house begins to feel stifling.

When Patrick comes back in the late afternoon, Jessie is sitting beside the fire. A new notebook is open on her knee, but the pages are all still blank. Patrick is brisk and cheerful. He has only come up to deliver the milk and change into his jeans.

'Dafydd is going to Betwys to pick up a pony,' he says. 'I said I'd go with him. Is that OK?'

'Of course. You don't have to ask me.'

'I wasn't really asking,' says Patrick. 'I was just checking. You might have had other plans.'

She sighs and puts down her pen. 'What other plans would I have?'

Patrick sits on the arm of her chair and rubs her head, then reaches down to lace his boots.

'What does Dafydd want with a pony, anyway?' says Jessie.

'It's a mare in foal. He's going to breed them. He says that they fetch a bomb if they're registered. He thinks it's what we should be doing.'

'Breeding ponies?'

'Yes. Can you see it? Bringing the kids to gymkhanas in their britches and velvet hats?'

'No,' says Jessie, 'I can't.'

'Nor can I. But it might be worth considering, all the same. We don't really have enough land for sheep or cattle.'

He tightens his lace and stands up, then hesitates in the middle of the room like a ship suddenly becalmed.

'Are you off straight away, then?' says Jessie.

'Yes. I'll bring the bike in case I'm home late.'

'You'll go for a pint, then, afterwards?'

'Is that a problem?'

'No. Be careful in the mist, though, won't you?'

'It's only there for the first hundred feet or so. The valley's quite clear.'

'See you later, then.'

But still he waits. When Jessie looks up to see what he's doing, he is just standing there looking at her. 'Is something the matter?' she says.

'No.'

She turns back to the fire, and after a minute she hears him behind her opening the drawer of the dresser. It is the first time, she realises, that he has ever taken money from it in her presence.

That night Jessie lies awake, trying hard not to listen for the sound of Patrick's bike climbing the track. She sees no reason why Patrick shouldn't do as he pleases, and is appalled by the idea that the two of them should be everything to each other and have no independence. She is glad that Patrick is making new friends and getting such a lot out of life. But for all that she cannot shake off a sense of betrayal that grows stronger with every passing day. And no matter how much she despises herself for it, she cannot shake off the anger that she feels at having lost him, somehow, to a world of drink and male camaraderie that she can never join. When he comes in she pretends to be asleep, but lies awake long after he begins to snore and is awake again before him in the morning.

She has breakfast on her own, and then, as happens more and more often these days, she goes out to feed the chickens. The wire that Patrick put up hangs slackly across the yard, a shabby obstacle to be crossed every time she goes out to the new freezer or the tool shed. On weekdays they take it down in the mornings until the post has come, then put it back up and let the chickens out. Jessie stands beside it for a minute or two, wondering what particular insufficiency in Patrick it represents, then decides that she has had enough of it. Inspired, she unhooks it from its moorings at the feed-shed side and swings it round so that it runs along the top of the bank above the garden, between the pigsty and the gatepost. She fetches tools and cuts another piece of wire which she ties across the gate, making it chicken-proof, then fetches the car and parks it in the gap where Dai Evans usually turns, between the studio and the feedshed. Feeling well satisfied, she closes the gate, puts the tools away, and lets out the chickens for their breakfast.

The wire is the first thing that Patrick sees when he gets up and looks out of the bedroom window at the day.

'Jessie!'

His voice makes her jump slightly, and a small puff of flour explodes from the bowl in which she is mixing dough.

'What did you put that wire there for?' he says, as he comes into the kitchen, barefoot, buttoning his shirt.

'Good morning, Patrick,' she says.

'Good morning. Why did you move the wire?'

'Because I thought it was a better place for it. It keeps the chickens out of the garden and it doesn't block the yard.'

'And what's Dai going to do? Now he'll have to open the gate every time he comes with the mail.'

'So what? He has to get out of the van anyway. Now he doesn't have to bring it into the yard at all and he can turn much more easily outside the gate.

For a moment Patrick glares at her, then he says, 'But it's ugly, Jessie. It spoils the view.'

'It's not going to be there for ever, is it? It's only for the time being.'

'Listen. There was wire there when we came, remember? We took it down because it looked awful. Now you've put it back up again. I don't see the wisdom in that.'

His tone is indignant, as though Jessie had moved the wire just to insult him.

'You can get rid of it as soon as you've finished fencing the garden,' she says. 'It's not going to do any harm for a day or two.'

'I'm moving it now,' he says. 'I'm not looking out of my studio window at that.'

Jessie stares at her hands, still mumbling away at the dough on their own. She knows she shouldn't say it. 'You're never in your studio these days, so how can you look out of the window?'

There is a silence, during which, for the first time, Jessie is afraid of him. Then he says, in a voice that is suddenly, horribly calm, 'Sorry about that. I'm not living up to your expectations, am I?'

Jessie tries the computer again, but it is still on strike. Listlessly she flicks through a typescript on the desk. It is an easy one, and not urgent. It can wait. With a sickening feeling, Jessie realises that the work has failed to live up to its promise. It has no power to draw her mind away from the problems she is having with Patrick. The relationship with him is as central to her life as were the failed ones of the past. And now it seems to be heading in exactly the same direction as they did.

She meets Patrick at midday over hot bread and butter in the old kitchen.

'I'm thinking of going to London for a few days,' she says.

'Oh?'

'The computer has gone down. I'm going to take it with me and see if Gregory can sort it out.'

'Can he fix them?'

'Sometimes. Depends what the problem is.'

'Good for him. There's more to Gregory than meets the eye.'

The bread breaks as Jessie cuts it. The innards are spongy

and steaming. Patrick loads them with butter which slides around as it liquefies.

'Go easy,' says Jessie. 'You'll give yourself a heart attack.'

'Rubbish,' he says. 'That's yesterday's theory. Tomorrow's will be that it's a cure for cancer.'

Jessie laughs and takes her plate of bread over to one of the fireside chairs. 'Do you want to come?' she says.

'To London?' He hesitates, momentarily unsure about the prospect of being alone in the house. He has had some unsettling recurrences of his old fears recently. 'I don't think so,' he says. 'There'll be nothing for me to do there, really, will there?'

'Oh, I don't know. We could go to a play or a film. Look up some people.'

'I'll think about it.'

He pours tea and brings it over to her chair, then sits in the other one. For a while they eat in silence, then Patrick says, 'Will you be driving?'

'I'll have to. I won't be able to take the computer on the train.'

'That's great,' he says. 'It means you can bring back the TV.'

The bread seems to stick to the roof of Jessie's mouth. Abruptly, from nowhere, another argument is rising and, dimly, she sees more of them forming behind it, like lines of dark waves rolling in towards the rocks.

'Can we talk about it later?' she says.

'Ah,' says Patrick, 'I see. There's something to talk about, is there? I thought you said September.'

'I said we'd talk about it in September.'

'That's not what I remember.'

Jessie puts down her plate, the bread half eaten.

'Still,' Patrick goes on, lifting his eyebrows playfully, 'it's after September, isn't it? Let's talk about it.'

Jessie feels as though she is being backed into a corner. 'What do you want it for?' she says. 'You haven't missed it, have you?'

'Not much, but I will in the winter. There's nothing else to do around here.'

Jessie has tried so hard not to mind, but the words come out despite her. 'I hadn't noticed you having trouble filling the time. You spend most of your life in the pub.'

'I don't, as a matter of fact,' says Patrick, 'but I will if you want me to.'

Jessie stares at him. Calmly, he mops up melted butter with his last crust of bread and pops it into his mouth. He takes his time to chew it, then slaps his hands together to shake off the crumbs and leans back in the chair. 'It's your decision,' he says. 'Your TV, your house.' He smiles at her sweetly. 'Your man.'

Jessie looks down into her tea, unable to believe what she has heard. She is struck by a forceful memory of the ambivalent feelings she had towards him when they first met, and the sense that he was somehow dangerous. What is happening has begun to frighten her.

Patrick stands up and takes his plate and cup into the kitchen, then goes out through the back door behind the studio into the yard, but he has no purpose in being there other than to escape. He no longer understands Jessie. One minute she is as she always was, warm and understanding, and the next she is cold and critical, seeking to control him. He doesn't know which of those images is the real one, and it confuses him, brings up an anger inside that speaks with its own voice to the extent that he often doesn't know what he is

saying until after he has said it. It is all too familiar, and the
outcome all too inevitable.

To keep his mind off the problem, Patrick spends most of
the day clearing out the feed shed, and he brings Jessie the
dusty treasures that he finds there: a goose-feather hearth
brush, a hand-made bird cage, a rough wooden picture frame.
Later he cooks, and resists the temptation to go down to the
pub. But as they sit by the fireside that evening and read,
little is right between them.

Jessie leaves for London the next day with the computer
wrapped in a blanket and strapped into the passenger seat of
the car. For the first part of the journey, rain pounds out of a
sky so dark that a lot of drivers are using their sidelights, but
at Shrewsbury, where Jessie stops for lunch, it lets up and the
rest of the journey is dry.

She doesn't realise how much she has missed London until
she arrives in it, and instead of going straight to Camden as
she had planned, she spends the rest of the day visiting friends
and catching up on the news. By the time she meets up with
Gregory for a late meal at a Greek restaurant, her troubles
seem to have evaporated, and she and Gregory make a pact
not to talk about their men.

But the next morning she phones Patrick and gets no reply.

'He's probably sleeping,' says Gregory, 'or feeding the
chickens.'

He has restored the computer's confidence and also
installed a new word-processing package, better by far than
Jessie's old one.

'I don't know what's happening to him lately,' she says, as
they sit over coffee and croissants in the kitchen of the
Camden house.

'Why? What's up?'

'He's changed all of a sudden. He's become tetchy and argumentative. He's always going down to the pub. Sometimes I wonder if he's got his eye on another woman.'

'I doubt it,' says Gregory. 'It's probably hormones. I'm feeling that way a lot myself these days.'

He has still not got over James. He is still drinking his way out of it.

'It's the male menopause,' he goes on. 'The mid-life crisis.'

Ah, yes. The mid-life crisis. Don't knock it. It is the second teenage, another chance for mortals to dissociate themselves from the gods and to change their allegiances. It has many of the same features as the adolescent confusion which seems to have been left so far behind, but in one important respect it differs. The adolescent will fall back again among the gods and reassume their powers as his own. But in mid-life, when the gods draw back, individuals get a chance to differentiate between what belongs to them and what belongs to the gods. And among the attributes that they will find does not belong to them, and never did, is immortality.

But on this occasion, Gregory is wrong. Neither he nor Patrick is going through mid-life. Not yet.

'Do you think that's what it is?' says Jessie. 'It seems to have come on rather suddenly.'

'It does,' says Gregory. 'Believe me.'

Jessie looks at the television, sitting blank-faced in the corner like an overweight cretin.

Patrick has stayed the night on Dafydd's couch, following a long and hard-fought darts match. He goes home after breakfast and spends another listless day pottering around the farm. In the evening Dafydd drives up a few cattle to graze off the meadow which he never got round to cutting, and Patrick gives him a lift back down on the back of the bike. The rap band are playing in the village again.

This time, Bronwen has no difficulty in persuading Patrick to dance. He doesn't recapture the ecstatic excitement of the first time, but he enjoys it all the same, and stays out on the dance floor for much of the evening. When the bar closes and the band begins to pack up, Bronwen comes over and slips something that feels like a folded note into Patrick's hand. He watches her as she heads out towards the toilets at the back, then glances down surreptitiously. It is not a note. It is a condom.

Patrick looks round the room, but vaguely, careful not to catch anyone's eye. Then he makes his way towards the toilets and past them, out to the car park. There is no sound out there in the darkness, and for a moment he is afraid that she has made a fool of him. But she comes out behind him, from the Ladies, and leads him over to the trees.

Chapter Twenty-One

When Dionysus broke out of the dungeon, Pentheus determined to send his armies out to slay the maenads who were still having a ball in the surrounding countryside. But Dionysus persuaded him to spy on them first, and disguise himself as a woman so as not to be recognised.

The maenads were not so easily fooled. They spotted Pentheus, dragged him down from the tree where he was hiding, and tore him to pieces.

∽

When Jessie gets home, Patrick is building a wall. The chicken wire that he has returned to its place across the yard distresses him disproportionately every time he sees it, and he has at last come up with a compromise. He has begun to move stones from the derelict building behind the sheep pens and bring them out into the yard. So far, he has built to the height of a foot and a half along the top of the bank.

When Jessie sees it her first thought is that a wall will obscure Patrick's view far more effectively than chicken wire, but she keeps it to herself. He is coming to meet her, his eyes full of pleasure, and as soon as she is out of the car, they hug one another. It is he who prolongs the hold.

'Jessie,' he says, breathing the familiar scent of her hair.

'What?'

'Nothing. Just Jessie. What you are. I love you, you know. I missed you.'

She sighs in a flood of relief against his chest, and gently tightens her hold. He doesn't look into the car before they go together into the house.

It makes it easier for Jessie when, later on, she asks him for a hand to unload the TV.

Jessie doesn't ask Patrick where he was on the occasions she tried to phone, even though she is under strong pressure to do so. She doesn't know Hera's name, but she recognises her none the less, and is doing her best to resist.

For something of the same reason, Patrick doesn't tell Jessie about his knee-wobbler among the trees with Bronwen. Although he doesn't feel any guilt about it, he is sure that Jessie wouldn't understand. It was a celebration, a natural climax to the evening's dancing, and beyond that it meant nothing to either of them. Bronwen hasn't the slightest intention of taking Patrick from Jessie. A relationship is the last thing she wants. As far as she is concerned she has merely, with Jessie's implied consent, borrowed him for a few minutes.

But the next time Jessie sees them dancing together, she is very aware of how at ease they are with each other, how comfortable.

The rap band has become a regular fixture in the Bell on

Friday nights, though it might not be for much longer. They are growing in popularity around the area and are beginning to be in demand.

Patrick comes back to the table, flushed and happy. There is a brief, agonistic encounter between him and Mel before Mel moves aside and allows him to sit next to Jessie.

'You're not dancing?' he says, slightly breathless.

'Not after last time.'

'Oh, come on. It won't happen again. You can't spend the rest of your life on your arse.'

Jessie laughs. 'You asking?'

'I'm asking.'

'I'm dancing.'

He takes her hand and leads her out among the others as the band counts down into a new riff. Jessie is aware of his ease out here, and envies his ability to relax and enjoy himself. There were times when she could dance with as much abandon as he, and many a man, and woman too, have found themselves entranced in the past, watching her lithe body and the swing of her liquid copper hair. But over the years she has lost that assurance, lost the ability to throw aside her seriousness and let go.

It is one of the reasons why those who are governed by Hera are so often attracted to Dionysus. The gods engage in struggle within the individual mind as well as between different ones. It is those who are over-controlled, within as well as without, who tend to seek refuge in Dionysus.

Jessie dances lightly, carefully, hiding behind her hair. And as she does so, her body begins to rediscover forgotten networks of movement. She begins to cover more ground, advancing and retreating, swinging and turning, all of her actions centred around Patrick.

But not all of his are centred around her. He is interacting constantly with the other dancers and they are interacting with him. It seems to Jessie as she watches that he knows everyone there in the room. He winks at the girls as they pass and occasionally swings one around. He nods to the men and the boys and enters into comic engagements over their partners.

And why shouldn't he? It's all in fun, after all. But Jessie begins to lose her enthusiasm and with it, her rhythm. She has the impression that everyone there is dancing together while she is dancing alone. She lasts until the end of the number, then returns to her seat.

Patrick goes to the bar. Jessie has had the two pints she decided upon but Patrick has bought her a third.

'I didn't want one,' she says. 'I told you that.'

'Leave it, then. I'll drink it.'

They sit out the next dance, chatting with Dafydd and Mel. Jessie sips her pint reluctantly, trying not to enjoy it. Patrick and Mel are clearly beginning to take a dislike to each other, and Dafydd is keeping out of their conversation. He looks over at Jessie and shrugs.

When Patrick asks her to get up again, Jessie shakes her head, a little sulky. 'I don't think I will.'

'Why not? We were having a great time just now.'

Jessie procrastinates, waiting to be pressed. Patrick turns round to look at the band and is instantly swept into the fray by Bronwen.

Jessie sags. Beside her, Mel sighs and slides his pint a little closer to hers. She turns, instead, to Dafydd.

'How is it you never dance?' she says.

'I can't,' he says. 'Tone deaf.'

'What has that got to do with anything?'

'I can't hear the music,' he says. 'I don't know what to do.'

'I'll show you, then,' says Jessie, taking his hand and dragging him to his feet. 'Listen to the drums.'

Dafydd, indeed, cannot dance. But it doesn't matter to Jessie. She dances fit to burst, flirting with Dafydd outrageously and sending her hair flying around her like an electric storm. But the only time she notices Patrick, he is giving her a thumbs-up of delighted approval.

When the number is over, the band takes a break. Jessie watches them, noticing how confident they have become. There is something intriguing about the drummer, who is gazing distractedly into space as though listening to something that no one else can hear.

Patrick doesn't come back to the table. Another of the pub regulars has bought him a drink and they stand together on the other side of the room, leaning against the wall and smoking cigarettes. Jessie watches him. She has never seen him smoking before. He is at home here, relaxed and secure among friends, but she isn't. Mel is sitting too close to her, singing a Welsh ballad in a small timid voice, waiting to be asked what it is. Dafydd has disappeared. The last time she saw him he was dancing, ineptly, with Bronwen.

'Another pint?' says Mel, though she is not yet half-way down the last one.

'No, thanks, Mel.' She stands up and crosses the floor to where Patrick is standing and taps him on the shoulder.

'I think I'll go home.'

'Why?' he says. 'What's up?'

'Nothing. I've just had enough.'

She turns and goes out through the bar. Patrick raises his

eyes to the ceiling for the benefit of his friends, then follows her out into the street.

'Had enough of what, Jessie?' he says. 'Are you feeling all right?'

'Yes. My head is fine. Perfectly clear. I'm just not really enjoying myself.'

'Why not?'

'I suppose I'm a bit tired, that's all.'

Patrick stands deadlocked, looking at the road. He is in his shirtsleeves, still hot from dancing, and the wind is cold from the west, blowing straight along the street. The ash trees behind the car park are hissing like waves on a beach. Jessie puts on her jacket.

'All right,' says Patrick. 'I'll see you later, then.'

She turns away to hide the disappointment in her face. 'See you.'

As he watches her go, he is saddened for a moment and then, inexplicably, angry. There is a quiet malevolence in his voice as he calls after her.

'Enjoy the rarefied air!'

Jessie walks wearily back up the side of the valley. The calm serenity of the surroundings might lighten her heart if she let them. There is poetry here, lying like mist among the dozing gorse and mountain ash but Jessie doesn't hear it. She has not yet learnt how to.

At home, she lies awake in the darkness. The motorbike is shut up in the cow-shed but she is still listening for it. Occasionally she thinks she hears it but each time it is only the stream splashing down the crag.

She is still awake when Patrick comes home. It is late, but it would have been much later if Dafydd hadn't given him a lift. He thinks that Jessie is asleep, and makes rudimentary efforts not to disturb her, but he fails and lands rather heavily on the bed. Jessie waits. She has nothing to say.

Patrick undresses and rolls underneath the covers, snuggling up against the warmth of Jessie's back in the darkness. Then he stirs, remembering Bronwen, and slips his hand beneath her nightshirt.

She lies quietly, but in spite of the drink Patrick senses the rigidity in her stillness and moves away with a sigh. For a while the stream tries to lull them with its unique syncopation, but at last Patrick says, 'Why did you leave?'

'I told you. I'd had enough.'

'You didn't tell me enough of what.'

'Enough of you ignoring me and flirting with everyone in sight.'

Patrick is silent, and Jessie senses danger behind her and turns on to her back. The night is too pure here for her to be able to see him but she knows that he is staring up at the ceiling.

'You spend too much time in the Tardis,' he says. His voice, the strangeness of what he has said, fills the room like an unwelcome guest.

'What do you mean?'

'This place. The Tardis. Old and innocuous from the outside, but crammed full of technology.'

'What do you mean, technology?'

'Computers, fax machines, washing machines. Fridges, mixers, blenders. Hair dryers, for god's sake.'

'TV,' says Jessie.

'I haven't turned it on, yet.'

'We haven't got an aerial yet.'

'Whose fault is that?'

Now Jessie is staring at the ceiling, wondering how he does it, how he manages to turn everything she says around and use it against her. More and more lately she finds herself walking on eggs, terrified to say anything in case it is the wrong thing. The stream tries again, fruitlessly.

'It's a bubble, Jessie. A little, private pleasure dome set into the side of a mountain. Like a chunk of London that fell out of a passing magazine and got wedged underneath a big rock.'

The eloquence of Dionysus. He has the ability, at times, to charm even me.

'We can't go on living like this,' he says. 'It's a fantasy. Can't you see that?'

'No.'

'But what are we doing? I'm fiddling around with stones like a kid playing with Lego. You're gathering quaint little stories for your fictionalised anthropology. What's the point of it all?'

'Does there have to be a point?'

'I don't know. But I do know that you'll lose your marbles if you don't start getting around a bit. That's the reason I go out to the pub so often. It's the best way to become part of the community, you know? We can't just cut ourselves off on our own. We'd turn into a couple of pale crabs, scuttling around in the shadows.'

Jessie listens, slightly breathless, aware of the terrible truth in his words.

'It'd be different if we had a family. There'd be a reason for it, then. The house would be a home, not just a luxury office.'

The children again. Jessie falls back into conflict. Patrick is silent beside her for so long that she thinks he has fallen asleep. Until he speaks again.

'But you're not going to have children, are you?'

Jessie doesn't answer. She still doesn't know.

'You're not going to have children because you don't need them, do you? You've got what you want, haven't you?'

'I don't know what you mean.'

'Don't you? Don't you see what you're doing to me? Managing my life?'

'But I'm not! I've done everything I can not to manage your life!'

'Rubbish. You have me perfectly organised, all set up with pencils and paper in my playroom. Can I go with you into town, mum? Can I have a shilling for lollies?'

'It's not like that, Patrick, and you know it!'

'Yes it is, it's just like that. Wowee, a surprise for my birthday. A new bike! Look at me for god's sake. Going around every week in a new set of woollies and fancy rompers.'

There is nothing Jessie can say. After a while, Patrick turns on to his side, away from her.

Hera has been confronted. Even Aphrodite is fast losing interest in this issue.

But she is Jessie's only defence. The harder Patrick tries to destroy her, the more she loves him. She turns now, desperate to make everything all right, and runs her fingers gently through his hair. But he is asleep.

When misery finally exhausts itself and lets her go, Jessie has a dream. She is in her parents' house, and it is the way it was in her childhood. Patrick is sitting at the table with her parents, who are alive and well and vigorous. They seem to be getting on well with Patrick, who is at his social best, charming and attentive. Jessie watches from a distance. She is not involved in what is happening at all.

After a while, her sister Maxine comes in and joins the party. She too is at ease with Patrick, and soon all three of them get up and go outside. Jessie knows that all her friends are waiting there, and that everyone is going off for a walk and a picnic. It isn't until after they are gone that she feels a sense of disappointment at having been left alone.

In the morning she tells Patrick the dream when she brings him coffee in bed. He listens with a reserved curiosity.

Jessie attempts to interpret the dream according to a Jungian method that she learnt during a series of lectures a few years ago.

'The parents and the members of the family refer to different aspects of myself,' she says, 'and the friends, I suppose, represent different stages of development that I've been through. You know the way you like different kinds of people at different times of your life.'

'So what does it mean?' says Patrick.

'I think it's a great dream. My parents wouldn't have approved of you, in many ways, and I suppose there would be some part of myself that would have been influenced by them, you know? But I think the dream is saying that I've accepted you. Every part of me has accepted you, just as you are.'

Patrick smiles and strokes her hair.

If I had hair, even hair like she has, I'd have torn it all out long ago. I have given her the simplest of messages, and look what she does with it. The dream could not have been clearer.

Patrick is taking over her life.

And how. She never sees him take money from the dresser drawer, but it decreases more rapidly as the weeks go by. She despises herself for not standing up to him about it, but despises herself more for desiring to start keeping an account of what he is spending.

The new Frances Bailey has arrived, but Jessie finds that she can't concentrate well enough to read it properly. She can manage more simple editing as long as she can do it while Patrick is out. But whenever she hears him moving around the house, she becomes tense, afraid that he will call her from wherever he is with some new complaint.

Living with Patrick has become like living with two different people. At his best, he is more delightful than ever, funny and thoughtful and sensitive. But although he has never come close to physical violence, he is beginning to scare her. His virulent verbal attacks on her and all women are becoming more frequent and there are times when she stays silent for hours, even days, rather than risk saying anything that might provoke him. She is frequently reminded of the eight of swords, the card that represented her past relationships in that first reading all those months ago. She is there again, somehow; oppressed, besieged, on guard.

And it's not only Patrick that she's on guard against. There are times when she says things that she doesn't intend to say, or when something that was supposed to be innocent comes out all wrong and sounds like criticism. When that happens she can understand why he goes out so much. But when he does go out it is almost always to the pub and the sense of relief that Jessie feels at his departure is invariably followed rapidly by resentment at his absence, his spending, and his preference for company other than hers. No matter how often she thinks about it and how hard she tries, she can't see any solution. She doesn't know if it is some inherent darkness in Patrick that is causing the problems or whether it is herself, but she does know that any attempts she has made to talk about the things or improve them in any way has only made the problem worse. She feels increasingly helpless, a swimmer against an impossible tide.

And Patrick, too, is lost and afraid. The aerial that Jessie eventually bought can't get a decent reception up there among the hills, and the television is useless. The mornings have begun to gape at him, all their previous promise lost. If Jessie doesn't wake him, he sometimes gives them a miss altogether and gets up in time for lunch.

And he cannot account for the way he is behaving. He doesn't want to be hurtful to Jessie. He loves her and can't bear to see her face fall yet again as he suddenly loses control. There are times when he longs to reach out to her and ask for her help with whatever it is that torments him, but he is afraid of her scorn. Everything she says seems to eat away at his diminishing confidence. The only way he can escape is to reach for a drink.

He is caught between the devil and the deep, blue sea.

Chapter Twenty-Two

Aphrodite, as might be expected given her nature, has many, many children. With her illicit lover Ares, she bore Phobus, Deimus and Harmonia. Poseidon fathered Rhodus and Herophilus. And then there's Hermaphroditus, as everyone knows, the result of her union with me. But despite her assumed association with Dionysus, she resisted him for a long, long time.

She did yield, however, eventually. Their son is called Priapus. He is a gardener and carries a pruning knife. He spends a lot of time in pear trees. But mostly he is recognisable by his enormous genitals.

∞

On a clear day in January, Patrick pauses in his work and looks up at the sky. Some elusive and beautiful quality has entered the light. Intrigued, he leaves the building of the wall and goes into his studio.

The drawings on the walls are beginning to curl, just slightly, but apart from that there is no sign of damp. The weak winter sun has been shining against the window all day and the atmosphere in the studio is warm and inviting. The cockerel still has dominion of the drawing board and in the new light, Patrick dares to approach and examine him again. In his mind, the image of the drawing has reduced itself to a most appalling childish mess and he is surprised to find that in actuality it is not so bad. What is wrong is mainly the colour. The chalk pastels were too soft. They have failed to capture the clarity of the live bird and the brightness of the blue-green feathers around its neck. The problem fascinates him and he ponders it for a long time, thinking about different materials and how that marine iridescence might be reproduced. In the end he lets it go but the cockerel is no longer so threatening now that he has discovered what is wrong with it. He takes it down with a sense of liberation and lays it on top of the others. Then he takes out a clean sheet of paper, pins it to the board and begins to draw.

The lines he draws are shorter than the free-flowing ones of the early summer but he soon knows what he is doing and begins to move in on the details. When he stands back an hour or so later he is a little disturbed by the image he has produced, but as far as the quality of the drawing goes, even he can have no doubt.

Satisfied, he locks up the studio and goes into the house. Jessie has also noticed the strange light and has been sitting beside the window in her study looking out across the abandoned wall towards the gorge. Now she hears Patrick come in and tenses, waiting to find out what his mood is. She isn't aware that she has made an unforgivable omission.

Patrick has decided to celebrate his successful return to the studio. The whiskey bottle is nearly empty so he opts for a quick visit to the pub before dinner. As he changes out of his boots it occurs to him that the new drawing will fit perfectly into the old wooden frame that he found in the feed shed. He decides to go to Bangor with Dafydd one day and get some backing card and glass, then give it to Jessie as a present.

'Jessie?' he calls from the hall.

'Yes?'

'When's your birthday?'

'October,' she calls. 'You missed it.'

'Did I?' he says, peering quizzically round the door. 'What a shame.'

She smiles, relieved, off guard. 'Why? What are you up to?'

'Oh, nothing. I'm just nipping down to the village. Don't cook, will you? I want to do the mackerel.'

'All right.'

He goes into the old kitchen and over to the dresser. There is nothing in the drawer apart from a handful of loose change.

Patrick walks into Jessie's study and stands thoughtfully on the Persian rug in the centre of the room.

'Are we bankrupt, sweetheart?' he says.

'What?' says Jessie.

Patrick's voice is mock gentry, comical, but extremely threatening. 'It was bound to come sooner or later, I suppose. We shall just have to sell the silver, that's all.'

Jessie's mind is flitting like a trapped bird, seeing nothing clearly, neither the enemy nor the way out.

'You may put away the car, Bradshaw. Madam has decided I shall not be needing it. And you may tell Elsie to light the fire and set up the Scrabble.'

'Oh.' Jessie lets out a long-held breath. 'Is there no money there? Do you need a few quid?'

'A few quid? We don't deal in few quids, do we, dear? Don't we deal in nobler currencies? In art and literature and ideals? Nothing so base as few quids, surely? Or evenings in front of the TV, or shitty nappies.'

'Oh, leave off, Patrick, will you?' She gets up and goes into the hall for her shoulder bag. The money is there. She has just forgotten to take it out. He is suddenly friendly, himself again.

'Am I spending too much?'

Jessie sighs. She can retreat, lie, tell him that of course he is not, or she can tell the truth and bear the consequences.

'Yes,' she says. 'You are. But what can I do about it?'

'Just what you have done, I suppose,' he says. 'Don't leave it lying about.'

'What, ration you, you mean? Give you pocket money?'

'Why not? You'd like that, wouldn't you?'

'Don't be ridiculous.'

'Yes, you would. Another way to control me.'

'Patrick, I wish you could hear yourself, sometimes. There's no middle ground with you, is there? It's all or nothing. There's never any room for negotiation. You're spending too much money, yes. But I don't want to control you.'

She walks into the old kitchen, the bag in her hand. 'Sometimes I think it's what you want, though. Someone who will take responsibility for you. The way you're behaving these days, it's obvious that you don't know how to take responsibility for yourself.'

Patrick has been waiting in the hall but now he follows her into the room and stands behind her. 'Ah,' he says, 'I thought we'd get round to that one, sooner or later. It always comes up.'

'What do you mean, always?'

'With women! I'll never understand them. First of all they're all over you and you can do no wrong. Then all of a sudden you're not good enough. They're trying to change you into something else.'

'I'm not trying to change you, for god's sake. I liked you the way you were. If there's any changing going on, you're doing it all by yourself. I don't understand what's happening.'

'What way would you like me, Jessie? Out in the garden in my wellies? Sitting beside the fire every evening, smoking a pipe? Would that make you happy?'

Jessie stands with her back to him, feeling absently around in the bag. 'I don't care what you do, Patrick.'

'But you do, don't you? You manipulative bitch. You fancied me as an artist, didn't you? I'm surprised you didn't get me a beret and a smock. You're wrong, I'm afraid. I'm not an artist. I never was and I never will be. And I'll never be happy up here on Mount Olympus, either.'

'Go, then.'

Dusk is falling. The magic light has gone and the gloom has settled back in around the unlit fire. The drawer of the dresser stands open like an outstretched palm.

Patrick is trembling slightly. For a moment they stand silent, their eyes averted from one another.

It is an opportunity, if only they knew. In moments like this, as the gods regroup, mortals have the chance to be friends, to retract ill-directed blame and reveal their own form of love. But it requires the rarest and most painful of the human qualities to do this. It requires honesty.

Jessie finds that she has a sheaf of notes in her hand. In the circumstances it is obscene, and she stands looking at it in helpless confusion.

A match. A match. Patrick hears me, blast him, but he never listens.

The matches are sitting there beside the fire. Jessie would have let him do it, too, the way she's feeling. They could have stood together and watched those fivers and tenners go up in flames, a little joint sacrifice, a chance to break out of the roles they've been cast in. They might even have laughed.

But Patrick doesn't look. He doesn't see. Instead he goes through into the kitchen and gets the mackerel out of the fridge. As soon as he is gone, Jessie drops the notes into the drawer and closes it. The *status quo* is resumed.

Dinner is a civilised affair, with as much small talk as the two of them can muster. The bottle of wine has settled Patrick's nerves but Jessie is drifting in a state of vulnerability, unsure where to turn. She senses that she has dealt badly with the crisis, that it was an opportunity for some change to be made and that it has passed by without her taking advantage of it. Out in the kitchen as they are finishing the washing up, she says: 'If you fancy a pint, I wouldn't mind coming down with you.'

'Yes, you would,' says Patrick. 'But thanks all the same.'

He goes out to the yard to shut the hen-house door and Jessie fetches a book and sits beside the fire. When Patrick comes back he refills his wine glass in the kitchen and comes in to join her. She puts down her book, hoping for communication, but he stands looking into the flames.

Jessie watches his face. Everything is so fragile. There can

be no more arguments. This is either the end or the beginning.

'Do you remember,' he says, 'the time when we first slept
together? When you came into the room in your dressing-
gown?'

Jessie is not confident enough to laugh. This could as easily
be a launch into a new attack as a fond memory. 'Yes,' she
says.

'God, it was great.' Patrick turns slightly and looks at her.
'You don't feel like taking a bath now, I suppose?'

Aphrodite halts in her exodus and flings herself back into the
fray.

Now Jessie laughs. It is the beginning. She stands up and kisses
Patrick gently, seductively, on the lips. 'I'd love to,' she says.
'A bath is just what I'd like.'

As she goes up the stairs I try to foil her and she trips on an
overhanging stair board and almost falls on her face.
Downstairs, Patrick grins to himself. 'Hey,' he calls. 'Don't
fall at the first fence. Take your time.'

'It's that bloody floorboard again,' she calls back. But she is
embarrassed, and remembers her dignity.

But it seems that everything I do just now is playing straight
into the hands of Dionysus.

Because Jessie, remembering her dignity, takes her time in the
bath. And that gives Patrick plenty of time for what he is
doing in the bedroom.

Or Dionysus. Because Patrick hardly knows what he is doing,

or why he is doing it. He himself has been charmed, as Pentheus was charmed before him.

Jessie gets out of the bath and slips into her dressing-gown. She takes off the bath cap and goes into the bedroom to brush her hair. But Patrick is not there. She carries on brushing her hair until she can brush it no longer but still he doesn't come. She puts on a little make-up, just a touch, and goes to the locker to get her diaphragm. It isn't there. She hunts underneath the bed then sits on it for a while, racking her brains.

There is still no sound from Patrick. Puzzled, Jessie goes downstairs into the old kitchen. The light is off and the curtains are drawn against the night. Patrick is standing in front of the fire as he was when she left him earlier, gazing down into the flames. But he has changed into the white shirt with the puffed sleeves that he once refused to wear.

'Don't switch the light on,' he says. 'The firelight is lovely.'

Jessie feels that she ought to be pleased that he is wearing the shirt, but she isn't. It is her shirt now, and seeing him in it makes her a little uneasy. 'Have you seen my diaphragm anywhere?' she says.

He points to the box and the tube up on the mantelpiece beside his wine glass. Jessie breathes a sigh of relief and lays a gentle hand on his arm. The fabric is soft beneath her fingers. Patrick turns to her and she looks up into his face.

It takes her a moment to realise what he has done. His eyes, normally dark, are darkened again by eye-liner. Jessie stares at him, her mouth open.

'What's wrong?' he says. 'This is what you wanted, isn't it?'

Now it is Jessie who is caught in the Zen master's wobble, torn between mortal fear and the desires of the gods. The effect of what Patrick has done is more powerful than he could have imagined. Jessie knows now where the images that haunted her came from. The Hindu gods, male and female alike, have eyes like that. It gives them, as it gives Patrick, a treacherous sort of beauty.

He slips his hand beneath her hair and kisses her lightly on the lips, as she kissed him so recently. But now it is he who is seductive and she is being drawn into something she has never experienced before. She has no impulse to hold him. What stands before her now is not her property.

He lowers his hands to her waist, unties the cord of the dressing-gown and draws it out of its loops. Her eyes remain fixed on his face but he doesn't look at her. Instead he watches the gown as he slides it from her body and drops it to the floor. Jessie reaches out for his waist but he stops her arms, runs his hands along them up to her shoulders then down again, pushing them gently behind her back. He is still holding the cord.

'Don't, Patrick.'

He has moved closer to her now, his body against hers as he winds the cord around her wrists and ties it. The smooth fabric of the shirt smells of herself, smells of nothing. He lifts her face, looks down with those kohl-rimmed eyes. 'You're not afraid, are you? You like games, don't you?'

She does. Her resistance is nominal, produced by an irritant nagging in the back of her mind. It is not a resistance against him, but against the desire which has taken hold of her body and deprived her of her own will.

What is happening here is between Aphrodite and Dionysus.

He moves her backwards and presses her down on to the

edge of the armchair. She yields; yields further as he pushes her shoulders down against the backrest. As he stands above her and opens his fly, the small voice is twittering, calling out for the diaphragm, but it has no place in this room.

He steps towards her and leans forward. The arms of the chair creak in submission beneath his weight. As he takes the use of her body, the power in his eyes is like that of the moon. Distant. Indifferent. Ancient.

So Aphrodite yielded, yields, will yield for ever to the charm of Dionysus.

PART FOUR

*H*ERMES

Chapter Twenty-Three

Messenger of the gods, guide of souls, guardian of travellers, tricksters and thieves. Some of my titles, not all. I am Hermes Trismegistus, he who the Egyptians called Thoth, god of all scholars and scribes. It was I who invented the alphabet, taught mortals the uses of language, sign and symbol. When The Church tried to banish me I was rescued by the alchemists, who called me Mercurius and remembered that I was, am, and always will be, patron of all the arts.

∞

Afterwards, Jessie cannot look at him. She goes to the spare room and lies on the unmade bed waiting for sleep, but sleep is a long, long way off. What has happened repeats itself again and again in her mind. It makes no sense in relation to the Patrick that she knew during the summer, but it makes perfect sense in terms of what he has become, and of that lurking darkness which she has become aware of lately.

The stream is closer to this room than to their bedroom, almost outside the window, and from time to time the sound of it seems to grow to a roar and drag her out of her thoughts. Each time it happens it is a small relief. Her mind is following spiralling tracks, going nowhere purposeful. She can see no solutions, no return from this.

The sound of footsteps on the stairs sends a shock of fear through her bones and she lies with her eyes wide open to the darkness, holding her breath. With one half of her heart she fears him and dreads the sound of the door handle turning. With the other half she longs for him to come in; to apologise and explain what happened and tell her that it's all going to be OK.

The steps pass by. She hears him go into the bathroom and piss, then he comes out and goes on into her room. Surely now he will come, to find out where she is, to talk, to look for comfort and to give it. He does not. There is no clock in the room but the stream tumbles on and Jessie knows that time passes and continues to pass. Still he doesn't come. Jessie's fear and hurt begin to turn to anger. If he can treat her like that and feel no remorse, then things have gone too far. For the last few months she has been living in fear, and it can't go on.

She lies still and listens carefully to the house. There is no sound of movement. Carefully, quietly, she gets out of bed. The dressing-gown has become distasteful to her, but she has nothing else to wear so she puts it on and opens the door of the room. Still there is no sound. The landing light is on and so is the hall light below, but she is sure that Patrick is in bed. As quietly as she can she creeps downstairs and into her study, where she brings the Tarot cards out of a long concealment at the back of the filing cabinet.

It's cold. In the old kitchen the fire is still burning. On the mantelpiece above it is an open cigarette packet, and two empty wine bottles are standing on the brick hob. Jessie picks them up and brings them through into the kitchen where she puts on the kettle. Then she throws a few sticks on the fire and sits down with the cards. She shuffles without ceremony and deals.

This time, she gets what she wants. A set of five delightful cards, her favourites, all with wonderful associations. The Star is there, representing inspiration, and the three of wands, the boundless spring of creative energy. The Papess turns up, head declined in contemplation of her feminine wisdom, and the Queen of Cups, emotionally replete. And in the middle of it all, holding the ebb and flow of the universe between his outspread hands, is the Magician. The air around his head is full of mysterious symbols. His eyes are dark and capricious. Jessie loves him, always has, but here? Among yet another set of her ruins?

She shakes her head, looks over the cards again, can find nothing in which to believe. It is almost as though they are mocking her. A kind of convulsion begins in her abdomen which might be laughter and might be howls of rage and grief. She stops it before she finds out, and with a sudden deft certainty gathers up the cards and drops them on to the fire, where they produce quick flame, as colourful as themselves. She watches them for a while, without regret. She doesn't need cards any more. She knows what she has to do.

Patrick doesn't move as she comes into the bedroom. He is still dressed, half under the covers, and snoring deeply. Jessie changes out of the dressing-gown and into jeans and a sweatshirt before she leans across the bed and shakes him.

He wakes with a start. 'What? What?'

'We have to talk.'

Patrick looks up through bleary eyes. The eye-liner is still there, hardly smudged, but the only effect it has on Jessie now is to make her feel slightly saddened, slightly disgusted.

'Wake up,' she says, 'come on.'

Patrick lifts his head and then drops it again, falling back to sleep. He smells strongly of stale alcohol and tobacco and fills Jessie with repugnance. Now that she has made her decision it seems obvious what the problem is, and she is amazed that she has taken so long to realise it.

'Patrick!' She shakes him again.

'What!'

'I want to talk to you. Will you wake up?'

'There's nothing to talk about. Will you just leave me alone?'

'No, I won't. But you're going to have to leave me alone.'

'I don't have to do anything.'

'You do. You have to leave, Patrick. I can't take things the way they are.'

'Right.'

Jessie looks down at him. His eyes are closed again. Her heart feels hollow as she says, 'Is that it, then?'

But there is no answer and she doesn't know whether or not he is awake.

'Patrick?'

He pulls the covers up over his head. Jessie goes back to the spare room.

In the morning she is woken by the sounds of Patrick moving around the house. Her first thought is that he is making tea. He will bring her some in bed. She dozes off again.

And dreams of the hideous child with the pruning shears and the enormous genitals. He is in her arms, and over her shoulder someone is saying, 'And his name shall be called . . .'

The front door closes. Jessie opens her eyes and discovers that she is in the spare room. Maybe Lydia is staying, or Gregory, otherwise why . . .

'Priapus!' I yell at her. 'Priapus! Aphrodite's son by Dionysus!'

It all comes back, in stark horror. Jessie sits up, her dream forgotten. She is still in the clothes she put on last night. She remembers the burning cards.

The sun is streaming in through the window. One of the shed doors in the yard is opening. Patrick must be feeding the hens. Jessie gets up and goes into the bedroom for clean clothes. There are inky tearstains on the pillowcase, still wet. As Jessie looks at them, she hears the bike being kicked into life and purring away down the track.

She stares at the square white dazzle of the window. She didn't really believe that it would end like this, despite her resolutions of the night before. He can't really be gone.

He is, though. I could have worked wonders with Patrick. I could have taught him, with time, how to capture that elusive iridescence and know when to use it in his work. I could have shown him how to paint the magical light that I sent that day, and the shifting moods of the mountains. I could even have taught him how to portray the nature of the gods without giving them the faces they don't have. He is one of the few who could have listened.

I can move in two directions at once, no problem. I can move in a million directions at once if I want to, but there's no point in following Patrick. He is utterly deaf to me now.

There is plenty of dark, silent water in Wales where a man pursued by Bacchus might, or might not, turn into a dolphin. There are also roads which lead to Manchester and Shrewsbury and London, and there are ferries which cross over the sea to Ireland. There are pubs, too, and maenads, and more lonely women like Jessie. Given time he may find one who has all the good qualities of Hera and none of the bad ones. Given an eternity.

Let him go with Dionysus. Why shouldn't he, after all? What difference does it make to him which one of us he chooses to ally himself with? None of us can offer what he's looking for.

In any case, I'm not going to squabble over him any more. I have other business to attend to.

Jessie has not ignored the Priapus dream, even though she doesn't know what it means. She is already at the dressing table, covering the dreadful face that pleads from the mirror with a mask for a new day.

She drinks coffee, then drives to the Family Planning Clinic in Bangor to get the morning after pill. The doctor there, to her relief, is a woman. And Jessie's meticulous make-up hides nothing from her.

'There's no problem about letting you have the pill,' she says. 'You just give this to the woman in the dispensary in the waiting room.' She smiles. 'We get a lot of burst condoms around here.'

She writes something on her pad but instead of handing it across the desk between them, she comes around to stand beside Jessie and puts a gentle hand on her shoulder. 'Is there anything else you'd like to tell me about?'

The accent is musical and comforting, and Jessie is brought

close to tears by unexpected concern. But she shakes her head. 'It was just an accident.'

'Are you sure? The police are much more sympathetic these days than they used to be.'

'No. It's nothing like that. I haven't been raped.'

But there are times over the following weeks when she feels it might have been better if she had been. She could have despised Patrick, then, instead of despising herself. What she is left with, for a while, is the awful belief that what men say about women is true. They want to be raped.

But she is wrong. They do not, any more than men want to be flogged within an inch of their life by any woman, known or unknown, despite the submissive fantasies they might indulge in. Fantasy is one thing. It is the interplay of the archetypes within the human psyche; the dramas of the gods, perhaps, as they vie for supremacy. Actuality is something else. The two should never be confused.

Jessie returns to the house on the hillside in a state of total confusion. She feels that she has duped herself into acting without proper consideration. If she had known that he would put up no resistance, that he would just go and never look back . . .

She makes lunch for herself from Patrick's home-baked bread and one of the rare winter eggs but she has to force herself to eat it. Her mind is overwhelmed with images and the strongest of them, the one which returns time after time to haunt her, is the look that was in Patrick's eyes as he leaned above her the night before. It was a look of complete objectification.

*

Only the gods can see a human being as an object. It is their prerogative. For how can one person in possession of their own senses look at another and fail to understand that they are of the same stuff and involved in the same pathetic struggle for autonomy? All the fear and rejection, the scorn, intolerance and worse, all the murder and torture and exploitation is the work of the gods, let loose among a succession of generations that have no resistance to them.

Jessie has failed the gods, failed all of them, and they are angry. They have failed her, as well, but they are not gone yet. Jessie, with nowhere to go and no one to turn to, is helpless in their midst, torn between them as they carry on their ceaseless squabbles.

Aphrodite loves Patrick, and when she gets the upper hand, Jessie loves him too, desires him, longs for him despite all he has done to her. But Hera hates him. He has escaped her clutches yet again, and allowed Dionysus to make a fool of her. So Jessie hates him as well and can't understand how she ever came to be taken in by him. And Dionysus is there, too, lurking in the shadows, berating her for having spoiled everything by manipulating Patrick, disapproving of his drinking, dressing him up, trying to turn him into something that he wasn't. Jessie swings among them all in a desperate arc between love, bitterness and guilt. The only comfort is a voice which emerges and recognises the human weaknesses that gave rise to all the problems. It allows her, briefly, to forgive both of them for what has gone. But the voice comes rarely. The voice is still small.

The mists roll in and out of the valley and the days do, too, and the nights. The last of the year's growth of weeds remains in the garden among the cabbages which rot on their stalks in the damp air.

When Dafydd comes looking for Patrick, he finds Jessie making a bonfire on top of the compost heap.

'Hiya, Jessie.'

'Hello, Dafydd. How are things?'

'Fine, fine.'

As he watches, Jessie takes a dressing-gown out of a plastic bag and throws it on top of the books and papers that she is burning. There is something about her attitude that he finds unsettling.

'Everything all right, is it?'

'Yes, thanks.'

'Good. I was looking for Patrick. Haven't seen him about for a few days.'

Jessie adds the plastic bag to the fire and watches it as it shrivels and turns into a waxy puddle. Then she sighs. 'Patrick's gone, Dafydd,' she says.

'Gone? Gone where?'

Jessie shrugs.

Dafydd stand awkwardly for a moment, then crosses to the other side of the fire and pokes it with a pitchfork. The dressing-gown hasn't caught light yet. It looks perfect to him and he wonders why she is burning it. Jessie looks fixedly at the flames that spring up from the papers beneath.

'You've split up, then?' says Daffydd.

'Yes.'

'Is that all right?'

'Yes. It was inevitable.'

The dressing-gown begins to burn. They both watch it in silence, and Dafydd feels that there's a purpose to the burning which he can appreciate even if he doesn't exactly understand.

'If there's anything I can do,' he says.

Jessie nods. 'Thanks, Dafydd.'

He goes back to his Land Rover and drives away, leaving Jessie alone with her pyre.

Most days, Jessie goes into town for provisions and remembers to feed herself. She keeps the fires lit and the house in some sort of order, but that's the extent of her work. Patrick is gone, the gods have no use for her, and now it is her turn to suffer the pain of withdrawal.

This is what the tool-maker suffers on being made redundant, the businessman on going bankrupt, the young soldiers on returning from Vietnam to find that in their absence, their god has been deposed. And the sailor returned from the sea, the proud housewife widowed, the sportsman retired, the philatelist robbed of his stamps.

Jessie is doing cold turkey. She sits in her office with a manuscript in her lap and stares at it blankly, without comprehension. She lies awake at night, staring at the walls, listening to the stream mimicking the sound of Patrick's motorbike. At times she brightens and thinks of walking in the mountains. Once she gets as far as the door in her jacket and boots before she realises that she cannot leave the house in case the phone rings. She knows that Patrick will not come back. But she still believes that he will.

When the phone does ring, a week after Patrick has gone, it is Lydia, wondering what has happened to her manuscripts.

Jessie sighs. 'Everything's a bit of a mess, I'm afraid. You may have to get someone else to do them.'

'Why?'

'Patrick is gone.'

There is a long silence, during which Lydia feels unaccountably guilty. 'Are you all right?' she says at last.

'Yes, I'm all right. I just can't really concentrate. I'm not sure you weren't right all along.'

'Don't say that, Jessie. You seemed to be doing so well. You seemed to be made for each other. What happened?'

'I don't really know. It just did.'

The silence which follows is so long that Lydia eventually says, 'Jessie?'

'I'm here. There isn't anything to be done about it. But it might be best if I sent the manuscripts back to you. Can you get someone else?'

'Of course, but I'd rather you did them. Shall I come up, do you think? Talk about it?'

'No. There's nothing to talk about.'

There is, but where to begin? Jessie struggles on, staying alive. Bereft, terrified of facing the awful fact of being merely mortal, Jessie clings to Aphrodite as hard as she can. If she can only serve that dimly perceived goddess well enough, believe in her totally, then surely she will bring Patrick back. But Aphrodite has no more use for Jessie. The harder she clings, the harder Aphrodite pushes her away. Jessie's longing and loneliness cause a pain which is physical in its intensity. It is only a matter of time before it will reach the point where she will not be able to hold on any longer. Then she will have to let go.

Gregory comes, driving a small hired van. Jessie breaks down when she sees him and weeps for four hours with her head in her hands over the kitchen table. He makes tea and coffee and dreadful jokes, and periodically he takes her in his arms and hugs her.

She sleeps soundly that night for the first time since Patrick left, while the stream remembers old melodies from her childhood.

Gregory takes command and Jessie allows him to. He is taking her back to London, at least for the time being. It comes as a salutary realisation to Jessie that she has nothing to stay in Wales for. Nothing at all.

Together they pack the most necessary things into the van. There are no boxes and Jessie at last knows why she was so covetous about plastic bags. Gregory, with his dynamic energy, makes short work of the packing but the problem arises of what to do with Patrick's things. There is only one key to the house and Gregory advises Jessie against leaving it under the stone in the yard while she's gone. For a while they work to the plan of leaving the stuff with Dafydd but then Jessie remembers the studio. Patrick has taken his own key with him, but there is a spare one hanging in the kitchen.

She brings a few bags of clothes out into the yard and around to the studio door. Inside it is as bright as the day. Jessie feels that she has stepped into some kind of mysterious space.

She has. My space. It's unused now, of course, but I still have special power here, as I do in certain other fragments of the mortal world. There were times when some of the people knew that and marked such places or enclosed them. My names were different everywhere but by whatever name I was called, you will still find my monuments. Stone circles, fairy forts, the ruins of ancient shrines. Even churches, some of them, were built upon ancient sites which belong to me.

Listen for me if ever you are passing such places. Some of them I have abandoned, but not all.

Listen for me.

Jessie's eyes fall first upon the cockerel at the top of the pile of drawings and she experiences a moment of disillusionment. It is not a good drawing and she wonders how she could ever have believed that it was. Was he right? Was his ability a figment of her imagination that she tried to make into reality?

Her eye roams around the room and comes to rest on a pair of envelopes that are lying in one of the alcoves. Intrigued, slightly guilty about invading Patrick's privacy, she approaches them. One is unopened, a brown vellum one with a window. Inside is a final reminder to send in the change of ownership form for the bike. The other envelope contains the birthday card she gave him, the unsigned form, and nothing else. The three blank cheques have gone.

In sudden anger Jessie turns back towards the door, but as she does so her eye is caught by Patrick's last drawing. The anger descends as rapidly as it arose, and Jessie walks over to look at the picture. It is of a man turning into a dolphin.

It is a fabulous drawing. The two beings are both clearly represented, not half and half but interwoven, each of them somehow complete in its features and yet barely formed. The figures are interdependent, emerging from each other, neither of them dominant. It is one of the most powerful images Jessie has ever seen. It bristles with my power and for a moment Jessie feels herself being sucked in towards it. There is another world there. The symbolic image is trying to tell her something that she is almost ready to understand.

But not quite. She pulls back, clings to Aphrodite, who fills her heart once again with love for Patrick, then slaps her down to the agony of his loss. Jessie retreats, back to Gregory's cheering activity. But the next time she comes with a bag of Patrick's things, Jessie rolls up the drawing and finds a safe place for it in the van.

On the way back to London, Jessie tells Gregory as much of the story as she dares. There are certain things that are taboo, even between the two of them. Gregory, in turn, tells her about James. He has come to the conclusion that she was right and that James just enjoys playing with people. He has put the whole business behind him and stopped drinking. His mid-life crisis seems to have passed.

They unpack as soon as they get back, in the dark. Gregory is keen to take the van back before morning so they leave all the stuff in the hall for the time being. Jessie is slightly horrified by the amount of it. She hasn't the energy for organisational work of any description. All her energy is elsewhere, at the moment, turned inwards.

Gregory drinks tea with her and then leaves with the van. Jessie sits at the table until she begins to fall back towards despair. She is exhausted.

Her old hot-water bottle is still underneath the sink, so she fills it and goes upstairs. Gregory is using her room, but she doesn't want it back. It holds too many memories to be comfortable. Instead she goes into the spare room and makes up the bed with clean sheets.

As she washes in the bathroom, the face that looks out from the mirror is haggard and worn. It doesn't surprise her that Patrick left. It surprises her more that he was ever able to look at it and find it lovely. Perhaps he didn't. Perhaps . . .

There is no point in going through it all again. She is too

tired. Back in the spare room, she goes over to close the curtains and looks down for a moment at the garden. The sundial is hidden by darkness, but closer to hand there is another reminder of the early days of her relationship with Patrick. Beside the window a drainpipe runs down from the guttering above her head, and something has snagged on one of its joints, brought there by the wind or dropped by a nesting bird. It is tangled now, and jaded by the weather, but there is no doubt that it is the same little circlet of her hair that appeared like an omen that autumn day, more than a year ago.

It is too much. Jessie wavers and clutches at Aphrodite's robes in desperation. But Aphrodite has had enough. She shakes Jessie to the core, determined to teach her the results of her foolish vanity. Jessie clings even harder. The goddess turns, reveals herself at last.

'At least there is Gregory,' Jessie thinks.

And lets go.

Chapter Twenty-Four

I am Hermes, messenger of the gods. Without me, none of the residents of the immortal world can carry on their business. I have credit with just about everyone, and that includes the Muses.

One of them is ready now, whispering, waiting to be heard.

∞

What Jessie has perceived is the soul of an immortal revealed for what it is: an infinite, insatiable vacuum. The desires of the gods are without limit and humans who row in with them may never discover that contentment comes only to those who cease to search for it.

Jessie is falling, tumbling helplessly towards the abyss which lies between human expectation and the will of the gods. She is terrified, utterly lost, aware only of a darkness which gapes like a black hole among the stars.

Jessie is falling, and this is the moment I have been waiting for. As she drops she catches a glimpse of my golden staff, and